GW00858973

The boy with a

violet eyes

Feroz Patel and Gerard M-F Hill

Black Bud Books

First published in the UK in 2011 by Black Bud Books

ISBN 978-0-9568961-0-0

All rights reserved. No part of this publication may be reproduced in any form by any means, stored in or introduced into a retrieval system, copied or transmitted, without the prior written permission of the publishers.

© Feroz Patel and Gerard M-F Hill 2011

Feroz Patel and Gerard M-F Hill have asserted their right to be identified as the authors of this work in accordance with the Copyright, Designs and Patents Act 1988.

Camera-ready copy produced at www.much-better-text.com
Printed in Britain by lulu.com

You can visit Meena and Jack at www.jackandmeena.com

Contents

1   Who knows? 1

2   The quest 6

3   A small world 11

4   Seeing is believing 19

5   So you say 23

6   Ardunya 32

7   The twelving 39

8   Hindsight 45

9   Dr Meena's medicine 54

10 A kink in the learning curve 63

11 Found 69

12 Just Jack 77

13 Unlucky for some 83

14 In the forest 90

15 The pilgrimage 96

16 The bottom of page 9 106

17 The nadir 111

18 Fireworks 123

19 The monster in the swamp 133

20 Crystallised 141

21 I never did 149

Science makes sense of things. Stories make sense of people.

Science is about asking questions, and questioning the answers.
Life is one long experiment.

1 Who knows?

Far, far away from Macron, on another little planet called Earth, in a galaxy few people ever visited, it was time for Jack to get up for school. But Jack was trapped in another world.

"Go away! … NO!"

Whichever way he turned, the thick, dark fog was all round his head like a cloud of midges, stinging his face and hands. He lost all sense of direction. He couldn't see and the fog blotted out all sound apart from his thumping heart, until he heard it laugh – a deep, nasty laugh.

Jack began to run blindly, scared of crashing into something, but much more terrified of the demon in this evil, stinging mist. He had to hold onto the crystal, and there wasn't much time. The deep, rumbling laughter was louder now, all around him, making him panic, until he tripped and began to fall, banging his knees, hips, arms, elbows, tumbling over and over.

——— § ———

The laughter faded to silence. He had stopped falling. A scuttling noise made him shiver and look up. Two green eyes glared at him. No cat likes to have ten minutes' stalking wasted – Galileo certainly didn't.

Jack found himself upside down at the bottom of the stairs, bruised and cold, heart pounding. That nightmare again. Why? Jack looked at everything scientifically, but what was scientific about a nightmare? Each time it got longer and scarier. This time he'd ended up sleepwalking, fallen downstairs and woken his mum.

"Jack."

The first call was barely audible; the next was more desperate.

"Jack!"

He picked himself up, climbed the stairs and padded along the landing to his mum's bedroom. The sunlight through the thin orange curtains seemed to give her a sun-tan; even so, she looked pale and feverish. She had wrapped herself in her duvet, but she was shivering.

Anita Cooper had short, light brown hair, emerald-green eyes and a few freckles across her pale cheeks. She was in her late thirties and very attractive, with a lovely smile when she was well – but Jack's mother was a sick woman and she wasn't getting any better. Her illness had brought on a stroke, leaving her too weak even to manage the stairs. Unable to go out any more, her world was reduced to their small house. She relied on Jack.

The district nurse wanted her admitted to hospital and kept threatening to arrange it; Jack and his mum, fearing she would never come home again, were determined to prove they could manage. So every weekday she was up and dressed, sitting in an armchair, with a cheerful smile to keep Nurse Dixon at bay.

To her credit, the nurse insisted that the council send a home help, so three mornings a week Mrs Whale (a small, wiry person) came to do housework. That left Jack to put out the rubbish, do the shopping, feed the cat, cook, wash up, tidy his room, cut the grass – and look after his mother. He worried that otherwise she would go into hospital, he would go into care and they would lose their home. So he did his chores willingly.

Even when he was doing his own stuff, Jack had learnt to stop every so often to check on his mum and her medication. She needed so many little things. Anita Cooper's illness was being managed, but that seemed to be all her doctor could do.

Jack went over to the bedside table and checked her tablets. She should have taken the last one hours ago but, sure enough, there were still three left in the box. He got her a glass of water, sat on the bed and began to feed the tablets to her. She swallowed and gave a groan. While he waited for the medicine to take effect, Jack filled up the box with her tablets for today. His thoughts wandered back to his dream.

What did it mean? He had nightmares when he was six or seven, but he'd long since grown out of them. These were just as terrifying. Now he dreaded going to bed, but he couldn't talk about it. A 13-year-old having nightmares? People would laugh, even Mum. Yet he was tormented: this was the third night in a row he had tried to get through with the crystal, only to be trapped on the strange planet by a sinister, stinging black mist. He shuddered, lost in his thoughts. A look of anxiety came over his mum's face.

"Jack, what's the matter? You look worried."

"Er … you're imagining things, Mum. It's those pills."

There was a silence. She could tell he was hiding something. "You're growing up. A boy your age should be enjoying life." Mrs Cooper, stuck in bed, couldn't help him. Frustrated, she began to weep.

"Stop it, Mum, you'll only make yourself worse." He'd started the day upside-down, and this was all upside-down too: mothers don't cry. He put on his no-nonsense-mum voice: "I mean it. I'll call Nurse Dixon … then you'll be sorry!"

His mum burst out laughing and wiped her tears away. "All right, I'll be good. And you'd better get dressed."

Jack couldn't help laughing too, clearing away the awkwardness. He got up from the bed, tucked the duvet around his mother's shoulders and took her empty glass. As he closed the door, he heard her getting up.

Entering his bedroom, Jack came face to face with himself in the cracked mirror on the wardrobe door. He saw a 13-year-old boy with violet-coloured eyes, just like his father's, in pyjamas that were a bit small – a rather skinny boy with a new bruise on his forehead just below his tousled brown hair. It was getting rather long, but he couldn't afford a haircut just yet.

He looked around his room. It was very plain, with a moth-eaten rug, tired paint, the teddy-bear curtains he got for his fifth birthday, a single bed and a bookcase doubling as a bedside table, stuffed with books and a few gadgets. On top was Meena's book. He'd only read it to please her, but he'd enjoyed it. He must remember to give it back. There was a small desk littered with tools, bits of apparatus and a book on fireworks. That was it: no television, no computer games – no computer, even – plenty of reasons not to invite friends round. Apart from Meena.

Jack never complained. At least he and his mum had a house, though they were alone in the world. They had just scraped by since his father died, when Jack was 16 months old. He had often wondered what it would be like to have a dad around – to play with, do things together, talk to. All he knew of his father was the little his mother had told him: that he was a joiner, she never met his family and his death came out of the blue.

Yet Jack *had* met his father – though he'd never told anyone – in dreams. Exciting dreams, too, where his dad did magic or made fireworks – like another world. In one dream, his father had led him to the desk downstairs and pressed a button that opened a secret drawer: in it was a crystal, quite unlike any crystal in science books. It was bigger than his hand, many-sided and sparkling, with the shape of a black flower at its heart.

Early the next morning, Jack had run downstairs to search for the crystal in that special drawer. Instead he found a large lump of rock, bright blue and very heavy. It was now at Professor Shreddon's laboratory, where Jack was experimenting with it. He hadn't told Meena yet; she'd be excited! Experiments were fun. You never knew what would happen.

Twelve years ago, when the professor needed a joiner to fit out his lab, he had asked Mr Cooper. They found they shared an interest in chemistry; Jack's dad was fascinated by fireworks. That's what he was making at the lab when he suddenly died. After that, Paul Shreddon took an interest in the boy's welfare; he was like his next-of-kin and guardian angel rolled into one. He had come to have a high regard for Jack. Every so often he would visit Anita Cooper too, to see how she was.

——— § ———

Jack glanced at the clock and two violet eyes opened wide. It was quarter to nine, he still had chores to do before school and his form tutor wasn't called Attila the Hen for nothing.

"Oh no, she'll go hyper!" he muttered.

The boy with the violet eyes

He quickly dressed. His blazer and tie were nearly new, but his trousers were worn at the knees and barely reached his ankles. His newly washed school shirt was a dull cream, and one sock had a hole where his big toe poked out. He struggled with his tie; he wasn't good at knots. He rushed to the bathroom, threw soap and water on his face and hands, half rinsed and dried. He brushed his teeth like a maniac, wiped his mouth and went downstairs two at a time.

Mrs Gutten was going to chew his ear off, but mum's breakfast came first. Why was the kettle so slow? The toast would have to be very lightly toasted. There wasn't time for his own breakfast. He went to the door to get the milk, followed by Galileo – Leo for short. Jack named their kitten before he found she wasn't a tomcat. She had one ear torn and some fur missing.

"Whoa, Galileo! Who did you upset?"

If you push your luck, you're bound to get hurt, thought Jack.

Going for the margarine, he got a nasty shock as a fat spark leapt from his finger to the fridge door. Why didn't this happen to Mum or Meena? Was he positively charged, and they were negative? Or just generally highly charged? His arm tingling, he filled a saucer with milk, poured some into his mum's mug and put the rest back. As he gave Galileo her milk, he heard water running down the bathroom plughole. He rushed upstairs two at a time, dashed into his bedroom to grab Meena's book, jammed it in his waistband and ran to his mother's door.

"Slow down, Jack!"

She was leaning on the doorpost, her tablets in one quivering hand. Jack put his shoulder under her arm and they made their way slowly downstairs and into the lounge. Putting the book down, he gently helped her into an armchair. As the clock cleared its throat to strike nine, Jack got in first.

"I'll just bring your breakfast, Mum, and I'm off."

A minute later he was back. He put the breakfast tray down beside her, leaned over to give her a kiss, then shot out into the hallway. He tied his shoes with some difficulty, picked up his bag and bolted for the door.

"Bye, Mum!"

He banged the door behind him and ran down the path.

———— § ————

School was a good quarter of an hour's walk away, but he could do it in half the time running. He pelted along Hornbeam Avenue past high hedges and trees, beautiful gardens and empty driveways. Everyone had gone to work or school. No one was about. He turned to look before crossing the road.

As he paused, he heard a single footstep, then silence apart from the cars on the main road in the distance. He looked both ways: there was nobody to be seen in the whole length of the road. Everything seemed normal. Yet he was

4

sure he had heard a footstep and – now he thought back – before that, somebody running. Was somebody playing a game?

Jack was about to go back and look, when he remembered how late he was. He set off again, crossing the road onto the common. Apart from a few trees, it had no hiding places. This was where he used to pretend to be Agent 006 in enemy territory, trying to reach the safe drop before the other side could intercept him and capture his message. Was he being followed? He stopped behind a tree, leaned on it and peered round. In one of the gardens he'd just passed, a branch twitched and a bird flew out.

Had he imagined those footsteps? This was just like the nightmare where he was being chased. Doubting himself, Jack looked back one last time, but there was nobody there. Agent 006 raised an eyebrow, shrugged and set off again. This time he didn't run. He was out of breath, and he wanted to show he wasn't frightened. But he knew he was.

He listened tensely for footsteps, but now they would be on the grass, so of course he wouldn't hear them. Anyway, why would anybody follow him? There were supposed to be people who gave you sweets and tried to kidnap you; but he was too old for that. Anyway, his mum once said he was more likely to fall in the canal than be kidnapped. He still avoided the canal.

Could it be Tom Atkinson the troublemaker? He'd begun to take an unhealthy interest in Jack. But he wouldn't hide: he and his gang had Jack down for the job of getting them cigarettes from Mr Patel's shop. Jack glanced back again and saw no one. The experiment hadn't yet produced any results, but he was convinced something was going on.

He heard light footsteps on the road and quickly turned, but there was no one there. The experiment had gone on long enough. As much bewildered as frightened, Jack sprinted fiercely across the grass, not once looking back until he reached the main road. He ran straight across, dodging the traffic.

Reaching the safety of the school gates, he stopped to get his breath back and go over what had just happened, like any scientist reviewing the evidence. He had heard footsteps three times; he had seen no one and nothing to make the footsteps; yet he was convinced he had been stalked. Why? Who would bother? He had hardly any money and no mobile phone.

Anyhow, he was safe for now – though not from Mrs Gutten. First, Jack went to the secretary's office. She tut-tutted over getting the register out again, but after that she took no further interest in him, and he set off to his first lesson. But if Jack thought this was the last of his nasty surprises for today, like Galileo he was in for a nasty surprise.

2 The quest

There was a clear sky that night, and the desert was almost as bright as day. The red sand dunes were bathed in the light from the two moons, one high in the west, the other beginning to dip towards the eastern horizon. Every few minutes, meteors blazed across the purplish-blue sky where thousands of stars twinkled. Might two of those stars warm another planet with intelligent life, like Ardunya?

In one place, red rocks rose out of the dunes to form crags and cliffs, full of shadowed crevices. Above them were the vast, bare slopes of a solitary, humpbacked mountain. There was no sign of plant life in this desperately forbidding place, and yet there *was* life. This corner of the desert was now occupied, but underground; the surface was too hot for survival except at night. To reach this remote spot, your animals had to be fast enough and tough enough to cross the uncharted desert in a night, or roast along the way.

A group of weary travellers warily approached the mountain and stopped under an overhanging rock. Their leader rode up to the cliff face and disappeared in the shadows. When he emerged again, some bat-like creatures high above saw him beckon his men to join him. They rode up to the cavern mouth where, standing on horseback, they began to unfasten their packs from their massive beasts of burden. An earthling might have taken these for white elephants, except they were far taller and had humps on their backs.

The horses were muscular with large, square hooves; their jagged teeth suggested they were carnivorous. A few men untied bundles of firewood and lit a fire in front of the cavern, while others unpacked supplies and carried them inside. Their drawn, dusty faces showed how long and far they had ridden.

Their leader was tiny compared to his men, yet they feared him. He stood apart, ignoring them, the hood of his cloak shadowing his face as he studied a scroll. After a minute he looked up at the cliff, turned around, picked out a few men and sharply ordered them to follow. He never once looked back as he led them under a crag and up a shadowy, rock-strewn ravine. Clambering over boulders, the men had eyes only for their next footstep until they found the gorge closed by another, bigger cave.

Seeing darkness ahead, above and around, they froze with fright, heartbeats pounding. This was an evil place and they had no fire to drive the evil away. They feared the devil in this cave, but they feared their leader more. He was a real, immediate threat; the evil forces might be just stories. Reluctantly, they lit their torches and followed him, their footsteps echoing.

Deeper in, the cavern roof became visible high above, and every so often they glimpsed the sides of the cave, though it was still large enough for two of their massive beasts side by side. The floor began to slope downwards, and in the flickering torchlight they saw sharp rocks just above their heads. Was this some kind of trap? Fear smouldered in the men's eyes. Their leader never spoke, but pressed on down the tunnel, silhouetted in the light of his torch.

The men had heard whispers about mines deep in the desert, and a nameless raksas. Probably these man-eating demons were just stories, but Sharfeat told them nothing. All they knew was that life was cheap to him. He left men with sunstroke, and horses that went lame, to die in the desert.

Sharfeat was marshal of the army of Macron, the greatest kingdom of Ardunya. Iron-willed and determined, he demanded utter obedience and had no use for failure. He never discussed his plans, not even with Galman, his second-in-command. No one dared ask why they were here; they kept quiet, did exactly as they were told and hoped to get home to tell the tale.

A whisper of wind brushed their faces. Where had it come from? The men exchanged worried looks, the torches flickered wildly; one went out. The wind whipped their faces again, more sharply this time, and blew out all but one torch. One man panicked and turned, but fell heavily in the dark; one screamed with fright; the rest began to pray. Unmoved, their leader got out a flint and re-lit his torch. Suppressing their fear, his men did the same. They set off again.

A minute later, they came to a split in the tunnel. Sharfeat gave his torch to Galman, got out the scroll and examined it again. Torchlight flickered on Sharfeat's sharp nose and pointed beard. Smiling grimly, satisfied at last, he took the left passage, his men huddled behind him. Their boots left no mark on the rocky floor.

———— § ————

At first, they did not hear the footsteps, but then the sound quickly got louder. Silently the men cursed their leader. It was one thing to fight fairly in the open, sword to sword, quite another to face an unseen enemy deep underground. The noise became so intense that the cavern shook; loose rocks fell with a great crash. A wave of heat rolled over them.

The pick of Macron's army trembled with fear, welded to the spot, awaiting their fate. Marshal Sharfeat stood twenty paces in front, calm and confident, feet apart, hands on hips. Round the corner ahead of him lumbered a monstrous figure twice his height. Was it a giant? an ape? It stopped in its tracks and gave a low growl. The soldiers froze in terror; some ran to crouch at the cavern sides, where the monster could not go. It watched them scatter.

Sharfeat never turned. All he said was "Cowards!"

In the flickering torchlight they saw that it shambled like a gorilla, but then it reared up on its hind legs like a gigantic bear. Its leathery hide was dark red and it had a horn like a rhinoceros' between eyes as big as dinner plates. Yet its face was intelligent – or cunning. Its skin was red: it was radiating intense heat.

The beast glared, and each eye became a tunnel of fire whirling round. Then, to their horror, it spoke. "What want?" Its voice was heavy and menacing.

Sharfeat replied in calm and civil tones. "I wish to speak with your master."

"No."

"He will like what I have to say."

The creature growled. "You say. Better be."

At that moment, the wind blew in their faces again, carrying the same eerie whisper. The monster looked back into the blackness, gave a muttered grunt and turned to go. Sharfeat ordered his men "Wait here" and set off after it.

As Sharfeat followed, the beast's hide began to glow so brightly that it lit the whole cavern. It seemed it could control the heat and light emanating from its body. The marshal, stubborn and proud, was so unfazed that he might have been following a footman. In reality he was following a plan.

The high, winding corridor finally opened out into a high cave, its dusty floor empty apart from a pile of bones. The brute led him to the centre, roared once, then retreated to the side, the light from its skin rapidly dimming.

Sharfeat looked around. "Where is Black Mist, your master the raksas?"

"Kneel!" rumbled the beast.

Anxious not to make a false step on his road to power, Sharfeat reluctantly knelt. A thick black fog collected in the darkness to form a massive face hovering in front of him. The face was a mass of shadows apart from the narrowed eyes – red eyes with blank white pupils.

"Speak!"

"I seek your permission, my lord, to rid Macron of its unworthy ruler, descendant of your ancient enemy. The king sent me here, because he believes you can end the famine, but secretly he is plotting to destroy you."

An eerie whisper came from the mist. "He is a fool, but so are you! What makes you think you can replace him?"

Sharfeat pretended to be surprised. "That idea never occurred to me, my lord. Naturally *you* will become supreme ruler, but I would deem it a privilege to be your chief minister. My lord, King Jonda believes only in doing 'good' and worshipping his pathetic god. He does not understand power."

"And you?"

"I worship only you, my lord, most powerful and most worthy," Sharfeat replied smoothly, "My coming here testifies to that."

"LIAR!" Black Mist bellowed, "Your coming here shows that you need my help." The fog began to swirl around him, painfully stinging his face.

"You are all-wise, my lord, and see through me. I came to offer my service in ridding you of your enemy but, as you rightly said, I do need your help."

At these submissive words, the mist retreated. Sharfeat wiped acid from his face and hands.

8

"What help?" said the voice from the black mist.

"My lord, you have rid Ardunya of the coopers, and their crystal no longer exists, but the king is still protected by many holy men and an apothecary. With your blessing, great one, I shall crush them, as one would crush a cockroach, and then seize the Nawab's Gem."

"And I?"

"Your victory will be sure only when the king is toppled. For that, I need a certain noxious liquid taken from the seven-headed snake that people call King Shesha. Give me enough to paralyse the king, that monster of virtue. Then the people will see wonders."

There was a silence. Part of the black mist formed into a fist, holding out a tiny vial of dark liquid. The spirit spoke in a nasty tone.

"Take this souvenir of your visit and give it to the king. He will find I have not forgotten."

"Thank you, my lord. It would be good also to have a gift I could show him, to prove that I did my duty well."

Black Mist chuckled nastily. "You are cunning. Very well: take Khabish. He will obey you."

The beast began to glow, bowing its head humbly to acknowledge the command.

Sharfeat replied with satisfaction, "Thank you, my lord ... you will not be disappointed, I promise you."

"Keep your word. I have a special place for traitors."

Sharfeat did not seem to take this as a threat. His face showed relief, as if a tremendous battle had been won. This was his first step to real power.

"My lord, you will soon see how faithfully I serve you. Farewell." As he followed the beast out of the cave, he thought *You will see. This is only the beginning!* The raksas Kábandha, reading his thoughts, was well pleased at this eagerness to serve him. *This planet has enough walking food to feed all my shadow soldiers, and this villain will find more.*

———— § ————

With just one torch alight, Sharfeat's men were glad to see him reappear, but they shrank back from the beast.

"The raksas has given me Khabish as a token of friendship," said Sharfeat.

"Some friend!" muttered someone.

They trudged towards the mouth of the cave until they caught sight of daylight, then lay down to sleep until nightfall.

As soon as the first moon rose, they set off across the desert with their pack animals and the beast called Khabish. The soldiers were wary of him, though some soon relaxed, knowing he was now on their side. Their general looked at ease too, but he was no fool. For one thing, the beast was many times

Sharfeat's size and strength; for another, no demon would choose their servant for mere brute force, certainly not Black Mist, the most powerful raksas in the whole galaxy. There had to be more to Khabish than strength.

Sharfeat decided to find out more, but he chose a peculiar way of going about it. He was the master, and Khabish had to obey him, as Black Mist had ordered. The general turned to the brute, lumbering along beside his horse, and set out to provoke it.

"So, your master thinks you can be useful?"

The beast looked down at Sharfeat and grunted "*Our* master."

"Yes, yes … that's what I meant. You're big … is that all there is to you?" Sharfeat sounded unimpressed.

"Like see?" the beast growled.

The men riding behind were unsettled. What was the general thinking of, talking to such a mighty beast in this way? With its massive fangs, it could easily take a bite out of him, or flatten him *and* his horse. Yet Sharfeat showed no fear; he was the boss, stamping his authority.

Khabish also had a point to prove. He reared up, picked Sharfeat from his horse with one paw and looked upwards. The general dangling in mid-air and his men on horseback gazed up at the violet sky and fell silent, overcome with astonishment. High above, hundreds of large, bat-like creatures were following them across the desert, steadily keeping station, a silent aerial escort filling the sky with moving black shapes. Sharfeat was as awe-struck as his men.

"They obey," Khabish growled, before lowering Sharfeat onto the sand as nervous chatter broke out among his men.

The general picked himself up, remounted his horse and turned to the beast. "And now they will obey me. I see why our master chose you." His men looked suddenly more confident. "You see, men, what power I now control! I took risks; I made my own luck; with Khabish and his mighty force, I shall achieve what I promised. This marks the beginning of a new age, when we who understand power, and value it, claim our right to it. We shall decide the destiny of this world."

The men cheered Sharfeat, while Khabish looked on and the shadowbats circled silently overhead. As far as any eye could see in the moonlight, there was no one else to hear this declaration of war; but Black Mist heard it. The general and his force set off again with new vigour, towards civilisation.

The kingdom, tranquil and modestly prosperous for centuries, was about to be devastated by two equally terrible forces. The people of Macron slumbered quietly, deep in dreamless sleep. King Jonda dreamed that one of his envoys had returned just in time, with good news. Sharfeat, wide awake, dreamed of re-writing the history of the worlds. Jack was in another world, dreaming of the breakfast he had missed.

3 A small world

Wellington Spa School was just an ordinary secondary school next to a housing estate. It wasn't new, it wasn't really old, and its exam results kept a low profile near the bottom of the league tables. Those who could, sent their children to a private or faith school, but that meant money or the right piece of paper. Jack went to Wellington Spa.

It was the autumn term, and he and Meena were in the top set again for maths and science – admired by some, ignored by others. Year 9 was housed in a massive Victorian pile, set among trees and tired lawns. Behind it were the 'new' blocks, even more worn-out, though in the 1960s they gave the school a modern look, more classrooms and new laboratories. Beyond were bleak, muddy, featureless fields.

The teachers were a mixture: some were really interesting; others just earned their pensions. Still, there was always the professor's lab. Jack and Meena went there every Saturday to do their homework, to see what Professor Shreddon was working on and try experiments of their own. Meena was researching how often Jack realised he was being teased, recording her results each week on a graph; it hadn't yet occurred to Jack to study people.

Meena and Jack were never bored. At home they had jobs to do and their minds were constantly busy, but they looked forward to school because of their friends – who were fun and full of ideas. They were all a bit different. What made them friends was probably that they didn't mind being different.

Among them Jack stood out, and would have stood out from the best and brightest 13-year-olds anywhere. His teachers had never known anyone grasp an idea or pick up facts so quickly. Some said he was a genius, especially in science. Four-year-olds are forever asking 'Why?' Jack was one of those rare people who had never stopped asking why. Often he would analyse a problem, ponder a moment, check something and bang: he had the answer.

——— § ———

Just now, though, Jack didn't want to stand out. He scurried along the corridor, glancing up at the clock: it was 9.20. Even school assembly was over. He was very, very late and there would be trouble ahead. Friday lesson one was art with their form tutor, Mrs Gutten. Reaching 9G, he slowly and silently opened the door, at the back of the art room; he might get to his desk in the back row without being detected.

Mrs Gutten didn't look like an art teacher. She was a tall, skinny woman in her forties, with a sharp nose holding up small, square glasses. Her brown hair was tied behind in a knot; her clothes were businesslike. She was writing something on the board about Vincent Van Gogh, her back to the room, but the class was quiet and even mildly attentive. People didn't mess about with

The boy with the violet eyes

Mrs Gutten. Jack inched along behind the back row, getting a sympathetic smile from David. He was just sliding into his seat when Tom spotted him.

Tom Atkinson loved school, for all the wrong reasons. He was big for his age, bursting out of his clothes, with a ham-like face, hardly any neck and thick, curly brown hair. He was a bit fat actually, but to Tom this was an asset. It gave him power, and he enjoyed power because he could make bad things happen to people. He was a bully, who despised children like Jack.

He would pick on anybody who was too small or too clever for his liking, even someone with the wrong clothes or hairstyle or skin. Basically, anyone who didn't resemble Tom was asking for it. If their parents or older brother intervened, Tom moved on to another victim.

He'd already done his homework on Jack, who was definitely asking for it: his dad was dead, his mum was ill, he didn't have a brother or sister, he was too clever by half – and he had those stupid purple eyes. He also delivered papers for Meena's dad, so obviously he could nick things: Tom had ordered cigarettes. All this clicked into place in his mind as he saw Jack creeping to his desk. Tom coughed exaggeratedly.

Mrs Gutten turned to see what the fuss was, and her piercing eyes fell on Jack, sliding to a halt. Tom smirked and leaned back, waiting for trouble and ready to enjoy it. Mrs Gutten laid her marker down and put her hands on her hips, looking stern.

"Jack, you'd better have a good excuse today." She sounded calm, though her eyebrows were twitching.

"I slept in, miss." Jack spoke quietly.

Mrs Gutten was not going to let him off so easily. "This is three times running you've been late." She waited for a response, her foot tapping the floor. "Well?"

The eyes of the whole class were fixed on Jack.

"Sorry, miss … couldn't help it."

This sounded pretty weak to the others, but it convinced Mrs Gutten, who knew his circumstances at home. He didn't look as if he'd slept very well.

"You'd better come and explain yourself after the lesson."

Tom was gobsmacked. Why had she let Jack off? Tom wanted Jack in trouble, caught stealing into the classroom or stealing ciggies, so he could enjoy watching him suffer. That was Tom and his twisted mind. Well, Jack might have escaped punishment from Mrs Gutten, but he'd get it from Tom, who was furious at his plot being thwarted.

Unaware of Tom's malicious plans, Jack sat down and tried to pay attention, but his mind was elsewhere. *Who was following me? Why? I was chased in my dreams; maybe I just dreamt I was chased down the street. Maybe I'm paranoid?*

Mrs Gutten scanned their dull, motionless faces before asking: "Can anyone name a painting by Van Gogh?"

It went even quieter. Some people screwed up their faces and gazed at the board as if thinking intensely, the way you do, some pretended to write something down when actually they were doodling and the rest looked genuinely blank, until a shy girl sitting next to Jack raised her hand. She was small, with long, straight, shiny dark-brown hair and a short, delicate nose separating her hazel-brown eyes. Mrs Gutten's roving eyes came to a halt at Meena Patel.

"Yes, Meena?"

"*Sunflowers*, miss," she said proudly.

"Very good, Meena. And I hear you did well in your maths test. You lot could learn from her."

If Jack was far ahead in science, Meena was top in maths, though she did well at most subjects. He admired her ability, though he never said so. To the other girls, Meena was rather strange – and not very girly. She had never shown much interest in clothes, make-up or magazines, but she loved shapes, patterns and numbers. She was quiet and serious, yet assertive and brave, enthusiastic and stubborn. It was no accident that she sat next to Jack, but there was nothing soppy about that. They had been friends for years.

Mrs Gutten explained how Van Gogh painted his portraits. Then she got the class to sketch each other, using pastels. Meena enjoyed drawing, but she'd never tried a portrait. She studied Jack's face, and in the end her sketch did look a bit like him. It gave her a funny feeling every time she looked up, to see him gazing intently at her face. No doubt he did his best, but his drawing made her look like a witch.

At the end of the lesson, Jack explained to his form tutor that his mum had been ill and that he'd stayed until she recovered, which was sort of true.

Mrs Gutten not only let him off, but wanted to help. "You've done very well up to now, Jack, but I think looking after your mum is getting too much for you. Nurse Dixon visits, doesn't she? I'll have a word with her."

Jack protested, but Mrs Gutten insisted. Why did she have to stir trouble? How could he stop Nurse Dixon putting his mother in hospital?

——— § ———

David, Andromeda, Lloyd, Jack and Meena always brought a packed lunch and sat at the same table. David, a modest boy with freckles, was a good listener. He liked music and quickly tuned in to other people. Andromeda liked to read people's palms and tell them their fate. Her father, an amateur astronomer, had named her after a star; he was horrified when she inherited her mother's belief in astrology. If anyone asked Lloyd why he was so happy, he would grin and say "Man, I'm saved!" He and his mother went to a Pentecostal church and he didn't care who knew.

Lunch was a bright spot in the day for these five classmates: they enjoyed their food and conversation. Their table was in one corner and usually nobody bothered them. Across the room, Tom and his mates were busy swapping rude jokes, unaware that Kyra and her mates were busy laughing at *him*.

Jack pretended he wasn't hungry, but nobody believed him. Meena was happy to share her lunch. David offered him a cheesy snack, Andromeda shared her drink and Lloyd gave him a plum. Jack asked Meena whether she knew what shape the flight of an arrow made.

"A parabola."

"Do you know the formula for a parabola?"

"There are lots of them, Jack! Why?"

"To work out how far an arrow would travel."

"But you haven't a bow – have you?"

"No, it's just an idea."

"Well, an arrow takes the same time to fall whether you fire it or drop it. The time is $\sqrt{2h/g}$ – so the distance depends how tall you are."

Jack wrote the formula on his hand for later.

Meena asked if he'd enjoyed her book.

He blushed. "Sorry, I forgot to bring it." But he had some questions about it, and everyone had an opinion. They'd all read it except Lloyd, who asked to borrow it. As Jack wolfed down a sandwich, David was explaining that actually Alice was a pawn in a chess game, when Meena noticed Tom's lot getting up from their table and coming over. Tom stopped behind her, opposite Jack, who glanced up, then resumed his conversation with David.

"Sucking up to Miss again?"

Jack tried to ignore Tom and asked David something, but David had gone pale and wasn't listening. Meena knew that Jack wouldn't tackle the bully: he wasn't brave like that. Tom knew it too. Well, maybe Jack wasn't interested in a fight now, but Tom could change that.

Meena stood up and spoke in a loud, clear voice that carried across several tables. "Go away, Tom. Pick on somebody your own size."

She didn't mean anything bad by this, but Tom took the mention of size personally. He took both Meena's cheeks in one big hand and squeezed, forcing her lips into a circle. He was so close, she could smell his breath. At the end of the table, Lloyd stood up. Tom let go of Meena's cheeks and pushed his fist up against her nose.

"Keep your sniffer out of this, nerd. I'm talking to your boyfriend."

Most of Class 9G were aware that, to Meena, Jack was nowadays a bit more than just a friend, though he was quite oblivious of it. She flared up

14

angrily and knocked Tom's arm aside, ready to take him on. Tom took a step back, then disguised his retreat by marching round the table to Jack. His gang stood as if frozen. Lloyd opened his mouth and closed it again.

Jack was nervous, but he couldn't just sit there; he had to stand up for Meena. He stood and faced Tom. "Leave it out, Tom. I was late, Mrs Gutten let me off. What's the big deal?"

Tom smirked and took two steps closer: too close. He spoke in an undertone. "The deal is, you get me fags from your girlfriend's shop – simples – if you know what's good for you."

"I'm not nicking from Mr Patel." Jack was genuinely horrified.

"Course you can. He'll never know."

"I can't, Tom. You do your own dirty work."

"You—"

"Stick it, Tom!" shouted Kyra across the room, "Don't let Jack push you around!" She and her mates collapsed in giggles.

The teacher on lunch duty spotted the confrontation. Seeing Mr Collins moving in, Tom decided to let it drop, for now. His gang moved off, sniggering. Jack sat down again and Tom gave him an unpleasant smile.

"See you later, Jack … take care."

Mr Collins went back to patrolling the dining room.

Meena turned to Jack. "Ignore him. He's a jerk."

"Not much of a career, that," said Lloyd.

David chipped in. "Best to stick to what he's bad at!"

The joke was feeble, but it broke the tension. They laughed, got up from the table and cleared away. Jack caught sight of the red marks on Meena's cheeks, and his violet eyes widened. "You've got guts, Meena. You stand up to people. I can't."

"You just did. And he did back down." Meena hadn't heard the talk about the shop.

"I was just about to deck him," added Lloyd, unconvincingly.

"His stars are bad this week anyway," put in Andromeda, "I worked out his horror-scope. You can't escape Fate."

Andromeda's quaint ideas made Jack smile, until he recalled the events on his way to school – like any scientist reviewing the evidence. It wasn't Tom following him: he was in class first. *So who – or what – was stalking me? Fate? Is there such a thing? Fate sounds like luck to me, and I don't believe in luck. That's sad: I could do with some. All I know is, I'm scared. And I can't tell anyone: even Meena and Mum would just laugh.*

———— § ————

That afternoon, it was science in the new block with Miss Quigley. When 'Squiggly' had run through the theory of acids and metal oxides – and mentioned fun uses for salts, like laxatives and gunpowder – she made boys pair up with girls, which wasn't generally popular, though everyone got more work done. Jack and Meena had a bench facing the window, overlooking the playing fields. Today they were making copper sulphate. Jack had done this before, but it was no good saying so. Schools aren't meant for people who know things.

He was about to pour the solvent from the glass beaker through a filter when he glimpsed a face at the window. He glanced up. Someone, in what looked like oriental clothes, was staring in, searching for someone. Their eyes met, as if they knew each other. Then the face slipped below the window sill.

Astonished, Jack froze. The beaker slipped from his hand and hit the floor, shattering into tiny shards on impact. The whole class stopped and stared. Jack, in shock, was unaware of them or the smashed beaker. Meena, with no idea why he had dropped it, was just as confused.

"What's wrong with you, Jack?" Miss Quigley snapped. She didn't like anything out of the ordinary, especially during practicals. "Mrs Gutten said you interrupted her art lesson this morning, and now look at the mess you've made!"

"Miss?" Jack was still trying to make sense of events.

"Just leave what you're doing, Jack, and go and see Mr Williams. You too, Meena."

"But, Miss, I—"

"Both of you, NOW!" Miss Quigley pointed to the door.

Meena was embarrassed and indignant, but she wouldn't answer back. Jack was hardly aware he was in trouble. Tom wasn't in their set, but one of his sidekicks would tell him the good news. Mrs Gutten had ruined Tom's little ploy this morning, but Squiggly was making up for that. The pair picked up their bags and walked to the door; the class watched them go.

Miss Quigley had not quite finished. "I suggest you do the experiment again at home. You can do it together – I happen to know you have all the equipment you need."

Everyone erupted in laughter, one of Tom's goons leading the way. Miss Quigley turned and said coldly, "Would you like to join them?" The class fell silent.

———— § ————

Jack began striding down the corridor. He wanted to get this interview over, so he could find whoever had been watching him. Meena ran past him, turned and stopped.

"Thanks for getting me in trouble, Jack. What was that about?"

He tried to explain as they set off again. "It wasn't my fault."

"What are you on about? Nobody knocked you." Meena was vexed, but baffled too.

"Somebody stared at me."

"And that made you drop the beaker?"

"Well … yeah."

"You didn't mind me staring when we were drawing portraits," Meena said, half-teasingly; Jack went red. "Miss Quigley's right: you *are* acting weird today."

"Don't *you* start!" Jack raised his voice, just as the head of Year 9 came out of his office.

"Jack? Meena? I'm surprised to see you two here, of all people."

Mr Williams led them into his office. Jack wanted to get his side of the story in first.

"Sir, there's been a misunderstanding between us and Miss Quigley."

Meena stiffened at the word 'us'. Jack didn't notice.

"We didn't do anything wrong, sir—"

"That's one side of the story," Mr Williams interrupted. "Did Miss Quigley do something wrong? What do you say, Meena?"

"Jack dropped a beaker because he thought someone stared at him. Miss Quigley was angry."

"I'm not surprised! Jack, you're one of our best pupils, but you can't afford to dream. I only want to hear good things about you. Miss Quigley is an excellent teacher; if you annoy her, you can expect trouble. Is that understood?"

Jack nodded. Meena spoke for both of them: "Yes, Mr Williams."

Finding they had been given extra homework, he let it go at that.

As they left the office, Meena breathed a sigh of relief. "That was close. Good job Mr Williams was in a good mood."

Jack hardly heard. The face at the window must belong to the footsteps that followed him, but it still didn't make sense. And he couldn't tell anyone: they would think he was weird. Miss Quigley probably did already. Actually, if he was hearing and seeing people who weren't there, the evidence suggested he *was* weird. Perhaps he could design an experiment to test for weirdness.

Meena, seeing herself ignored again, caught his shoulder. "You're unbelievable, Jack, you know that?"

Jack was surprised. "Oh, thanks!" Then he saw she looked agitated; he realised he hadn't quite understood. "You mean you don't believe me?"

"I don't know what to believe. You say someone stared at you – but you were facing a first-floor window. You need to sort this business out before we get into any more trouble." She waited for a response – after all, she *had* said

The boy with the violet eyes

'we' and she *was* hoping to do the sorting – but Jack's thoughts seemed far away. She liked him being different, but not weird. "Are you even listening?"

"I'm sorry, Meena, I need to think this out. Okay?"

She opened her mouth, but her voice was drowned by the din of the school bell. It was home time, and they headed for the cloakroom. All at once they were engulfed by a flood of people – shouting, running, jostling. Meena and Jack struggled to collect their coats, said goodbye to David and Andromeda, returned Lloyd's cheery wave and headed for the door, to some rude comments from the jokers. Jack didn't notice; Meena was too proud to.

Since Jack delivered the evening papers for Meena's dad, they usually walked together to the shop. She hoped he wouldn't notice if anyone stared at him on the way.

4 Seeing is believing

They made their way silently down the steps through the usual deafening mob. They turned right to cross the school fields, past the pitches and the running track. Beyond that, the ground dropped away into a little valley, a pretty spot where a back gate brought you out on Toft Lane, the shortest way to Meena's father's shop.

The noisy crowd had fallen behind. Jack and Meena, each wrapped in their own thoughts, walked down the slope to where the school fence followed a line of old trees by a stream. School was lost to sight beyond the slope. As they neared the gate, Jack began to feel uneasy. Were they being followed? He sensed something was about to happen.

——— § ———

Meena's warning came too late. Several boys seized Jack from behind and wrestled him to the ground. Jack dropped his bag and tried desperately to wriggle his way out of their hold. Each time he tried to stand up, they pushed him back into the mud, laughing nastily.

He was trapped, pinned down. Two others grabbed Meena. She shrieked and kicked, trying to break free, but the boys were stronger and held her, twisting her arms tightly. Two of the gang dragged Jack to his feet. From behind an oak tree, out stepped Tom, smirking, swaggering, fist cracking against his palm. Jack cringed and closed his eyes, waiting for the first punch or kick – but none came. He looked up. Their eyes met.

"Listen, geek, I gotta job for you."

"I ... I've already told you—"

"Yeah. Mummy don't like you getting your hands dirty."

Meena jumped in sarcastically. "Looks like *your* mummy doesn't mind."

"Shut it, shorty. Okay, wimp, go get the ciggies."

While Jack was wondering what to say, Meena said, "You can't buy cigarettes at our age, fathead!"

Jack admired her nerve. She might be small for her age, and the gang might be pinning her so she couldn't move, but she wasn't intimidated. He knew she was annoyed with him – getting her in trouble, not explaining – and she looked angry. Not with him though: with Tom.

Despite his size, Tom wasn't slow. In a few steps he was in front of Meena. "Who said *buy*? You keep outa this." With one big hand he squeezed Meena's cheeks again, forcing them in until she was red in the face. Tom liked hurting girls – his interest in them ended there. Still grasping her face, he thrust her away and she fell sprawling beside the tree.

"Leave her alone!" Jack was angry now.

Tom sniggered, signalling to his mates. One gave Jack a hefty push and sent him crashing into the fence. The broken wire caught his shoulder, ripping his blazer and sawing at his skin. Tom grabbed Jack and half-wrestled, half-dragged him over to the oak. He forced him up against the tree trunk, one fist in Jack's stomach, the other gripping his collar.

"I told you nicely a pack of twenty – seems you don't like nice." His tone changed from sarcastic to menacing. "Now get down that shop now and make it forty … OR ELSE!"

Jack wondered what 'else' might be. He could say he'd get the cigarettes, only Meena might believe it. He wanted to look good in her eyes – but even in his dreams he wasn't a hero: she was. She still hadn't got up. Maybe if he let them beat *him* up, they wouldn't touch *her*. He couldn't face her dad if they did that. He'd have to give up his paper round – but what he earned, little as it was, helped make ends meet. *What should I do? Class tests have answers; life is a test where there aren't any answers – or you don't know them.*

"I'm waiting, wimp. What's it gonna be?"

Jack was still thinking.

Tom decided he needed a little encouragement. He brought his fist back, ready.

"No!" said Jack.

Don't hit me, he meant, but Tom took it for an answer. He rammed his fist into Jack's stomach. Meena cried out in anguish; the gang ignored her. Tom landed another punch and after that the rest joined in, kicking and punching Jack, cheering each other on.

Jack had no idea how to fight. He cowered, trying to fend off the hail of blows. They kept on until he subsided to his knees, choking, bruised. Tears started, tears of pain but anger too – anger at the unfairness of it all, anger with himself that he didn't fight back, anger that Meena had seen him beaten up. The yobs, still jeering but losing interest, began to drift off.

Meena stood up. Jack was on his knees, gasping with pain. She helped him up. He had a swelling under his left eye, mud on his trousers and shirt, a rip in his blazer. The gang looked back to admire their handiwork. The smirk on their faces vanished at the sight of Jack standing up. He should have stayed down until they had gone.

——————— § ———————

Tom couldn't let his gang see this show of defiance. He strode back, disgust on his face. Meena stepped forward, but Tom pushed her aside. As he drew back his fist, a whirl of leaves and dust shot between them. Jack was confused by the roaring noise. Some grit lodged in one eye, so he shut them both, trying to stay upright, expecting the worst.

The others also shut their eyes to keep out the swirling dust and grit that was sandpapering their faces. They were knocked about by gusts of wind that nearly lifted them off their feet. Jack had no idea what was going on, until the noise died away again and he cautiously squinted through one eye, wondering why Tom had not hit him. Tom was not there.

Now the sand and leaves were settling, the rest opened their eyes. They stared, baffled. There was just a space where Tom had been. Then they heard a far-off cry like a young seagull that had lost its way. Someone pointed. High up, falling from a blue sky, was the increasingly recognisable shape of Tom Atkinson.

Jack stared. *How did he get up there?* It seemed impossible. He would not have believed his eyes, except that the others could obviously see what he saw too. The gang, fascinated and horrified, gaped as Tom crashed into the topmost branches of the oak. A flurry of leaves and twigs descended, followed by an ominous pause.

Tom's main sidekick, Alec, a tall, wiry boy with red hair, screamed "The tree's got hold of Tom! It's spooky!" It was as good an explanation as any – good enough for the yobs. Forgetting Tom, fearing they might be next, his so-called friends scurried back up the hill.

When the tough guys had run away, there was an eerie silence. Meena straightened her clothes. Jack still looked shocked and bewildered, so she began to clean up his face. Pulling himself together, he took a few tissues from her and got the worst of the mud off his hands, then tucked his shirt back in. Both breathing more easily, they backed away from the oak tree, fearing that the tornado, or whatever it was, might return. Instead they heard leaves rustle, branches splinter and twigs snap. Tom Atkinson was falling heavily from branch to bough, finally landing with a loud splat in the mud.

He had blood running from his nose, his face was battered and his torn clothes revealed several nasty cuts. He was trying to get to his feet, only to keep slipping, falling over and rising even filthier than before. They couldn't help feeling sorry for him, though he had got what he deserved. Dizzy, shocked and scared, Tom at last found his footing. He never looked at Jack or Meena. He made a desperate run for the gate, limping badly and whimpering. They let him go.

———— § ————

Meena was pondering. Was Andromeda right, and it was all in Tom's horoscope? Was it fate? Was it magic? Could Jack offer a scientific explanation?

Not at the moment he couldn't. Jack's faith was shaken. He had always believed in a logical, scientific reason for everything, but he had no explanation for what he had just seen. He had read that the sky sometimes rained frogs or fish, but not boys – though it sucked a girl up in the sky in *The Wizard of Oz*.

The boy with the violet eyes

Was that real? How could the wind throw Tom high in the air? Why hadn't it taken Jack too? There had to be a reason.

Unnerved, they walked to the road in silence. Jack's watch said 3.52pm, not too late for his paper round. It was calm and pleasant. The sun shone, birds sang and no boys fell from the blue sky, only the first leaves of autumn. They looked back several times, but saw nothing unusual. Everything seemed normal – until they faced the road again. In the middle of Toft Lane was a figure.

Seconds ago, there had been no one in sight in any direction. This creature had silently appeared. Jack controlled his fear, wanting to make sense of this new situation. Astonished, Meena drew in her breath, ready for whatever threat they faced next.

The new arrival was quite a spectacle. Jack observed a human figure almost his own size, smooth-skinned and slightly tanned, with blue, leaf-shaped eyes but no eyebrows, pointy, elfin ears and a small, flat nose, wearing what looked like traditional Indian garments – anyone from the nearby estate would wonder where the wedding was.

Meena noticed first the blue bundi, heavily embroidered with gold and jewels. This long waistcoat was worn over cream shalwar kameez, a loose top and trousers, made of some very fine fabric. The serious, intelligent face was framed by long black hair topped with a domed turban. He didn't seem much of a threat. If anything, he looked apologetic, with hands clasped and eyes downcast, sneaking glances at them from under long eyelashes while standing calmly in the middle of the road.

"W ... What ...?" stammered Jack.

"Fret not. My name is Aseem," said the stranger. He sounded anxious.

He had expected a more respectful welcome. His journey had gone well, but after that things had gone from bad to worse. This boy Jack was unpredictable and this planet seemed almost as disorderly as the one he had just come from.

5 So you say

"Who?" Jack tensed, ready for any sudden movement.

"I am Aseem, from the planet Ardunya in the galaxy Hexades. I am prince of Macron." He spoke easily, as if expecting to be taken seriously, but also as if he had rehearsed his lines.

There was an awkward pause. Jack did not feel equal to this situation and stepped back; Meena did the same and Aseem followed. In formation they edged towards the school fence. Jack's mind began working again. He was intrigued by this odd figure, while wanting to laugh at the odd way he spoke.

Meena's reaction was to challenge him. "What do you want, Aseem?"

Aseem pointed at Jack, who took a step back. "I was searching for you," said the boy, responding to Meena but gazing straight into Jack's eyes.

It's rude to stare. Is he trying to hypnotise me? Jack felt apprehensive: this was like a bad dream. Maybe it *was* a bad dream? Maybe it wasn't even time to get up yet, and he wouldn't be late for school after all. He put a hand up to his face, and flinched as it touched the swelling below his eye. No, this was real. It was the strangest day of his life – followed, watched, twice in trouble, ambushed, Tom in the air and now this ghostly prince – but apparently it was all real.

Could this Aseem, if that *was* his name, really be from another planet? It would explain how he had apparently dropped from the sky and landed in Toft Lane. Yet why on Earth was he looking for Jack? Jack wasn't sure he wanted to know, though he was very tempted to ask. Abruptly he decided not to get involved: strangers meant trouble. Easier just to walk away, keep a low profile and pretend nothing had happened – except this weirdo might follow him. You can't keep a low profile with an alien in fancy dress stalking you.

———— § ————

Was he following me to school? As Jack asked himself this, Aseem answered.

"It was I followed your footsteps. I used my inward energy to scare away those bandits also. I much regret alarming you. I have come far to seek your aid."

If he can read my mind, I can't outsmart him. If he shot Tom up in the air, I'm not safe. Fear can make you nasty. Jack lashed out: "You followed me? I've heard about people like you."

"I am not an earthling. If I seem strange, it is because—"

"You're weird!" finished Jack.

Meena gasped and felt her face flush. She had never heard Jack be deliberately rude, and she didn't like it. Anyway, did he want another fight? He couldn't be thinking straight.

Aseem did not understand Jack's words, but he knew a sneer when he saw one. He stood straighter and his tone changed. "I am crown prince. I am unaccustomed to insolence from a commoner. It is honourable to serve the crown, and even the simple can be courteous."

Jack thought this was some kind of wind-up. "Get real! Crown prince? What are you on?"

Luckily, Aseem had no idea what sarcasm was. He was out of his depth in this strange culture, so far from home. He took a deep breath and spread his arms diplomatically. Meena saw that each hand had six fingers.

"Please outhear me," he pleaded.

"He's lost it," Jack whispered to Meena, raising his eyes in mock-despair.

Meena was embarrassed, but she tried to be fair: if Jack had been tailed by an alien and beaten up, no wonder he'd lost his grip. She was also very curious: what did this strange, serious boy want?

"How can Jack help you, Aseem?"

Jack too was curious. Aseem seemed pretty clueless, just as if he *had* dropped in from another galaxy. His language was sophisticated, if odd and old-fashioned, his voice cultured, just as if he *were* a prince. His manner was princely too.

Seeing he had Jack's attention, Aseem answered Meena. "My land is imperilled and my father is petrified. We have searched and searched for one of Jack's family to save us. Unless you are his sister, he is the only one left."

Jack tried to take all this in: danger, fear, last of his family. His mother was alive: this must be his father's family. He knew nothing about them, not even the names of his father's parents. Why had he never asked? Other people had normal lives and families; why couldn't he? Why did his father visit his dreams? He went pale and silent; he felt as if the ground was subsiding under his feet.

Meena spoke. "I'm Jack's friend. What is your father petrified of?"

"Of stone ... he is now but a statue. Let me show you the tree."

He brought out a small cotton bag, untied the string round its neck, thrust in his hand and pulled out some tatty, rolled-up paper. He brandished it.

"It is your lineage!"

They stared, bemused. Meena voiced Jack's question for him. "His what?"

"His genealogy ... his pedigree."

Jack couldn't see what the study of rocks had to do with dog food, or what either of them had to do with him. He was out of his depth here.

Aseem looked exasperated, and exposed the middle of the scroll. It had short lines running across and down, joining words and phrases in some unusual calligraphy. Beside each word was a picture. Meena went closer to get a better look.

"Meena!" This had to be a trick. Was she being sucked in? He didn't want anything to happen to her.

"It's all right, Jack," she said, gesturing to him to calm down. He muttered a rude word, making sure she couldn't quite hear what it was. "That's impressive, Aseem," said Meena encouragingly, "Could I see a bit more?"

The boy nodded gravely and began unrolling it further. The parchment was very old and creased. Meena gently took the foot of it and rolled up the scroll as the prince let the top unroll. Unsure what she was meant to see, Meena looked closer. She couldn't read the writing, but it looked rather like the Devangari script in the Hindi newspapers and Sanskrit storybooks at home. It was some kind of diagram; she wondered why every word had a tick through it.

At length, they reached the top, which was even more tattered than the rest. Meena's eyes widened and her mouth fell open. She looked at Jack, then at the scroll; then she turned to gaze at Jack again. Her hazel eyes searched his violet ones.

——— § ———

Jack stood, startled. This wasn't like drawing portraits in art class. Meena had never stared at him like this before. He had once or twice imagined how it would feel to be the centre of her attention. In daydreams, it felt delightful; now he felt uneasy.

Jack broke the tense silence. "What?"

Meena was still blatantly staring, first at Jack, then at the scroll.

"Why are you staring at me like that?"

"It's you!" Meena said.

"What is?" replied Jack, more baffled than ever.

"This picture at the top, it's you ..."

One eyebrow raised in disbelief, Jack strode up and grabbed the scroll. The next moment, a look of fear froze his face. His lips parted, but no sound came. At the head of this clearly ancient parchment was a pen-and-ink drawing, lightly coloured in, slightly faded but clear enough, of him – or a face with a staggering resemblance to his, right down to his violet eyes.

"What's my face doing on this scroll?" he demanded, as face stared back at him.

"You are he whom we sought! How else is this portrait here?"

"Maybe you drew it." Looking for a way out, Jack said the first thing that came into his head.

Meena wanted to find a way forward, but she tried to make it easier for Jack. "What's this language, Aseem? Can you read it?"

"Who cares?" said Jack.

"Stop getting stressed, will you? Give him a chance." He had to listen: this document was about him. Even if *he* didn't want to know what it meant, *she* did.

25

Jack saw it must be genuine, but he was scared. Wherever this Aseem went, strange things happened. Now he wanted Jack to help him. *What if I turn to stone or disappear? Mum would end up in hospital. If they think I'm chicken, tough. I can live with that.*

"Look, you've got the wrong guy."

"Jack, think! There has to be a reason for this picture. Course you want to know what this is all about."

She was on his side – and she was right. If he said 'I can't leave Mum', he'd sound feeble. He sounded feeble anyway: "But … we don't know what we're getting into."

"And we never *will* know if you don't use your head. I thought you were into science? You've seen Tom fly and Aseem pop up from nowhere. How come you're not asking questions?"

"Okay, how did you make Tom fly?"

"The bandit? I meditated to build my inward energy, then I focused it on him and let go," Aseem answered. Jack now had at least four new questions.

———— § ————

"Well, tell us more then. I haven't got all day." Jack felt sure he'd find a flaw in the story, so he could dismiss it, Meena would side with him and Aseem would go back where he came from. No hard feelings.

Meena felt sure curiosity would get the better of Jack. He *had* to know.

Aseem said, "I am glad you are no longer cantankerous. First: this is not a picture of you."

"But it is!" exclaimed Meena.

"So it was a trick," said Jack, vexed.

"Not so. This is a portrait of your ancestor Amal Barelas, made over a thousand years ago, in his lifetime. This is his family tree. Your name is at the foot; we had no picture of you, but we had one of your father, and your name, age and resemblance identified you."

"You've got a picture of my dad? Let me see!" Jack was suddenly eager.

"Of course. You wish to compare it with pictures you have at home."

"No. I've never seen a picture of my dad. Can I see it, please?" It was Jack's turn to beg.

"That is strange. One moment, please." Aseem rolled up the scroll at the top and Meena unrolled the foot, while Jack waited tensely.

Reaching the end, Aseem pointed to a name without a tick through it. "That is your name."

There was a pause.

"So you say. *I* can't read it, can I?"

"I am sorry. I was thinking your father would teach you to read."

Aseem was simply surprised, but Jack took his words for contempt. It was too much.

"I never knew him. He died when I was a baby. And I *can* read, but not this rubbish."

The violet eyes misted over. Suddenly he missed the dad of his dreams and everything they could have done. He tried to wipe his eyes, hardly aware of Meena gently putting an arm around him. She gave him another tissue and he blew his nose.

Aseem spoke. "I am much regretting that I chose my words ill. Hakeema says I can be most thoughtless. Please forgive me and accept my profound sympathy on the death of your father. If you will dry your eyes" – he offered Jack a fresh handkerchief of soft blue silk – "You will see your father's portrait." He pointed to a miniature at the foot of the scroll.

The coloured drawing was not much bigger than a postage stamp, yet it was far more than a sketch. It showed the head of a young man with lots of curly brown hair, slightly pointed ears, a neat beard, violet eyes and a serious – even sad – expression. The face was handsome, stronger and more assured – but otherwise it was Jack's face.

"Here is writ his name, Janardan Barelas."

"My dad was Jonathan Cooper."

"Say you so? Doubtless he changed his name, for he fled to your planet to elude the raksas Kábandha. Jonathan is very like Janardan, and Barelas is the same as Cooper."

"What do they mean?"

"Janardan is 'one who helps people'," said Meena, "And doesn't Aseem mean 'eternal'?"

"Indeed. Your friend has great learning," said Aseem admiringly, "They say your father was well named: he always helped others before himself – and Barelas means 'cooper'."

"What's a cooper?"

"In your language it is a barrel-maker."

"My father was a joiner!"

"So is a cooper!" said Meena, "But how do you know all this, Aseem?"

"Long ago, we had great lore and skill. Witches and wizards fathomed much that is now too deep for us. In the centuries after the barbarian times, their scrolls gathered dust – all but the Barelas tree. We knew it must be kept up to date, though we forgot why. When disaster threatened and even the wise knew not what to do, one recalled the prophecy on this scroll."

"What does it say?" asked Meena excitedly.

"A wise woman translated it for you, though she misdoubted certain words. One moment." Aseem gave the roll to Meena, reached into his cotton bag again and brought out a very small scroll. He unrolled it and read:

When black flowers the kingdom overwhelm
And rats devour the blossoms, crops and seeds,
When black shadows cross the royal realm,
Double darkness shrouding darker deeds,
Then is the time of famine, plague and treason,
Evil magic, slavery and war,
The end of things, but only for a season:
A barrel-maker shall the land restore.
 One who is named in this family history,
 Yielding rare power to the jewel of mystery,
 A youngster, mayhap – no hero, but brave –
 Only a cooper the kingdom can save.

There was a silence. Jack was thinking hard, so Meena spoke. "Is that metaphorical, or d'you ... is it actually ... I mean, have those things happened?"

"It is poesy, so all is not clear, but in Serpis the black flowers bloom, rats are eating the harvest, disease is spreading and people are starving, just as it said. The King's Marshal has turned traitor, and killed or enslaved innocent people. Only *you* can save us, Jack."

"Me?" Aseem's story was so extraordinary that Jack couldn't argue with it, but here was something he *could* argue about. "I couldn't even save *myself – you* did that. My only special skill is getting in trouble. Ask Meena." Here luck was on his side: he had the best friend in the whole world.

Though embarrassed, she rose to the challenge. "Well, Jack can be awkward and absent-minded, and he's a bit full of himself, but he knows what's right, he's kind and loyal, very clever, specially in science, and he's fun too. He's no hero, but he *can* be brave."

Jack was taken aback by this lavish praise, but he had to question the last bit. "Brave? How do you make that out? Those idiots hammered me."

"Yes, but look how many you were facing. And you didn't run."

"Nevertheless," said Aseem, "You are 'one who is named in this family history'."

"Yes, but there are lots of people on that family tree," snapped Jack. "I know most of them are dead, but I bet the rest are bigger and braver than me."

"Mayhap they were," said Aseem quietly, "But their names are struck through."

"I thought those were ticks," put in Meena.

"It means they have died."

"What, all of them?" Jack was shocked.

28

"All but you. The raksas Kábandha has been seeking out your kin and eliminating them, one by one. When the wise ones recalled the prophecy, we searched for a Cooper. Every time we tracked down one of your kinsfolk, Black Mist had got there first."

———— § ————

There was a pause, then Jack said slowly, "Did this Black Mist kill my dad?"

"Most like. He was still a young man when he died."

"Mum's never talked about it." *Why? Was she hiding something? There must be a reason.*

"My dad says 'What you don't know won't hurt', Jack. Could be she wanted to save you from getting hurt."

"She saved you from fear," said Aseem. He seemed older than them, as if he saw the bigger picture: motives, secrets, repercussions – like a prince, in fact. "It is a great thing our parents do for us. Imagine if you had known all your life that someone was hunting you."

"The way you stalked me today? That was well freaky."

"And *I* meant you no harm."

"You mean somebody wants to do me in? Seriously?"

"Yes. You have little time left, unless you act now."

Jack was wary. "You're just trying to scare me. How do I know this is isn't just chat?"

Aseem replied with a rhetorical question: "How else is your portrait on this roll?"

"Jack, think," Meena broke in. "That picture is old, but it's you; Aseem coming out of the blue; Tom going up into it: we can't explain any of this. It's like from another world."

Jack sighed. "Suppose you're right: what do I have to do?"

"Accompany me to my planet, Ardunya, and save my kingdom—"

"You what? How? And what do I do when I get there?"

"I thought you would know that." Aseem sounded tense, as if expecting an explosion.

Sure enough, Jack exploded. "How would *I* know? Look, if you're winding me up, it's not funny; if this is supposed to be real, it's impossible. Someone's out to kill me, and you want me to go and find them? You're crazier than I thought!" (Meena winced.) "What if I never come back? And what proof have you got? A picture of my father – so *you* say. I'm sorry, but that's not enough."

Aseem was stunned: he had never met a commoner so disrespectful as to question a prince or doubt his word. He could not imagine what lay behind Jack's constant arguing. Baffled and disheartened, he was beginning to give up.

"It is as Hakeema warned me," he said.

The boy with the violet eyes

"You mentioned her before," said Meena, fearing that Aseem would vanish and she would never get to the bottom of this. "My grandfather was a *hakeem*. It's a kind of doctor, isn't it?"

"A doctor of medicine, yes: an apothecary. She is my tutor and secretary, who looks after me and handles my affairs. She said you might not respect my wishes. Is it because I am strange, and do not resemble you, that you will not help?"

"Well, you *are* pretty weird," said Jack matter-of-factly, "But you probably think *we* are too. No, it's just so far-fetched."

Aseem didn't know what 'far-fetched' meant, though he wouldn't admit it. "It is true I have come far to fetch you. You are not convinced, yet you would like to be persuaded?"

"I think we both would," said Meena.

Aseem gazed at her thoughtfully. It was clear he took her words seriously, perhaps because she chose them carefully. Suddenly he brightened up and clicked his fingers. "It is simple. Why did I not think of it? I shall *show* you!" He beamed and walked into the middle of the road. "Please to stand here." Luckily, this end of Toft Lane led only to Toft Farm; very few cars came down it. In the distance, on the estate, they heard the chimes of an ice-cream van.

——— § ———

Meena looked encouragingly at Jack and tilted her head briefly, meaning *Come on, then*. She stepped into the road. Aseem, rummaging in the bag under his waistcoat, pulled out a purse with a drawstring neck and took out a white pill. Jack took a step and stopped.

"What's that?" he asked warily.

Meena looked uncertain, but her curiosity kept her there.

"It is strange matter," replied Aseem calmly. "You will see."

"Jack, we have to trust him." Meena stood next to Aseem. After a pause, Jack joined her. Aseem, eyes closed, began murmuring an incantation. This was creepy. Jack feared he might hypnotise them; Meena wondered if it was a magic ritual, but she kept quiet. Jack could not.

"I thought you wanted to show us something?"

"Cease questioning my every move," snapped Aseem. "Come close and cup your hands."

Jack and Meena edged closer, until their shoulders touched. They watched uneasily as Aseem crushed the tablet in his hand, the chalky residue spreading across his palm. He placed a little in their hands, gently rubbing it in, and kept the rest. Then he circled them three times, still muttering as he spread the dust on the ground in a ring around the three of them.

Meena and Jack shuddered as a cold, electric tingling shot up their spines. Next they were shivering too, engulfed by a wind so icy it took their breath

30

away, like jumping into a frozen lake. As the wind shrieked ever more bitterly, purple clouds whirled around and shrouded them in fog, blotting out the world.

They could no longer hear the ice-cream van, nor see the road, nor feel the ground under their feet. They lost all sense of space and time. The freezing wind seemed to go right through their clothes. They felt chilled to their bones and began to lose all feeling. A minute later, quite unexpectedly, the wind became warmer and softer.

The purple clouds began to clear, yet they could see nothing. Had they gone blind from that terrible cold? Then, all at once, the world around them sprang into focus. And what a world! They gazed in sheer astonishment.

6 Ardunya

Sunlight sparkled on a river below him. It wound across a wide valley of tiny, green fields, past a walled city crowded with houses around a great dome. Behind it, moorland merged into low hills. To the left, fields and grassland ended in forest that stretched to the horizon. To the right, bare mountains touched an indigo sky. Jack's mind took memories, like photographs. Below him were treetops: he was moving towards them fast, head first, yet he had no sense of falling.

A moment later he reached the foliage, disturbing twigs and flying things as he passed, until the waistband of his trousers caught on a branch and he lurched to a halt, dangling. He reached out for the tree, but missed. Either the waistband or the branch seemed to give and he sank through the greenery, frantically trying to grab anything that would halt his progress downwards. At last he slid to a halt, on a sloping bough wide enough to walk on.

He couldn't see far, but he heard forest-dwellers fleeing in alarm. There was an unpleasant smell in the air. The forest floor was hidden by what looked like bamboo, each spike carrying several little black buds. Had he fallen on a spike, he might now be dead. He looked around to tell Aseem he'd nearly killed them, but Aseem was not there. *Great! 'Trust me' he says. Trust him to drop us in it!*

"Meena?" His voice came out higher than he expected. "Meena!!!" No answer. "Aseem!" Silence. The birds began chattering again. He was alone, in a forest on another planet. He didn't know how he'd got here or how to get back. Fear, never far away, flooded his mind. He shuddered as something touched his face. A huge butterfly fluttered by. Taking a long, deep breath, he forced himself to think. This must be Ardunya.

The others would never find him in this undergrowth. So where would they go? That city he'd seen first – surely they would see it too? If he walked downhill, he would come to it. First he had to get down off the bough. If he jumped, he would impale himself on those spikes. It was no use heading for the trunk: it had no footholds.

Straddling the bough, he slid carefully along until it divided and he took the lower branch. He leant forward, gripping the wood with his arms and legs. It bent under his weight, and he slid smoothly round to hang like a sloth. He lowered his feet carefully between the bamboo plants and finally let go, dropping the last couple of feet.

Something touched his shoe. He looked down to see a large mouse scuttling away. He began to fight his way through the tall plants with the sinister black buds. The sickly smell came from them.

———— § ————

Did Black Mist know he was here? If so, he might die here, without finding Meena or saving anyone. Aseem had tricked them into it. It had never occurred to Jack that the prince would – or could – take them to his planet. 'Give him a chance', Meena had said. Some chance!

You took a chance too, Meena. Why? Aseem wanted me. Was she just curious? Too trusting? Over-confident? Or would she always go where he went? Maybe, though that sounded a bit odd. It was odd that the thought had even crossed his mind. Did she think he couldn't do without her? He'd show her he could manage! He might have to. There was no sign of Meena: maybe she never made it. *Better get moving.*

After ten minutes, he glimpsed daylight through the trees. The wood ended in pasture; a slight breeze ruffled the long grass. Jack cautiously looked out. There was the city, a mile or two away. In between were tiny fields, or at least different crops: there were no walls, fences or hedges. There were windmills, their sails gently turning. Pathways ran here and there between thatched houses – mud-huts really. It looked foreign and mediaeval. Every inch of land was tilled. The fields were as neat as gardens and the crops were lush, though wilting in the heat. *The crops should be in by now: it's the autumn term.* But the leaves were green, if a bit droopy. At home it was autumn; here it was summer.

He could see people digging in the fields, winding a bucket up from a well or tending animals, even a woman washing clothes in a stream. There were no cars or roads, no aerials or overhead wires, no aeroplanes or traffic, no phones, radios or music – apart from a man singing cheerfully in a field. It *was* the middle ages! This was strange, but not threatening.

There would be a palace in the city. Meena would head there to find Aseem; and *he* had to find Aseem too, if only to get home. But maybe the raksas was paying this 'prince' to betray him. Meena was the only person he could trust. He must be careful. His best bet was to look ordinary, but a school blazer and tie were not very mediaeval. He took them off, hid them under a bush and placed two twigs crosswise to mark the spot.

A creaking sound drew his eyes to a track crossing the grassland. A very large dog was pulling a crude cart. The man in the cart was not driving it; in fact he seemed to be asleep, despite the lurching of the cart. Its wheels were just planks joined together and shaped into a rough circle, but it was better than walking. Jack ran through the knee-length grass, down to the track. Even when he ran up to the cart, the dog – a Saint Bernard? – took no interest in him and nor did the man. Since his hood had fallen over his face, he probably hadn't seen Jack, who decided to hitch a lift anyway and climbed on the back.

It was hot; the sun was high in the sky over the city. Jack gazed around to search for enemies. Finding none, he looked back at the forest he had just come from and saw the sun, now much lower in the sky. He looked round wildly. The sun was still high above the city. This world had two suns!

He could not be certain of anything here. He glanced at the cart driver and wondered why he was wearing a cloak on a hot day. The skin of his hands was very white. As one cartwheel sank into a rut, his hood fell back. His face was covered in open sores; flies were feeding on them; his eyes were open, but only the whites showed. He was dead.

Jack jumped down and ran. The sad-looking dog tailed him slowly, the cart groaning and squeaking. People in the fields took no notice. He ran for half a mile until, out of breath, he slowed to a walk. Here, near the city walls, the people looked healthy.

Just before the city gate he caught up with a woman carrying two big baskets. If he followed her through, people might think he was her son. It worked a treat: the guards spoke to her in some foreign language, and she lifted the covers on her panniers to show them the contents. Avoiding their eyes, Jack stared at the baskets and saw that the woman had six fingers on each hand. So did the guards; they never looked at him. Everyone had Aseem's leaf-shaped eyes and ears too. It should be easy to spot Meena. He trailed behind the woman, trying to look fed up.

——— § ———

Beyond the gateway was a broad, cobbled street lined with wooden houses, one or two storeys high. There were no vehicles, though there were plenty of people about. They were dressed very simply in plain colours, in what looked like well-tailored sacks with holes for head and arms.

At a crossroads stood a tall obelisk. Jack climbed some steps to a sort of terrace. Every few yards was an iron tripod, taller than him, containing a boulder carved like a jewel. He tried counting the faces, but gave up at 36.

Below, in the side street, was a market; Jack walked past stalls selling everything from baskets, cloth and tools to weird fruit and vegetables, Persian-style carpets and exotic pets. People were shouting and haggling. It was like a bazaar crossed with a Sunday market. He walked around the end stall and set off down the other side, hoping to find Meena.

A little girl ran towards him, shouting at someone. Jack stopped to see what was going on. To his alarm, the girl ran straight at him, still looking elsewhere. Jack hardly felt her head hit his stomach; he swayed, but she carried on, right through him. A few paces further on, she slowed to a stop, bewildered – like Jack. Clearly scared, she pelted across the road and clutched her friend. Now Jack recalled a few minutes earlier someone almost bumping into him without apologising. He knew now why they hadn't noticed him, despite him looking so different. They couldn't see him.

34

Am I a ghost? Am I dead? If Meena was invisible too, how would they ever find each other? He had to find Aseem and sort this out … if he could see Aseem. He couldn't even ask anyone where Aseem was. He was cut off, alone and invisible in a strange land – and he might be walking into a trap. Black Mist, no longer just in his nightmares, was hunting him. The only thing he could do was find the palace. That wouldn't be invisible.

He made his way back to the obelisk and turned up the main street, keeping warily out of everybody's way. The street curved gently to the right as it climbed, ending in a grand square where ornate fountains made a curtain of spray that hardly seemed to fall. Behind, crowds were hurrying up a magnificent staircase of white marble, as wide as the main street, with balustrades surmounted by more of those polyhedral stones. The riser of each step was inlaid with script in red marble, in the same style of calligraphy Jack had seen on his family tree.

At the top of the steps was a parade ground backed by a high wall, pierced by three high arches. Guards in blue silk uniforms were scrutinising and controlling the crowds. Through the archways, so tall a giraffe might pass underneath with room to spare, Jack glimpsed the palace. A colossal stone dome, like a much grander Taj Mahal, rose above the other palace buildings, which extended far to each side. At the corners were four slim turrets, like minarets, topped by geometrical shapes.

To his left, an Arabian-style garden stretched into the distance. Spray from its fountains dazzled in the sunlight that came from two directions; trees with strange-coloured leaves bore exotic fruits, dangling at the end of branches as thin as twigs; strange, captivating animals grazed under the trees. Since he was invisible, he could go wherever he wanted with little fear. He was itching to go and explore this marvellous park, but he had to find Meena before his enemies found him.

Crowds were gathering, and the guards were moving them to the side of the gates. Loud cheering spread from spectators on the right, lining an avenue marked by trees. People surged in that direction; there were scuffles as some tried to get a better view. The royal guards had their hands full, but everyone seemed good-humoured.

One section of the crowd began chanting "Shar-feat! Shar-feat! Shar-feat! Shar-feat!" while others sang a patriotic anthem. Jack was intrigued by all this; he also hoped Meena might turn up in the middle of it. She was surprisingly attracted to trouble – well, excitement – so this was the place to find her. Jack moved around, scanning every girl's face, to no avail. Aseem would never have got him here without Meena's coaxing. And she had come because of him – so it was his job to get her home.

The boy with the violet eyes

Jack found the shade of a large tree. The two suns, one smaller than the other, were high in the purplish-blue sky. The heat didn't seem to bother people; no doubt they were used to it. The crowd kept on singing and cheering, waiting expectantly. Jack searched their faces.

The cheers redoubled as a mounted procession came in sight. Jack stared at the leading animals – elephantine creatures, the height of a house. Most were white, some were dark blue. They had two long trunks, one on each side. They came in their dozens, caparisoned in gold cloth and blue silk with an overlapping-rhombus pattern; each had three humps with howdahs between them, one for the mahout and one for the Very Important Person. The first VIP was wearing a cocked hat above his black cloak. Jack thought he looked remarkably small.

They were followed by a singular beast, more than twice the height of a man, its face full of cunning. It had a hide like a rhinoceros, muscles like a bull, a single horn on its forehead and a long snout covering a mouthful of sharp teeth. It seemed to glow, radiating heat as it passed.

At a safe distance behind it came eight tigers – at least, they looked fierce and had stripes, but they had six long, match-like legs and horsetails, and from their jaws protruded long canine teeth like a sabre-tooth tiger's. On their backs they carried patterned rugs almost touching the ground. They looked magnificent, though the crowd shrank back from them.

Next was a company of soldiers on what must be horses, despite their square hooves. Last came a number of large waggons pulled by oxen, which also carried rhombus-patterned cloths on their backs. Their horns were several feet in length and bent backwards in a curve to end in sharp points. Each waggon was heavily laden, though a cloth hid the contents.

The whole cavalcade passed under the three arches into the palace courtyard. Within minutes the cheering crowd had dispersed, leaving the place deserted. He hadn't seen Meena outside, so he'd better wait for her inside. Taking a deep breath, he strode straight past the watchful guards, under an arch and into the palace courtyard.

——— § ———

He sat down on a mounting block, with his back to the palace wall. Somewhere to his right he heard a faint voice.

"Jack!"

He saw nobody. But he knew that voice! He got up and frantically dodged about under each archway in turn, hoping literally to bump into her.

"Jack, it *is* you!"

Meena's head popped out, a beaming smile on her radiant face. He could see her! For a second, Jack thought she was going to fling her arms around him. The next second, she did. He didn't care. Ghosts can't be embarrassed.

36

Actually, he did care: he gave her a big hug back. It was a while since they'd embraced. He thought she seemed to have changed shape recently.

"It's so good to see you."

Then all at once he became self-conscious, forgetting that no one could see them. He sat down on the mounting block, embarrassed. Meena sat down next to him. He was annoyed with himself, which was silly, so he turned it into annoyance with her.

"Where've you been? I've been looking all over. And where's that Aseem?"

"He can't be far away. I've not looked for him yet. It's you I was worried about."

"Oh." Jack didn't know what to say.

"Do you believe him now?"

He could have just said 'yes', but he felt he'd been tricked into coming here and that annoyed him. "I don't trust him."

"Then why did you come?" asked Meena quietly.

Jack looked down, playing for time. The fact was he wouldn't have stood in that magic circle if it hadn't been for Meena, but he wasn't sure why and he wouldn't admit it anyway.

"Just 'cos," Jack muttered.

Meena was chuffed. Her intuition told her that he hadn't followed her just to see if Aseem was right. Now he was here, he could rescue her, which would be great as long as she didn't have to look pathetic, like some damsel in distress.

Jack was in unfamiliar territory here, in both senses. He knew he liked Meena, though he'd never said so; he knew he had to get her home, which worried him. He couldn't admit that either. In stories, the knight in shining armour is a man of few words, never at a loss, famed for derring-do – unlike Jack. He did the next best thing, a quick derring-think.

"I wanted to see if his story stacked up. Bit late now. He tricked us, and we fell for it."

Yet Aseem's story was evidently true. That didn't prove he hadn't tricked them, but he was hardly sinister: he had been kind and considerate, especially to Meena. Maybe he fancied her? That could help them survive, though maybe not get home. He had to defeat the raksas too.

Meena watched all these emotions cross Jack's face, though she guessed only half of them. She was thinking of the bigger picture. Where did Jack fit in? People might laugh, but that tiny picture on the scroll meant he was special, and not just to her. Maybe Andromeda was right about people having a destiny. Meena would have said Jack's destiny was to be permanently late, but now he had a chance to do something special; without her he'd mess it up. It was time they made a plan.

The boy with the violet eyes

Jack got up. He stared at the sky, shading his violet eyes.

Meena looked at him. "He's late. Seems you have something in common."

"You've got to be joking. I'm nothing like that weirdo!"

"Oh, I don't know. What about your big head?" She couldn't resist teasing him.

"It's not that big," he began indignantly until he saw her smile. "Oh … very funny. What's up with the sky?"

"I don't know. Why are we talking about the weather?"

"A few minutes ago it was bright daylight, and now look. Pretty weird, don't you think?"

Just then a rumble like thunder made them jump; they leapt back under the arch. Roaring towards them was a tall, thin, dark cloud, twisting vigorously, sucking up everything on the ground, creating a sandstorm that blotted out the courtyard. It swirled to a stop, still spinning, the sand and dust whirling around them. Out of the black mist, a figure began to take shape.

Jack's heart beat faster, he trembled and his legs turned to jelly. He was telling his feet to run, but they seemed glued to the spot.

"Pssst!" came a voice.

He could not locate it.

"Psssst! Over here!"

Jack turned to see Meena beckoning to him from behind a stack of barrels. He made a sprint for it. As he reached cover, the sand and dust settled, revealing an ominous figure.

"I see you!"

7 The twelving

They poked their heads around the barrels.

"Come, else you may miss the jollification."

She knew only one person who spoke like that. "Aseem?"

"Meena!" His inward energy spent, Aseem was his normal self again. His blue eyes danced.

Her relief and his welcome were cut short as Jack sprinted up to Aseem and grabbed his collar. They were almost rubbing noses. Jack's fear had turned to fury. Aseem did not flinch.

Meena cried out "Jack, stop! Are you crazy?"

Jack spoke through gritted teeth. "No, but this moron is, making us invisible. Okay, what's going on?"

"I regret we were parted for a time … but truly I never guessed we might be unseeable. Is it that you are addressing?"

"Don't give me that. You knew what would happen." Jack's anger turned to disgust. He turned away, the effect slightly spoiled by the fact he had nowhere to go.

"Aseem, we didn't know … I mean, that you would bring us here," began Meena, "It was quite a shock – to me, anyway."

"I was lucky I didn't get killed," Jack butted in, "I came down in a tree."

"I was lucky too," exclaimed Meena, "I landed on the grass in the park."

Just my luck, thought Jack. *She gets the red carpet, while I'm up a tree.* He felt resentful.

"We emerge from the timehole at other places," said Aseem. "I was consternated. It is the first time I travel so."

"Oh, great!" said Jack, not having a clue what 'consternated' meant.

"Excusing, not great, but needful to demonstriculate my tale."

"Dem- what?"

"He means 'show us', Jack. Aseem, why are we like ghosts?" Meena asked.

"Because we are not quite here," replied Aseem.

"Speak for yourself," muttered Jack.

"You know of worldholes – mayhap you know less of timeholes," said Aseem. Meena frowned. *He means wormholes, doesn't he?* "One end of a timehole is faster than the other, so we went back in time – half a day back. It is hindsight. We are only half here … as in a dream."

"Nightmare, more like," said Jack.

The remaining sun chose that moment to sink below the horizon. Like theatre lights going down, within sixty seconds it was night. No moon had risen, but it was as bright as moonlight, because the purplish sky was filled with glittering stars like tiny spotlights. The city was dark, just candlelight and firelight showing through window-panes. It was beautiful.

"How come it's dark so quickly?" Meena asked.

"Our days and nights are littler than yours," Aseem replied, answering a different question.

"Why?" Jack asked.

"It is some matter of the way our planet gyrates."

Jack had worked that out and felt superior; Meena had not come for an astronomy lesson.

"Aseem, you brought us here to explain how Jack fits into your story."

Jack was in no mood for stories. "Look, you've proved your point. Can we go home now? I've got homework to do."

"We are in dreadful peril – you most of all – and you wish to do housework?"

Meena was amazed that Jack could be so annoying and Aseem so restrained.

Jack took in her pointed silence. "Okay, maybe you're right."

Aseem already regretted his outburst. It was no way for a prince to behave. "Please, you are my guests. Welcome! I have something to show." He courteously gestured that they should go ahead, Meena first.

She turned to Jack, keen to include him now the upset was over. "Coming?"

Their eyes met, but Jack needed time. "You go ahead … I'll see you in a bit."

"Preferably do," said Aseem.

Jack was still resentful, watching them go. *Cheek! Meena is my friend, not his.*

Meena saw he needed a little time to himself; he'd soon come round. She glanced back a little sadly. Jack was walking away, under the arch.

At the top of the steps, he admired the twinkling lights of the darkened city. It was beautiful, but so far from home. *I wish I was home again. But I'm not going anywhere without Meena.* Anxiously he turned back. The courtyard was quiet, apart from echoing footsteps on the marble pavement. Were they his? He tiptoed, but the sound grew louder. A late guest strode past, the palace door opened and Jack slipped in behind him.

Inside, it was like a museum. There was a huge bronze polyhedron in the lobby. Behind it, two doors stood open, big enough to slide a house through. Jack entered and was startled to see trees. He looked up: the glass roof was higher than a cathedral; above it were the stars.

He was fascinated by this great indoor garden, its beautiful plants and varied landscapes – paths that climbed and dropped, steep banks and rock outcrops, waterfalls and shaded pools, groves of trees, glades with dappled lawns, bowers, grottos and gazebos. Further on, he heard strange, alluring music. The elephants, or whatever they were, were calmly eating exotic fruits. The six-legged tigers sat close by, yawning lazily. They seemed to enjoy the music too.

——— § ———

Above the music Jack could hear many voices chattering. It took some minutes to reach the other end of the garden, where two tall doors stood ajar. Here the music was much louder. In a great ballroom lit by flaming torches, a massive party was going on. Would there be fireworks?

Down the sides of the ballroom were marble columns, not round but octagonal, supporting arches. Up above were balconies like theatre boxes. Between the columns, partygoers sat on cushioned settles by low tables spread with food. In the centre of the room, sunk three steps down, was a dance floor of gleaming wood, crowded with people doing several different dances. At the far end, a band with odd-looking instruments played lively, haunting music. A bit higher, behind them, were dining tables and a blazing log fire.

Behind the columns, guests thronged broad side aisles with tapestries and tall windows. Waiters served food and drink from polygonal trays which floated beside them, and piquant aromas filled the hall. Acrobats dangled from turquoise scarves, unattached to anything, twirling in mid-air; jugglers juggled balls and balloons; clowns caught these and turned them into strange animals and birds, which came to life, strolling or flying around the room.

Jack was amazed and alarmed at this world of magic, though he knew Meena would love it. Where was she? He climbed a long staircase to a gallery above the fireplace, leaned over the balustrade and scanned the crowds, but he could not see Meena or Aseem.

He set off along a carpeted corridor, silent and unseen. The panelling, carpet and uniforms carried the same polygonal design. Guards shivered slightly as the young ghost passed. Beside each black door was a plaque with a miniature painting. One looked very like Aseem but much older; this must be the king's room. Jack was tempted to look in, but he had to find Meena.

The next door had a miniature of Aseem, with a drawing of a skull and crossbones tucked underneath. She might be here. Jack reached for the doorknob, but it felt squishy like a bean bag. The door dissolved as he passed through it. As Aseem said, he was 'not really here'.

It was a large, circular room with four alcoves. The opposite wall had a curved window-seat. To the left was a fireplace with a log-fire crackling; the wall on the right was sky-blue, with clouds and stars painted on it. With a wry smile, Jack couldn't help comparing this with his own small, tatty bedroom. *But where is Meena? Answer: Wherever the prince is. Why did I let them go? Answer: Because I was sulking. Sometimes I'm an idiot.*

41

———— § ————

Jack scurried from room to room, up and down staircases, searching. At last he found them, talking in low voices, just inside a large chamber. He was jealous: he wanted Meena to himself. Were they talking about him? Could he trust them? He was full of unscientific questions. They were watching a woman and Aseem – a tidier, more relaxed Aseem, opening presents. Yet next to Meena was the prince he knew, staring at this other prince. *They must be twins.*

Meena caught sight of him. "Jack, you found us!"

"It is most delectating you are here," said Aseem with a warm smile.

Jack cleared his throat awkwardly. "Is this what you wanted to show me?"

Aseem nodded. "This is my twelving ... my birthday," he replied, with a touch of pride.

"You never mentioned you had a twin."

Meena said, "No, Jack. It's Aseem, before he came to Earth ... we're watching the past—"

"I get it ... thanks!" Jack interrupted. He turned to the prince. "Just show us what happened, okay?" He wanted to push on now, do what he had to and get out. If this was the past being replayed like a film, Jack wanted to cut to the main action.

The scene was domestic, not dramatic. The prince was on the floor, opening cloth bags and wooden boxes, surrounded by toys and gifts. A large shaggy dog was harnessed to a neat little cart, with shiny green paintwork and yellow spokes. Aseem saw Jack staring.

"The hound and trap is a gift from the people of Serpis. They have few horses, so they use these dogs instead."

"I've seen one before. The man in the cart was dead."

Aseem looked startled. "Was he pale?"

"Yeah. Nearly white. And he had sores all over his face."

"It is the black-flower plague! It began in Serpis; I did not know it was so close. My father wanted to cancel this feast because of it, but Sharfeat said that might cause panic. Every child knows the tale about the plague, but we thought it was ... just a tale."

Jack jumped in. "You mean the black flowers are the cause?"

"Seemingly. The flowers bloom, the crops die, the plague follows. None knows why. The scrolls say this befalls but once in 1,024 years."

"That's 2 to the power of 10," said Meena, "How odd."

"I saw those flowers in the forest," exclaimed Jack, "Growing on sugar cane or something."

The young prince had finished opening presents. Now he was dressing up. A woman in her thirties knelt in front of him, helping him fasten the buttons on his shalwar kameez. She had shiny, straight, dark brown hair, falling just below her shoulders, like Meena's. Her features were smooth and delicate. Her nose could have been moulded in clay by an artist, so perfect was it. Her eyes were a twinkling blue. She wore a pale yellow silk sari with red embroidery in a striking pattern. Her hands and forearms were elegantly marked with a grapevine design in henna. She was very, very beautiful. Jack couldn't take his eyes off her. He had forgotten about pushing on.

Meena nudged him. "That's Hakeema … and it's rude to stare!"

Jack blushed and turned to the prince. "What happens next?"

"All will be revealed shortly."

Once Hakeema had finished dressing Aseem, she picked up a cloth bag and presented it with a teasing smile. "Here is my gift. Do not open it now … but put it on and read what I have writ before you leave the palace. Wear it at all times. It warns of peril."

Aseem felt it cautiously, but did not open it.

Hakeema frowned. "You might display pleasure … or thanks."

"I … I am grateful, it's j-just … I know n-not what it i-is. My thanks, Hakeema."

This hesitant expression of gratitude was all the excuse she needed to give Aseem a cuddle. Then she rose. "Come, we must rapidate. And mind, no folly: your guests will be watching. Especially if you spy a bonny one amongst them."

"Please desist, Hakeema!" Now it was Aseem's turn to go bright red.

Jack wondered if everybody here used this weird, old-fashioned language.

The shiny black doors were opened and the prince, tutor, pages and guards set off down the long corridor. They met a young man coming the other way. Neatly dressed in white, he looked the spitting image of Hanuman, the monkey god, with cheeks swollen as though full of air and a monkey's tail. In Hindu scripture, Hanuman with his mighty ape army helped Ram to rescue his wife Sita from the clutches of an evil raksas. This young man had a golden bow and a quiver of arrows on his back, a professional archer in formal dress. Hakeema stopped him.

"Ah, Indar – how is Aseem progressing?"

Aseem clasped his hands and gave Indar a pleading look, making sure Hakeema didn't see. Indar, pretending not to notice, replied with a grin. "He fares well … though his stance and action are a little clumsy. If he were to start earlier each morn, we could remend them. What say you, prince?"

The prince, judging by the face he made, didn't like the idea of getting up any earlier. Hakeema gave him a glance and turned back to Indar.

"I see no obstacle … I feel sure Aseem will be up early tomorrow."

Young Aseem gave Indar a disgruntled look as they moved on.

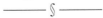

43

The boy with the violet eyes

Jack, Meena and Aseem followed the birthday boy down the marble staircase. A short, wiry, grey-haired man in a cloak was hurrying up the lower stair. His eyes were buried in an old leather-bound book. He flew round the corner and collided with Aseem. The book went flying across the floor.

"How dare you, you fool!" the man shouted angrily as he retrieved his book. Then he noticed Hakeema, helping young Aseem back onto his feet.

"Ah … pardon, Young Majesty, I did not see it was you. Such a rush – so much to do, people to see, favours to grant, problems to solve – a brat … I mean, a boy like you has no idea."

The man was hardly taller than Jack, with pointed nose, little beard and long chin; he had bags under his dark green eyes, bushy eyebrows above; his few hairs were combed back over his wrinkled skull. His robe was heavy and elegant, blue velvet emblazoned with an intricate design; it reached to the floor, seemingly made for someone taller. He looked different, an outsider. This man might be small, but he was dangerous.

Aseem was still getting his breath back, but Hakeema challenged the little man.

"Be careful, Sharfeat … men have lost their tongues for such insolence. Anyway, what is so urgent that it needs your attention this evening?"

The man called Sharfeat didn't seem to care about losing his tongue. "The king's marshal is never off duty … unlike *some* people."

"I think the king's marshal has *forgot* his duty."

"My duty is clear. Your position may be less safe, but I believe the post of clown will soon be vacant. You should apply."

Aseem was bursting with indignation, but his *ayah* patted him on the shoulder.

"Aseem, the marshal has cracked a joke; does it not make you laugh?"

Sharfeat rose to his full 4 feet 11 inches before striding off. Hakeema allowed him three paces before having the last word.

"If I need an assistant, Sharfeat, you'll be on the shortlist – the *very* short list."

The young prince burst out laughing. Higher up the stair, Jack, Meena and Aseem joined in, ghostly and lively laughter together. What happened next should have been impossible. Sharfeat stopped on the stair, turned and scowled, not at Hakeema or Aseem, but at Jack. It was an unblinking, menacing stare that singled out Jack until he had to look away. Finally the marshal stalked past them up the staircase.

Meena nudged him. "What's wrong, Jack? You look as if you'd seen a ghost."

"It's w-w-worse th-than that. A ghost saw *me*. That Sharfeat can see us."

8 Hindsight

"It cannot be," Aseem exclaimed.

"I know what I saw," Jack insisted. "That guy can see us – or he's got a sixth sense." Trembling, Jack turned to Meena and grasped her shoulders. "He saw me, Meena, I'm telling you. He stared right into my eyes. Let's get out of here. We should never have come."

Jack was in shock. He'd been flattered at first, discovering his family was famous on Ardunya, and he wanted to know why he was special. Now that he was specially hated and hunted, he wanted to be ordinary again. His natural curiosity had been killed stone dead.

Meena saw that Jack was shaken, but she wasn't ready to give up. She too wanted to know what made him special. However evil this Sharfeat was, she felt instinctively that he couldn't win, provided Jack did what he was meant to do – and, with her help, he would.

Aseem was frustrated. Jack had to see the terrible events that involved him too. He couldn't be just the frightened rabbit he looked; perhaps he didn't quite understand.

"Whatever Sharfeat does, you are absent. It is my past that you observe."

"Your past is a bit too real for me: I've already upset Sharfeat."

"But Jack, we're in another dimension. He can't touch you." Jack was not convinced. "Aseem will look after us: it's in his interests. Remember, he saved you from Tom."

The prince nodded. "Indeed so. I vow to allow no wickedness to befall either of you."

———— § ————

They stood by the balustrade. Dancing had stopped, the band was playing quietly and servants were filling goblets for the hundreds of guests. As the prince and his entourage appeared on the stair, the musicians struck up a cheerful tune and people started clapping. The young Aseem smiled as he made his way past two tables of youngsters. At the royal table, he was greeted by his parents and sat down between them. Hakeema was there too, and half a dozen other adults.

King Jonda looked like an older version of his son. He wore a royal-blue cloak with a crest sewn onto it, over an embroidered yellow bundi; his grey eyes twinkled and the light gleamed on his gold crown. Queen Radha was a mature woman with a strong, kindly and wise face, even beautiful in a way. She wore a sari, mustard-coloured with gold embroidery matching her ear-rings and necklace. A small red spot – the *bindi* – on her forehead marked her out as married. If the king had such a mark, it was hidden by his crown.

Meena wondered what was coming, and from where. She scanned the guests, searching for anything suspicious. What was that beast, lurking behind the pillars at the far end of the hall? Every so often it reared up, but even on all fours it was twice the height of any guard. It looked like some mythical creature, with a cunning face and snout below the horn on its brow, its leathery hide stretched over big muscles.

Jack had seen Khabish before, in the procession entering the palace gates. He waited for the tragedy to replay and wondered how Aseem had escaped. He felt immensely nervous now that Sharfeat had seen him, and seen him as an enemy. The marshal was hardly the party type, but he saw his small, cloaked figure descend the stair and move stealthily to the side of the dais.

The chatter was silenced by a blast of trumpets. A herald unrolled a parchment and declaimed in a powerful voice: "Ladies and lords … guests from all nations of Ardunya, … King Jonda … of Macron … bids you welcome … to this birthday feast … for the Crown Prince … on the day of his twelving. … On the prince's behalf … we invite our king … to say a few words … in honour of the day … and we thank him … for this magnificent feast. … His Majesty!"

There was cheering as the king stood up, grasping a goblet. He raised his hand and spoke. "Good people, I warmly thank you all for coming, but especially our guests from Serpis. It seems the black flowers have bloomed there, and they threaten us all. Serpians, be assured that we will help you. The royal bookwarden and apothecary are searching for a remedy.

"Howsoever, this is an important day. Our only son, Crown Prince Aseem, has reached double figures. Now he is twelve, his little childhood is over and his great childhood begins. He has much to learn, but he displays great promise at half age. From this day, the queen and I shall entrust weightier duties to the prince. I confide that, when we retire in twelve years' time, your new ruler will be wise beyond his years. Yet childhood must be fun, and a twelving means a party. Raise your goblets and join me in wishing our son the happiest of birthdays and many more of them, even to twelve times twelve!"

The whole hall gave a shout of "Twelve times twelve!" and drained their goblets. There was prolonged cheering and stamping of feet. Finally, the king called "Bring back the entertainers! Bring fresh food, clear the floor and let the band make music! Let fun and frolic resume!"

These commands were swiftly obeyed. People began dancing again, or eating, drinking and chatting, Queen Radha and her son fell into animated conversation, and King Jonda talked to Hakeema. A sudden, extraordinary thought came into Jack's head. He turned to Aseem.

"Your father speaks English, and so do you … well, kind of. We're not on another planet at all, are we?"

"English has been the speech of our court ever since the witch Jemimah came, three hundred aeons ago. It was she who taught us how to use worldholes. She never returned to Earth – in her day people were wary of witchcraft."

———— § ————

At the end of the first course, Aseem took a sack and went over to the other tables. He spoke to each youngster in turn, giving out packages from the sack and getting a hug in return. Jack noticed one girl about his own age give Aseem a kiss and a grin as well as a hug. Maybe he needn't worry about Meena and Aseem. People feasted or danced or watched the entertainers. When the prince had nearly finished handing out gifts, a herald approached the king. Jack heard a sudden intake of breath. He turned to see the ghostly Aseem, with a look of dread, cover his face and turn away.

In the hall, guests were whispering; a restless air spread across the room. They were looking at King Jonda, who seemed in severe pain after sipping his wine. He sat stiffly, gripping the stem of his goblet, coughing and gasping. Several guards, Sharfeat, Hakeema and Queen Radha were frantically trying to help him. The king gasped even more wretchedly and screamed in agony. He raised his arm to point, but the limb stiffened in that position.

As they watched, stone began to form around the king's right hand. It spread up his arm and crept across his chest. There were a few screams or groans from the guests, but most were silent with horror as they watched the stone carapace encase the king. He struggled desperately for life as petrifaction spread rapidly and silently to his throat. He choked on his last word.

"H-H-Hak—!"

She leaned close, to make out what he was striving to say. But the stone had covered his lips; only his grey eyes still moved, gazing at her in deep pain. Hakeema sent an assistant to bring a linctus, but it was already too late. The king was a stone statue, sitting bolt upright with his arm outstretched, pointing. Queen Radha and young Aseem clung to him, sobbing with grief, begging him to come to life again. Hakeema watched grimly. Whatever King Jonda had drunk from that goblet had been deadly.

Sharfeat looked straight at the beast Khabish at the back of the hall, where soldiers were massing, then he jumped up on a chair and spoke in a powerful voice.

"Attention! The king has fallen victim to an evil plot. This is the work of Serpians. I order the immediate arrest of all Serpian guests. I—"

Hakeema interrupted. "Sharfeat! You cannot – you have no authority, no evidence. I have not even begun to investigate what petrified the king."

But already, as she challenged the marshal, troops were dragging people aside and restraining them. Other soldiers closed around the platform and the royal party. The guests were unsettled. They pushed towards the doors in fear and panic.

Sharfeat saw that he had to do something about Hakeema – and the queen and prince. Her words must not reach the city. He signalled to Khabish and his soldiers to guard the doors and round up everyone in the hall. In response, the royal guard closed ranks around the queen and her household. A scuffle broke out as they clashed with Sharfeat's men. Swords and knives were drawn and there was hand-to-hand combat. Angry shouts and curses were mixed with screams of pain as men fell bleeding.

Seeing the royal guard forcing back Sharfeat's soldiers, Khabish lumbered over and began picking up guards in his huge paws, crushing them to death. The tremendous heat he radiated was burning some victims to charcoal before the life could be squashed out of them.

Pandemonium and confusion engulfed the hall. Hakeema, determined to protect young Aseem and Queen Radha, took out some powder and started throwing it at Sharfeat's men. It appeared to cause severe pain to anyone it touched, and men began retreating in fright. Sharfeat signalled for reinforcements.

Khabish reared up and a terrifying, high-pitched trumpeting erupted from his horn. The crowd froze, the fighting stopped. The sound echoed for a few moments, a few weapons clattered to the floor and a nervous silence followed. No one moved. In the distance a rumbling could be heard, like wild animals stampeding. It came closer and closer.

They smashed through the windows and doors, and flew across the hall. High-pitched screeches filled the air. The torches, flickering with the wind, cast an eerie light on the hundreds of invaders. Aseem had seen all this before. *If only …*, he thought. He glanced at the other two. Jack and Meena were awestruck.

The shadow soldiers were like giant hawks, with broad wings twelve feet across. Their muscular brown bodies and heads were sheathed in black armour, their beaks were as big as a man's head and their heavy talons half the length of a man's arm. The flying army of black knights crashed into the hall, some flying, some running, rounding up the guests without even a scuffle. It would have been futile to take on these powerful creatures. A few guards fled; a few fought their way through to join the royal family; the rest surrendered.

Jack noticed that no shadowhawks went near the dais, where the royal party were. But the hawks' victory freed Sharfeat's ordinary soldiers to join the fight on the platform, where they quickly surrounded and captured the remainder of the royal guard. Sharfeat, now in control, addressed the crowd again.

"Today we have seen what befalls a weak, do-good ruler facing a ruthless foe. The strongest will always win. Macron needs a strong leader; the times demand it. Therefore I declare myself King of Macron. I give Serpians a choice: surrender now without conditions or die in battle."

There was silence. Nobody had the stomach to face such a powerful army with such a ruthless leader. In effect Sharfeat was now ruler of Macron and Serpis. With such a swift and easy victory, and the forces of the raksas behind him, Sharfeat saw himself as sole ruler on Ardunya very soon. Once the planet had one ruler, there were other worlds. His imagination saw no real limit to his realm. Hakeema did, and said so.

"Remember, marshal, power is easy to acquire, but difficult to maintain."

"Ah," murmured Sharfeat, "The apothecary … who tells everyone how to do their job, but couldn't do her own. Your physic was not much help to the king, was it?"

"You couldn't stop soldiers dying either, and you had time to plan."

"If you imply I foresaw these regrettable events, that sounds to me like high treason. I shall deal with you personally. It will give me great pleasure." He rubbed his hands in anticipation.

The queen could restrain herself no longer. "If you lay a finger on Hakeema, you will suffer for it. You have no right to be king, Sharfeat! You swore to serve the crown, and Aseem is crown prince. He may be just twelve, but he knows his duty."

"Pah! Let the pretty little boy go and play with his toys."

The prince leapt forward angrily, but was caught by a soldier. Queen Radha, outraged by the marshal's insults and cunning, picked up a carving knife and lunged at him. He grabbed her wrist and twisted it sharply, making her cry out and relax her grip. He wrenched the knife out of her hand and slashed. The queen gave one brief scream as a thin line of blood spurted through the cut in her sari. She made no more sound as she slumped to the floor. Her body crumpled.

Young Aseem, seeing his mother now lifeless too, ran at Sharfeat and started hysterically kicking and punching him. The soldiers hesitated, unsure what to do. The prince, grappling with Sharfeat, shouted "If you have killed her, you will suffer! You shall not get away with this!" Hakeema grabbed the prince and pulled him away. Shocked and angry, she saw they were alone. The rest of the court had been taken away.

Aseem had lost both his parents in a matter of minutes. Jack wished now he hadn't given him such a hard time. *I didn't know. If only I could go back. He was so patient. I should have listened to him – and Meena.*

Sharfeat ordered two soldiers to take Hakeema and young Aseem to the dungeons, to be dealt with later. The city would be in turmoil when news got out. He needed to take control of the walls and gates, close down the temples and spread his version of events to establish his authority: fear would bring respect. Two of Sharfeat's men took a torch each and escorted Hakeema and Aseem towards the staircase.

——————— § ———————

Meena nudged Jack, and he saw that Aseem wanted them to follow. Jack was glad to escape from Sharfeat's fierce eyes. They descended the main staircase to the hall and ran round to catch up with the guards on the lower staircase, down to the cellars.

At the foot of the steps, guards and prisoners set off along the deserted tunnel, lit only by the two flaming torches. Their footsteps echoed against the stone; water dribbled down the walls, collecting in puddles. The passage sloped downwards, curving left. As Jack, Meena and Aseem watched, several men jumped out behind Sharfeat's soldiers, who were caught off guard, overpowered and hog-tied. They had been ambushed by the night watch, who had been lying low until they could do something useful.

Hakeema thanked them and asked them to follow. She had made it her business to know every inch of the sprawling royal palace, even underground. She had searched the archives and pestered the royal architect until she knew the palace's whole history, every building and rebuilding, every bit of lore; she knew of doors and passages long blocked up and forgotten, or never meant to be found. Now she put her knowledge to use.

She led them down a side-passage, just wide enough for two. It twisted and turned until they reached a heavy door. The night watch had a key that fitted; the door creaked open and on they went. Hakeema turned under a narrow archway on the right, and they followed her in single file up a flight of steep steps. At the top, the passage led to a door with four keyholes, one above the other. Hakeema took a large key from a cord around her neck and turned it in each keyhole in turn. One of the watchmen eased open the door, revealing a wall of ivy. They doused their torches.

This part of the city moat was dry and overgrown, but they edged along behind the ivy while the watchmen checked there were no sentries on the wall. There was no gateway on this side of the city. With only starlight to see by, they clambered up through the undergrowth until they emerged on scrubland.

——————— § ———————

They set off in the half-dark. They had gone only a few hundred yards when two shadow soldiers swooped on the watchmen up ahead. The night watch engaged these agile, powerful creatures, but what looked like deadly swipes and slices by the royal guards' keen-edged, well-crafted swords simply went through the shadowhawks. Their brave efforts were futile.

Hakeema tugged young Aseem by the wrist and they crept along under the bushes, constantly glancing behind as they fled further into the wilderness. The shadowhawks had eyes only for their struggling opponents.

Meena, Jack and Aseem stayed to watch the dreadful outcome of the fight. The shadow soldiers dived on the watchmen, lifted them bodily with their talons and flung them against the city wall, smashing their skulls. When only the captain of the watch was left fighting, one shadowhawk disarmed him. The captain raised his hands in surrender. The shadow soldiers stared at him without blinking. Then one moved slightly and all but vanished, leaving a deep shadow. The other remained motionless. Jack and Meena peered into the dusk, trying to see where the hawk had gone.

The shadow began to heave and spread, like a monstrous pool of treacle. It boiled and seethed, creeping sideways, edging around the captain, whose face bore a look of terror. It washed over his boots, surged up to grip his legs, then sucked him suddenly into a bubbling quicksand. He roared in excruciating pain as the heaving mass devoured more and more of him, until only his head and chest were left. Moments later, the captain's screams were cut off as last of him vanished. The black puddle of quicksand shrank, solidified and took on the shape of a shadowhawk once more. The two shadows flew off into the night.

They tortured him, thought Jack. *They made him die in agony, deliberately. That was evil.*

Meena sensed that Jack shared her horror at this gruesome scene. They let Aseem lead them up across the rough terrain to catch up with himself some eight hours earlier. Looking back at the city, they saw shadowbats patrolling the indigo skies, lit up by flames. They could see houses being set alight, soldiers loading barrels, sacks of grain and other supplies onto wagons, and people and animals being rounded up and led away, roped together.

——— § ———

They pressed on into the forest, still climbing. At the top they caught up the two fugitives stumbling down the far side of the hill. Young Aseem bubbled with questions for Hakeema.

"You said once: never run away from problems. So why are we fleeing? And whither?"

"Problems, you can solve; troubles, you cope with. These troubles could kill you, so I am taking you to my secret hideout. For now, endure."

There were no more questions from young Aseem, only a deep, thoughtful silence.

The forest floor here was clear, but rocky and often steep, the canopy thick enough to hide them. They clambered down into a ravine, so narrow that in places they had to jump from rock to rock in the foaming torrent. Edging around a shoulder of rock, they saw their way blocked by a broad waterfall. The noise of it bounced off the walls of the gorge.

Below the cliffs on the other side, on a ledge of rock 10 ft above the water, was a stone cottage. It had several windows, a stone roof and a chimney stack at one end, but they could see no door and no way to reach it. They saw Aseem follow Hakeema onto a ledge that led behind the curtain of water. It brought them out on the other side of the gorge, yards from the gable end of the cottage and its door. They went inside.

"This was my workplace before I came to court. I sought to complete Jemimah's last spell. Some in the city thought my alchemy wicked, so I came here … this became a refuge."

It looked like a scholar's den within an olden-day chemist's shop. Above the work benches, the walls had built-in drawers, small cupboards and shelves stacked with jars of potions and herbs. At one end, above a leather-covered desk full of scrolls, were bookcases. In the middle was a long table piled with books and more papers; in the one clear space were a chopping board, pestle and mortar, glass retort, beakers and pottery jars. Hakeema felt for the flint and lit two candles. She rooted through piles of papers, until she found what she was after – a scroll.

"Mind my every word, Aseem. There is little time. You recall that we went once through a worldhole to the planet Arkadel?" Aseem nodded. "I must now send you farther yet, through a timehole to the land whence came Jemimah. There you will find a boy with *this* face and *these* eyes." Hakeema pointed to the scroll; Jack recognised the picture Aseem had shown him.

"You recollect I spoke of the Barelas family?"

"I recall all you told me, Hakeema."

"It is well. This boy is the only Barelas still alive. He has strange powers and a crystal of rare potency. Mayhap he knows not he has these things, so do not flummox or fright him. Unearth him and bring him hither with the crystal. If Sharfeat or Black Mist finds him first, decent folk face only misery, terror and death."

Hakeema gave Aseem the scroll, tucking it carefully inside his bundi. She gave him some white pellets, instructing him how to use them. "Remember, these smaller tablets are for the timehole: be particular not to mix them up."

The prince was flabbergasted – a crystal, the land of Jemimah, the boy with violet eyes? His tutor was always sensible and reasonable, whereas this sounded like mumbo-jumbo. But he had faith in her. *Do as you are asked. Bring the alien back with the crystal. It is simple.* Aseem wasn't so sure.

"I also must journey to seek help. At your return, await me here."

Each saw how uncertain all this was. Even if they survived, what then? If one succeeded, the other might fail. If one came back, the other might not.

What was certain was, they would be hunted, and they knew what shadowhawks could do. No one would willingly brave this ordeal. But it was all the same now, whether they crossed the universe or just went home.

They snuffed out the candles and left the cottage. Downstream, there was a small beach. She embraced Aseem, holding him longer than usual, then sprinkled the white powder around him as she chanted. A breeze sprang up, making her eyes water. Aseem vanished into the whirlwind, setting off to find a land called Earth and a boy with violet eyes.

———— § ————

With Aseem, Jack and Meena watched Hakeema return to the cottage, and then they both spoke at once.

"How—?"

"What—?"

Jack tried again. "How did Hakeema know about my crystal?"

So he does have a crystal, thought Meena, *Why didn't he say? I thought we were friends.* She stopped herself. *If he kept it secret, there was a reason.*

Aseem spoke. "It has been in your family for over a thousand years. It was foretold."

Jack was speechless; Meena was not. "What does he have to do?"

"Hakeema will enlighten us. First, where is the crystal?" asked Aseem.

Jack answered awkwardly. "In the lab – I'm doing an experiment."

Aseem was aghast, realising he should have asked before. Meena believed in Jack, so the next step was clear. "We must go back and get it."

Jack nodded with more enthusiasm. "Yes, we'd best go right away."

Aseem's troubles had bubbled up and boiled over in a day; Jack's had been simmering unseen since he first opened those violet eyes. For two boys who never looked for trouble, they were coping with it remarkably well.

Aseem took a pill from his bundi, crushed it and placed the dust in their palms, murmuring under his breath. The two stood close together as he circled them three times – anti-clockwise, Meena noticed – sprinkling a trail of white dust around them, staying outside the circle himself.

In a moment the temperature sank, and they couldn't stop shivering with the terrible cold – Jack, without his blazer, especially. A fierce gale sprang up, whipping Meena's hair across her eyes, some gusts threatening to lift them off their feet. They clung to each other, hoping their combined weight would keep them on the ground. Through the whirling dust they saw Aseem more and more dimly. The cloud around them thickened until nothing could be seen or heard or felt. They flew through dark space – through the timehole, they sincerely hoped – until they landed on earth with a little thud.

9 Dr Meena's medicine

They were on Toft Lane, or what seemed like it. That wasn't scientific proof to Jack – to him 'seem' and 'is' were poles apart – but the chimes of the ice-cream van playing 'Twinkle, twinkle, little star' tipped the balance in Toft Lane's favour. Jack's watch said 3.53pm. They retrieved their schoolbags from the grass verge.

Everything seemed twice as real, like getting new glasses. Jack was so happy to hear the birds, smell the grass and feel the breeze. This was home. Ardunya was, literally, wonderful and exciting. But there's exciting, and then there's terrifying. Jack could cope with wormholes, invisibility, strange lands, even magic and replaying the past; but not fighting beasts, barbaric torture and living death. Worst of all was the hatred in the eyes of that tyrant Sharfeat.

Meena too was glad to be home, but she was unhappy: Aseem was desperate for Jack's help, and she wanted to be proud of him. Jack had disappointed them both. Now she had to get him back to Ardunya with his mysterious crystal.

There was a whoosh, and Aseem stood there, bowing slightly, hands clasped behind his back. Meena was pleased to see him. Jack was not.

"Why have *you* come back?"

"Without my help, you cannot return to Macron."

"We've only just got here. Tomorrow—"

"Tomorrow may be too late. Time is precious!"

Meena was shocked. "Jack, you said we were coming to collect the crystal – was that just a trick to get home?"

Jack squirmed. "Well … I need time to think."

Aseem looked aghast. "You saw what the plague can do, what Black Mist and his puppet Sharfeat have done. You promised to fetch the crystal. Does your word mean nothing?"

"If Aseem says you and your crystal can save Macron, you have to believe him, Jack. Why else did he come? Not to hang out with you."

Jack knew Meena was right, but he hadn't got around to seeing things from Aseem's point of view – and they didn't seem to have Jack's fears. *We got back this time, but what if we were captured? The shadowhawks would kill us – after torturing us.*

He envied Aseem his calm confidence. Now Jack had seen Sharfeat and the shadowhawks, he was scared witless. He was no good at fighting or leading, or handling people. He would look a fool: he had no idea why he was special or what he had to do and nobody could tell him.

"Okay, Aseem. How *do* I save Macron?"

Aseem looked at him dumbly.

"You don't know, do you? You just hope I'll find out before I die. Moron!"

Meena didn't like Jack's language, but she had to persuade him. "You promised, Jack. You can do it if you put your mind to it."

"Hakeema and I will help you."

But Jack wanted to kill the idea stone-dead. "You know how stupid you guys sound?"

Aseem looked desperate. "You must return with the crystal! We have no other remedy."

"You forget, I'm doing an experiment. If it works, you can borrow the crystal, but you won't get me back there. That place is dangerous!"

"Earth too is perilous. Ere long shadowhawks will hunt you by day, shadowbats will come for you at night and the raksas will track down your dreams."

In his mind Jack saw the final torment of the captain of the night watch. His fear doubled.

"Why? All I did was visit your planet. And that wasn't my idea."

Meena was about to lose her cool, but she bit her lip. What had happened to Jack? She couldn't forget what she had seen or the way Aseem had behaved – as if he was the eldest of the three of them, not the youngest. He was hopelessly honest, kind-hearted and forgiving, but she admired his quiet dignity after seeing his parents killed, his patience with Jack, his determination. He had taken their worries seriously and brought them home. How must he be feeling now? Meena felt ashamed. She went up to the prince and shook his hand. Aseem bowed and clasped her hand with both of his, then stood very straight.

"I am sorry, Aseem. It's a shame the one person you need is so pusillanimous."

"What's that mean?" Jack snapped.

"Why don't you look it up? You might learn something."

Meena turned in disgust and set off homewards. Jack looked uncertainly at the prince. Their eyes met for a moment, then Jack turned his back on him and ran to catch up Meena.

The prince stood alone in the lane, tears running down his face. Hakeema had trusted him to bring Jack Cooper and the crystal, and he had failed. He should have told Jack – too late now – that Black Mist had already tracked him down. If Jack tried to hide, his planet would be attacked with high magic.

Out of the blue, a wind sprang up. Bleak, grey clouds began to form with unnatural rapidity. A bolt of lightning shot across the sky, its fingers reaching to light up every part of the town. Thunder erupted, and with it a sudden deluge, like a monsoon. Aseem knew what it meant: wherever Jack went, sooner or later the demon would find him. The raksas was roaming the Earth to find the last of the Coopers, to kill him.

——— § ———

It was raining hard and the lightning flashes were followed within seconds by long rumbles of thunder. Meena and Jack walked on, hardly noticing, not speaking. Meena looked back once or twice but she couldn't see Aseem.

Ever since they had first met at age seven, starting junior school, she and Jack had got on well: they argued about things, played with ideas, did experiments, did everything together. They were fascinated by shapes and patterns, numbers and science, not much interested in gangs or fashions. They were on the same wavelength.

They weren't alike in everything. She was modest, but a bit bossy and never at a loss; he was rather full of himself, but awkward with other people and full of fears. She was organised, he was always late. People made fun of them, a boy and a girl being friends, but they had stuck together. Now Meena felt shaken. How could they be friends after this? What could she tell David, Andromeda and Lloyd? What would they say?

Jack too was thinking hard. Like a cloud of midges, questions kept biting him. *Can the shadowhawks find me? Is anywhere safe? How did Hakeema know about the crystal? What do I do with it? Can't Aseem do it? How come I have no picture of my dad? Why has Mum never talked about him? How much does she know?*

Jack was apparently destined to save Ardunya. Meena was probably destined to save morons like him from themselves. Was every baby born with a destiny?

He knew he should have gone straight back with the crystal. Aseem – no parents, no home, not much future – had been straight with him; he'd used magic, but not to trick him. And what had Jack done? He'd insulted and tricked Aseem, he'd deceived Meena and chickened out. Had she meant to go back with Aseem? Well, too late now.

She had tried to help, though there was nothing in it for her. People said how good he was, looking after his mother; but wasn't that self-interest? Today he could have helped a stranger and he'd walked away, because there was nothing in it for him. He felt bad.

Aseem was certainly an oddball. So what? Did that make it right to spurn him, sneer at him, leave him in the road alone on a strange planet, without even saying 'sorry' or 'goodbye'? What was he thinking of? Himself, mostly. Because he was afraid. He knew that now. He was scared, scared, scared. As Meena said: knowledge can hurt.

Their hurrying footsteps were the only sound. As they crossed the bridge, Jack glanced down. The swirling waters were dark, as if in spate, yet they were not muddy brown but purple, and the level was quite low. There were dead fish on the bank, but nobody was fishing; instead, fish were trying to wriggle out of the water.

He wanted to investigate, but there wasn't time: it was 3:55pm. He'd been waylaid by Tom's gang, yet he was only slightly late – as if he'd spent no time at all on Ardunya. It was pouring harder, raindrops bouncing off the pavement, streams running in the gutter. Jack felt rain trickle under his shirt collar and start down his spine. He glanced at Meena; she looked untidy, strands of shiny hair sticking to her cheeks, her blazer sodden. A breeze blew spray off the deserted road; they had to lean against the wind.

Near the row of little shops, Meena looked around for Tom's gang. No sign. They met Mrs Smith, Jack's next-door neighbour, struggling with an umbrella and shopping bags. She greeted him, nodded to Meena and looked them up and down disapprovingly, before stumping off. They must look a mess. He had no coat and was soaked to the skin; his blazer and tie were lying under a bush on Ardunya. How on Earth was he going to explain that?

——— § ———

The sign over the shopfront said 'Praveen Patel (Prop.) Newsagent'. Jack let Meena enter first. Mr Patel was tall, dark and handsome, with black hair and a handlebar moustache. His English-born wife, visiting her grandparents in India, had met Mr Patel, fallen in love and brought him back with her. Now he looked serious, as always, but happy to see Meena and disconcerted at the state of them. She went behind the counter and straight upstairs. Jack put his schoolbag aside, wondering why there were no lights on, until Mr Patel explained in his Indian accent: "Damn power cut." Just then his wife came bustling downstairs.

Rani Praveen Patel was a tiny woman who did everything at double speed. She beckoned Jack to follow her through to the back. The Patels' kitchen was warm and homely, with a gas fire. Jack knew it well; he was almost like family. As he closed the shop door, she burst into speech. "Meena's right. You are soaked! How could you be so careless, going out with no coat? Come upstairs and take off those wet clothes before you catch cold! The papers will have to wait."

He followed her upstairs, his feet squelching as he moved, and went into the bathroom. He took his shoes and socks off, then everything else. He dried himself quickly with the bath towel and arranged it around his waist. He heard Meena go past, then Mrs Patel appeared with a pile of clothes and thrust them through the door. Jack dressed, not caring what he was putting on.

When he came downstairs, Meena was sitting by the kitchen fire. She got up without a word and went out. Mrs Patel said "You should stay here by the fire with Meena, but I suppose you must deliver the papers." Meena came back with a duffle coat. Her mother seized it and gave it to Jack.

He mumbled his thanks and went out hastily, feeling ashamed, avoiding Meena's eye. She was tempted to say something, but chose silence instead. In the shop, he picked up his newspaper bag and glanced at the evening paper. He froze.

WHY?

TOWN HIT BY DISASTERS

The town of Wellington Spa is reeling from the effects of several unexplained natural disasters, all in the last hour. Rivers and streams are poisoned, rare diseases are reported, torrential rain is flooding homes and closing roads, high winds have brought down power lines and telephone cables, lightning has damaged several buildings and an earthquake has been reported.

The town is said to be almost cut off and many areas are without electricity. People have been told to boil water before using it. Police are warning people not to travel. Hospitals and surgeries are struggling to cope.

So far, areas near by are unaffected by these calamities. Experts are baffled. The county council is putting emergency plans into action, and the government may be asked for help.

Jack thrust the paper into his bag, put his hood up and set off.

Once outside, he began running as fast as his legs would go. It was like a bizarre relay race, with newspapers instead of a baton. He thrust papers into letterboxes as if his life depended on it; maybe it did. He hardly noticed the weather, partly thanks to Meena's warm coat, partly because his brain was in overdrive.

Aseem had said the raksas would find him. Jack hadn't taken him seriously, but now Black Mist was hunting him down – had maybe already found his mum. He sprinted from door to door, dodging the puddles. He posted the last paper and ran straight home.

——— § ———

When he unlocked the back door, everything was just as he'd left it: dirty plates in the sink, breadcrumbs and a used knife on the table, a glass with dried-up milk stains. They would have to wait. Galileo wouldn't wait, so Jack opened a tin of cat food and emptied it in her bowl. The kitchen clock said 4:55pm.

He crept upstairs and along the landing, and listened at her door. No sound. He tensed. If the shadowhawks had already been, his mum would be gone. If so, they'd be back for him. His heart pounding, he cautiously opened the door. She was there, alive and fast asleep. Feeling suddenly weak, he tiptoed downstairs again.

Jack was ravenous. As he opened the fridge, a spark shot from his finger. "Ouch!" He grabbed two pieces of bread, spread margarine on them and crammed the sandwich in his mouth. He heard a noise and turned in dread. It was his mother struggling downstairs with some plates. He quickly went to take them.

"Mum, what are you doing? I'm supposed to do that."

"I can manage, thank you. That sleep did me good." She sat down next to him. "Whose coat is that?"

"Meena's. I got soaked on the way to the shop."

"Yes, I heard the rain! You're so lucky to have Meena as a friend."

I was, he thought.

"You forgot to leave your newspaper bag at the shop."

"I came home first to see if you were all right."

"You worry too much. I know that doctor wants to write me off, but I'm too young to die – I want to see you grow up into a mad scientist first!"

Anita Cooper chuckled. Jack didn't, but then he had a mouth full of bread. She spoke brightly, seeing worry engraved on his face, but inwardly she grieved. *If only Jonathan were here, he would look after me and do things with Jack.*

Jack was shocked. They say 'Only the good die young' and his mother was good. *Not that she has much chance to be bad*, he thought wryly. *It's hardly being good if you can't be bad, is it?*

Mrs Cooper had meant to reassure her son, but she saw she had said the wrong thing. "You look bothered. Has something happened?"

"No, Mum … I'm fine." She gazed at him. "I've got to get back to the shop." She nodded. Jack stood. "Mr Patel will be panicking. Is there anything you want?"

She mentioned some groceries, then leaned over and gave Jack a kiss. He winced when she touched the bruise on his cheek.

"What's this? I knew it!"

"It was an accident – it's nothing."

Mrs Cooper pretended to believe him. "Off you go then – careful who you bump into!"

How did she … ? No, she couldn't know. He flashed a bright smile.

"You'd better do the same. Don't open the door for anyone!"

"Not even a tall, dark, handsome stranger?"

"Especially not him. I'll be back in a bit to cook."

"Sounds good. I might even make a start myself." She gave him another kiss and watched him go.

———— § ————

It was still teeming with rain, and the water now covered parts of the road. Jack was glad of Meena's duffle coat. It might be tricky making up with her: he should have told her about the crystal and he'd been pretty rude. Worse, he'd disappointed her by breaking a promise. Somehow he had to sort things out with Meena – only he wasn't good at people things.

The boy with the violet eyes

He found the shop dimly lit by various lamps. Mr Patel looked relieved to see him with an empty newspaper bag. "Why so long? Something bad is happening, yes?" Mr Patel's English was still very Indian.

"I popped in to make sure Mum was all right." He spotted Mrs Patel. "Is Meena around?"

"She should be. Wait here."

She was never usually so formal. A chill ran down Jack's spine. Mr Patel was now busy with a customer. Jack thought of buying a drink and fished in his pocket for money, then realised he was wearing Meena's jeans. Her mother came back.

"She's busy with her science homework and then she's going to bed."

Was that her idea, or her dad's? They were supposed to do it together at the lab tomorrow.

"I've got to see her," Jack insisted.

"You can bring her clothes back tomorrow."

"But I need to see *her*."

"Sorry, Jack," said Mrs Patel, shaking her head.

"Not possible," put in Mr Patel between customers.

Jack looked wildly from one to the other. Meena must have told them to send him away. He didn't blame her. Now it was even more important to see her.

"We had a row about something I said. Please could you tell her I'm sorry?"

Mrs Patel softened a little. "Very well, I will tell her."

"But I think Meena is not seeing boys any more," Mr Patel added rather stiffly.

Mrs Patel tut-tutted. "She does not 'see boys', Praveen, as you well know. Jack is different. He helps with her homework. Jack, wait – let me have a word with her." Shaking her head, she went upstairs again. Mr Patel started counting the till receipts. He didn't look up. Jack shifted from one foot to the other, feeling desperately awkward. After what seemed an age, he heard footsteps on the stairs and the door opened.

"Meena will see you now, in the kitchen," her mother announced. *It's like seeing the dentist*, Jack thought gloomily, as he went through.

————— § —————

The kitchen was half dark, lit only by the flickering flames of the gas fire. Meena sat in a high-backed chair beside it, her face mostly in shadow. She didn't speak. Jack sat down opposite.

What was she thinking? *He broke his promise to Aseem; he chickened out; he never told me about his crystal; he called me stupid. From Monday, I'll sit next to someone else in class; I'll stick with the girls at break; I'll walk home five minutes after him or cross the road;*

I won't give him a chance to even speak to me. What could he say to change her mind? They had never argued this seriously before and it felt horrible.

He coughed uncertainly, searching for words. Meena got in first.

"Suits you, that blouse."

"It kept me dry – thanks ... anyway, I ... I—"

"Just spit it out."

Jack took a deep breath. "Look, I've come to say sorry. I've been a total jerk."

"You said it. It's Aseem I feel sorry for. But there's no going back now."

"I wish we *could* go back. I wouldn't be so hard on him." There was silence apart from the hissing of the gas fire. He went on, trying to explain himself. "What he was asking was like Mission Impossible. Don't you see?"

"No," Meena flashed, "Cos I'm stupid, aren't I?" She looked to be enjoying this.

"Don't be daft, Meena. You're not stupid."

"Oh, I'm daft now, am I?"

"I didn't—"

"... think? No, I've noticed. Why not think before you speak?"

"I never thought." Jack sighed. He seemed to be making things worse. Then Meena bit her lip. Jack's hopes revived. Was she a bit sorry? He gave one more try. "From now on, if I'm acting like a jerk, you've got to tell me."

"Oh, I've *got* to, have I?"

"No. Look, I always seem to say the wrong thing. I don't mean it."

Meena liked to see Jack trying to get out of the hole he had dug for himself. She was still tempted to poke him back down. It was good she could blame Jack, because she was angry with herself too. "So when you said 'You won't get *me* back there', you didn't really mean it? It seemed clear enough to me."

The hurt showed in Jack's violet eyes. "I wasn't straight with you. I did mean to go back at first, but when it came to it, I just couldn't. And I shouldn't have called you stupid. I'm sorry."

Meena felt her anger ebbing away. She'd got what she wanted. Now it was her turn to feel bad, tormenting him when he was already miserable. How would *she* feel if she messed up? Nobody was perfect, right? *Not even me,* she thought sarcastically. "I'm sorry too."

Jack smiled hopefully. "Can we be friends again?"

"If you promise to be straight with me."

"I promise. I won't screw up again." Meena kept a straight face, but inside she was smiling too. "I've got to go and cook dinner. You will come tomorrow, won't you?"

"Yep! I want to see the crystal."

The boy with the violet eyes

"Okay, but remember it's a secret – and I don't know what will happen."

"You promised Aseem, remember?"

"He can have it. It's no good asking me to go. I just can't." At last he'd said it.

"I know you're scared, but running away won't help us."

"Hakeema said you could run away from troubles."

"You can run, but the raksas will find you, Aseem said. It's better to go back and face it."

"I'm no hero, Meena. Let's face it, I'm just not as brave as you, or as grown-up as Aseem."

"You don't have to be. My dad says bravery is not just about fighting; it's about standing up for what's right."

"Like standing up to Tom?"

Jack meant to be sarcastic, but Meena nodded firmly.

"You stood up for me and you never did that before. Now you have to stand up for Aseem. It's your crystal and you have to go back with it – tomorrow." But she wondered how they would find Aseem again.

———— § ————

The power cut lasted all evening, so Jack made a salad. He and his mother ate by candlelight, washed up in lukewarm water and went to bed early. He tried to recall everything he'd ever read about wormholes. Without the library or the internet he couldn't find out more tonight. He would ask the professor.

Meena did some finding out; luckily, her father didn't need batteries. Over a cold supper, she asked him about the *mautam* – the much-feared flowering of the bamboo in Assam. It happened once every 48 years, and with the flowers came rats, which ate the crops, followed by plague and famine. After that, events on Ardunya made more sense. She was looking forward to explaining it all to Jack, very slowly and carefully, tomorrow.

10 A kink in the learning curve

It was Saturday morning. Jack had not slept well, again. The power came back on about midnight and he had to get up and turn the light off; about 2am his mother woke, so he made her a cup of tea; and after that he was woken again and again by nightmares.

Cold and terrified, he was in a twelve-sided dungeon. Someone wanted to steal the crystal, and Black Mist was catching him up. Then he was running across a plain, pursued by horsemen, the sky darkening with a swarm of shadowhawks. There seemed no escape, until suddenly he was climbing a pyramid. In the darkness someone was coming closer. It was hot and stifling, and he was blinded by a brilliant light.

The sunlight was in his eyes. It was 8.45am, the blue sky promised a beautiful day and he had overslept. In 15 minutes he was due to meet Meena, to re-do their experiment, the one he had cut short by dropping the beaker. He'd done it before, but Meena hadn't. He didn't want to be in Miss Quigley's bad books again. And he wanted to ask Meena something.

He hurriedly put on some khaki trousers, slightly frayed at the knees, and a blue t-shirt, then went to see his mum. For Anita Cooper it wasn't a good morning. She was covered in duvets, with a towel across her forehead.

"Mum … you all right?" whispered Jack, kneeling by the bed to be at her level.

"I'm freezing."

Jack got out two thick blankets and spread them on the bed. He went to close the window.

"Leave it, son: I need the fresh air. Off you go. I'll be fine."

Jack decided sleep would do her good. He kissed her and whispered "Love you, Mum" before heading downstairs, yawning. Galileo was waiting, so he poured some milk for her and a glass for himself. He put the rest in the fridge, which gave him an electric shock as usual. He found a bacon sandwich, unwrapped it, cut it and put half back in the fridge, getting another shock. The door didn't close properly, but the fridge still worked. He drank his milk, munched his way through the sandwich and left by the back door, followed by Galileo.

———— § ————

The professor's laboratory was only 10 minutes' walk, if you cut across the common and through the wood. Meena was there, sitting on a boulder beside a tiny concrete hut. It had no windows, only a door with peeling blue paint and a rusty padlock.

She stood up. "Finally! I've been here 20 minutes."

The boy with the violet eyes

"I came as fast as I could."

"You mean you overslept. Never mind."

She got out her torch. He brought out the key and unlocked the door. They stepped inside. Meena locked the door behind them and gave him the key back. She shone the torch as they descended the steep stair. Unlocking another door, they entered the underground laboratory. The lab was warm, clean and dry. It had once been a secret military bunker.

Paul Shreddon didn't like fuss: local people knew him as plain Mr Shreddon, but he was a professor emeritus, which meant he still merited the title 'Professor'. He had retired to have more time for his own experiments, but sadly his wife had died not long after. Then he met Jack's father. The two found each other's ideas fascinating and planned experiments together.

Jack's father was a joiner; he had fitted out the the professor's lab with work benches, work-table, storage cabinets and a fume cupboard. Next door was a kitchen, and a study with desks, bookshelves, armchairs, computers and printer. There was even a dark room for developing films. Jonathan Cooper had also fitted two skylights, hidden by shrubbery, with glass so thick you could jump on it.

The professor equipped his laboratory with all kinds of apparatus – the latest just arrived in a tall crate, only half unpacked – and stocked it with hundreds of chemicals. The place was his pride and joy. Jack loved it too. Here he was free to create, invent, test, try out and dream of being a real scientist. It was like heaven.

The kitchen door opened and out came a man wearing a smart white lab coat, carrying a pencil and clipboard. He had white, curly hair, with tufts around his ears and a bald patch on top. He had the calm face of a man who has faced many struggles in life and learnt to live with the result. His skin was slightly wrinkled, with some pale spots on his cheeks. He wore rectangular spectacles perched on the end of his nose.

"Morning, Meena. How are you? Hello, Jack. How's your mum today?"

"One minute she's fine, the next she's ill again. She's never going to get better."

"She will! Is everything else all right? You look bothered."

That's what his mum had said. Was his mind transparent? Then he realised the professor was just being kind: he must know Anita Cooper's illness was incurable.

"I didn't sleep well – nightmares."

Meena glanced at him, worried. Paul Shreddon knew merely that youngsters often have bad dreams – he was concerned, but not worried.

"Sorry to hear that. You had science yesterday, didn't you?" he said, looking from one to the other, "Anything exciting?"

64

"We never finished the experiment, but it looked exciting. We're going to do it now," Meena said diplomatically.

"It's one I did ages ago. I don't know what's exciting about it."

Meena cringed: Jack sounded so cocky and patronising. He was quite unaware of this, too busy thinking about yesterday. He wanted to ask about wormholes.

"Professor, what's happened to Wellington Spa?"

Paul Shreddon tucked his pencil behind his ear and put down the clipboard.

"It's all very bizarre. Not natural, I'd say."

"That's what I thought. So what is it?"

"Who knows? Some say an act of God … someone put it down to that violent electrical storm. It's hard to believe all these inexplicable events are not linked, and yet I can't see any link. I'm sure somebody will find the explanation – perhaps you two!" With a twinkle in his eye, he added "But I guess you have homework to do first. I need a couple of things from the electrical shop, so I'll leave you to it."

"Thanks, professor," the two chorused, and smiled at themselves.

"My pleasure. I know my lab is safe in your hands." The professor put on his hat and coat and disappeared up the steps. Jack had forgotten to ask about wormholes.

———— § ————

Jack and Meena got out test tubes, a bunsen burner, a flask and other equipment.

"Let's get this experiment over. It's the next one I'm gagging for."

"The crystal? I really want to see that!"

"I'm making a rocket too." Her eyes widened, so he added "A proper firework rocket – I need you to calculate the lift-charge – but we'd best do this first."

Meena bit her lip. He was right: homework first. Who knew what might happen?

"Come on then, let's set it up."

He handed her the glassware, let her put it together and talked her through the experiment. She put on gloves and goggles, poured acid over the copper oxide and lit the bunsen burner.

Just then he remembered two things. He was a little apprehensive about raising either topic, but he could hardly ask *his* question before answering *hers* – which she tactfully hadn't asked.

"Meena."

"Yeah?"

"Sorry I didn't bring your clothes. I didn't have time to wash them."

The boy with the violet eyes

"That's okay." Teasingly she added "You can keep them if you like."

Jack went red. "No, I daren't! But thanks." He took a big breath; his ears remained red. "What do you make of this Aseem?" *Maybe she saw things I missed.*

Indeed Meena saw and understood much that Jack didn't – about Jack himself for a start. She knew his moods, habits, interests, even the way he thought. She was going to enjoy this.

He waited for her response. After ten seconds, he reiterated his question. "I wondered what you thought of Aseem? Did you believe him?"

Meena couldn't help giggling. "Sorry! ... Aseem? Oh yes, he's genuine."

"How do you make that out?"

"You asked for my opinion, and I told you."

"But that's too simple. What if he hasn't told us everything?" Jack was full of doubts. Real scientists are.

Meena sighed. "I know it's more complex than that, and you want all the facts. That's the way you are. I judge Aseem on his character, not who he is or where he's from. He's not all that clever; he's too honest to fool you. He was straight with us, wasn't he? He didn't play any tricks and brought us back, even though you were a pain and he needed you there. And all this after he's seen his parents killed?"

Jack didn't answer. Meena's reply seemed so mature. What she said was unscientific, yet it was valid. This was a new idea for Jack. Like a kettle coming to the boil, he now struggled to keep the lid on his admiration for her.

His silence puzzled her. "What's wrong?"

Jack couldn't explain and, not wanting to look a fool, didn't try. "But even if he's genuine, who'd believe us?" *Aseem's story is like a fairy tale. Everybody would laugh at us. They'd say we were just children trying to get attention.* "Listen, Meena, let's make a deal. We're not going to mention this to anyone. They'll just take the mick."

It sounded more like an order than a deal, but that was Jack.

Getting no response, he added "We don't want to get into trouble, do we?"

"But that's what you're good at. Miss Quigley and I are thinking of getting you a t-shirt saying Here Comes Trouble."

"Sometimes I think *you're* just taking the mick," said Jack slowly.

"Another major discovery for science!" Meena announced triumphantly.

———— § ————

Aseem felt like going home after his futile efforts to persuade Jack, except Hakeema had made it crystal-clear he must bring the earthling back. Mind, *she* hadn't met Jack. Aseem had never known anyone so difficult: sceptical, stubborn, selfish and very rude when he got angry, which happened a lot. He was no hero either, his violet eyes didn't seem to give him any special powers and he was very vague about the crystal. He couldn't even read. He seemed useless.

Now Aseem was outside the lab. He had crept through bushes and tall grass, hidden from any watchful eyes, and crawled under a small duct linked to the fume cupboard in the lab. It was a well-secluded spot where he could contemplate what to do next.

In the lab, Meena had done Miss Quigley's experiment and was writing it up. Jack looked through the glass door of the fume cupboard to check on his experiment. For the first time he told Meena about the dream that led him to the crystal that turned out to be a blue stone.

"That's odd. Did you know 'Meena' means 'blue stone'?"

"Does it? The weird thing is, I had it all the time."

"Because your dad put it there?"

"Yes. The crystal was in my nightmares, but it was in other dreams too. This kind voice told me what to do with it. I didn't recognise the voice, but what it said sort-of made sense. Next day I searched the web, but that didn't help; I couldn't identify the blue rock. That got me stressed, but finally I got some ideas. Basically I've done what the voice said. I daren't think what to expect."

He got a hammer and chisel, placed some thick mats on the workbench, put on protective gloves and goggles, and went over to the fume cupboard. Meena tried to see what he was carrying. Jack wrapped a thick cloth around it. Red-orange foam was spitting out from a clay mould, still very hot.

"What is it, Jack?"

Jack didn't reply: he was concentrating, being careful not to move the clay mould about. He carried it to the table and set it down, a little smoke still rising from the mould.

"Wait and see," he grunted, chipping away the mould.

Each shard that fell away revealed a little more of the shiny, many-faceted solid within. The sunlight caught it and dazzled them, refracting into a spectrum of colours that filled the room. It was beautiful. The more Jack chipped away, the wider the range of hues seemed to be.

Meena was mesmerised, admiring the dancing colours on the walls and ceiling. The dull white-and-grey lab had suddenly turned amazingly bright and impossibly colourful. When Jack had finished, the two just stared. There were colours they'd never seen before, and the complex shape was unlike anything they'd ever come across. The effect was indescribable.

Meena spoke. "Is it a kind of stellated icosahedron?" She knew about shapes.

Jack wouldn't know a stellated icosahedron even if he accidentally sat on one. "No idea, but is that a black flower in the middle?"

"Looks like it. I've never seen a crystal this big … I couldn't even name some of those colours."

"It's weird. I can see such a deep blue … a wonderful green … powerful yellows … lots of reds – but some of the others don't make sense. They're out of this world."

That was only half a metaphor, for it was literally true. This was something unknown to science, and unknown means dangerous. Doesn't it?

"That makes sense," said Meena. Seeing Jack's face, she lost her exuberance. "What is it?"

"You know that kind voice in my dreams? It was my dad. He had the crystal and they killed him for it. I'm scared, Meena."

Only now he was brave enough to say so.

11 Found

They heard movement above and looked up. Through the skylight, they glimpsed a hurrying figure. They looked at each other. Jack went pale.

"Did you see who it was?" His voice came out rather high-pitched.

"I think it was Aseem."

"You think?"

"It looked like his suit."

"Why didn't he just come and knock?"

"What, after the way you left him?"

Jack had no answer to that. "I suppose. I wonder if he knows what this crystal does." It was cooler now. With some difficulty, Jack shoved it in the pocket of his jeans.

Before they could speculate further, they heard a series of loud thuds on the roof, then scrabbling sounds. They faced each other, bewildered and anxious. Meena spoke in a whisper.

"That's not ... whoever it was – they can't be in two places at once."

"Who, then? Tom? Not after what Aseem did to him."

The noises stopped. There was a moment of silence, then a few thuds, and a drilling sound began. Everything started to vibrate: the table juddered, papers fell to the floor, apparatus rattled and crept across the workbench, a test-tube rack fell over, even their teeth chattered. Then the ceiling cracked.

Someone was determined to get in. It was surely just a matter of time before the roof caved in. Meena was never daunted by people, but this unseen, unknown danger unnerved her. She moved closer to Jack. "Let's get out of here!"

Jack didn't feel like hanging around either – but, though very scared, he couldn't help trying to make sense of what was going on. "N ... not yet. What if it's a set-up, to get us in the open?"

Her eyes on the ceiling, Meena now stood so close that they touched. She couldn't stand the drilling noise and the shaking. She couldn't think straight, but she wasn't going to make a run for it without Jack: they must stick together. For once she trusted his judgement over her own. She clutched his arm tightly and whispered loudly "Let's run, before it's too late."

"No, bad idea. Let's get a look at them first. We'd better hide – c'mon."

Jack could hardly move in Meena's vice-like grip, but he caught her eye and she let go. His first thought was the heavy wooden crate, taller than them, labelled HANDLE WITH CARE and THIS WAY UP. The top (actually the bottom) was open; jumping up, Jack peeked inside: the straw packing was a long way down; they might not get out again. Under the work-table were large cupboards full of equipment. He quickly emptied one, as Meena dropped the contents onto the straw in the crate.

Meena crept into the cupboard and sat down; there wasn't room to do anything else. After a brief struggle, Jack squeezed in as well. He had to tuck one leg sideways under the other before he got his feet inside. The crystal jabbed into his hip. Meena closed the doors.

——— § ———

Before the commotion started, even before the intruders came into sight, Aseem had been alerted by the gadget strapped to his waist, Hakeema's gift. First it became warm and then it began to throb, though he didn't know why. Now he knew, but all he could do was watch.

He was at once concerned for Jack and Meena and, let's be honest, the success of his mission. He moved hastily to some thick vegetation a little further away, where he could still observe. As he reached the shelter of a rhododendron bush, the intruders landed beside the fume duct. Had they seen him? Two of them came into view, searching the undergrowth. Aseem knew what they were, and shuddered. He had never dreamt they could follow him here from Ardunya; Sharfeat had sent them.

They were shadowbats, black all over apart from their large, red eyes. They looked like bats but much bigger, with elongated bodies – like a meerkat, only twice the height. They could fly fast with their batwings or walk on feet shod in what looked like metal boots. Shadowbats were vicious.

——— § ———

Squashed together in the cupboard under the table, Jack and Meena could hardly think for the drilling noise overhead, and the rattling and rumbling all around. The whole lab started to shudder, as though an earthquake had struck. They heard the roof above their heads groan ominously, as if about to give way. The table was several inches thick, so Jack felt they would be safe there even if the roof fell in; but it was getting airless in the cupboard, and that might be more of a danger.

He and Meena took turns peeking through the gap between the cupboard doors. Through the swirling plaster dust and rain of grit and particles, they could see a circular patch, roughly half a metre in diameter, being carved out in the ceiling. The edges of the cut were turning black, smouldering, the smoke lazily dissipating as the circle was completed. An instant later, with a loud bang, the circular slab of concrete fell to the floor. They glimpsed blue sky through the clouds of dust.

One by one, the creatures descended to the floor, tucking their bat wings behind their thin bodies as they landed. They began to move around the lab, searching. After a quick scan, the three creatures simultaneously eyed each other; it looked telepathic. Wedged in the cupboard, Jack and Meena didn't move a muscle, but it was only a matter of time before they were found. Jack knew why the creatures were here. Meena thought of Aseem, out there alone. What if the bats found him? She shivered.

The shadowbats began to throw, overturn or break everything in sight. Within a minute, the lab looked like a bomb site. A bottle cracked on the table above them and leaked onto the hot mould, starting a small fire before rolling off and smashing on the floor in front of the cupboard. Flames licked around the jar, fumes poured out and a pungent odour hit their nostrils. The flames shot down the trickle of liquid and ran across the floor.

If Jack and Meena came out of the cupboard, the shadowbats would attack them; if they stayed put, they would be poisoned or burnt to death. Not a great choice. Another bottle smashed and began giving off billowing clouds of thick smoke, like dense fog on a winter morning. They could see only a couple of feet, but Jack knew where to go. Professor Shreddon had made sure of that when he began using the lab.

Opposite their hiding place, about three metres away, was a low platform (in case of flooding, the professor said) and an emergency exit, installed when this was a high-security military command centre – and a good thing in a lab, where accidents are always possible. From the look on Meena's face, she was a nervous wreck. Jack nudged her knee with his elbow. "Follow me. C'mon!" he whispered.

"Okay." Normally she would insist on being told what was he planning – but now she was ready to do exactly what he said. She had no bright ideas, and discussion was impossible.

Jack cautiously opened the doors and awkwardly, with the crystal jabbing into his thigh, let himself down to the floor on his hands and knees. Meena did the same and started to crawl behind him, trying to avoid the broken glass and acid on the floor. They couldn't tell where the shadowbats were. The smoke was so thick that even Jack's head was a bit hazy to Meena, but his bottom was clear enough, and that was all she needed to follow.

As she crawled onto the platform, Jack reached up and pulled the metal bar to open the emergency door. Unused for a long time, it didn't open as smoothly as he had expected. There was a loud squeak. Within moments, the shadowbats closed in, standing or circling in front of them, red eyes fixed on them like laser beams, unsheathing their claws.

Meena had never felt such menace, even in nightmares, but she wasn't going to give up, even if she could see no way to divert the imminent attack. Jack let go of the door, and it closed with a sudden squeal. He got to his feet and put his hands up. Meena watched him, aghast.

One of the shadowbats flew straight at them, opening its nostrils wide. Meena put her arms out as if to grab it, and it swerved sideways and down through the flames of the little chemical fire; they heard a snort as it breathed out heavily, followed by a bang. The shadowbat had exploded. The beast was a mass of flame: within 20 seconds it had burnt to a blackened crisp. The rest paused uncertainly. Jack seized this moment to grab the bar on the exit door again.

———— § ————

Aseem had been watching the whole assault, at first from under the rhododendron. When the attackers dropped through the hole in the lab roof, he crept to the edge and observed the mayhem below. He couldn't see Jack or Meena; they must be trapped. What was he to do? Then, through the smoke, he saw them right below him, Jack surrendering. That would put them in Sharfeat's power – unless the shadowbats followed instinct and ripped them to pieces.

He could not go home without Jack and his crystal. If the earthling were saved, he might be able to show him how their destinies were entangled, like ivy round a grapevine. Aseem liked Meena, but that was irrelevant – it was Jack he needed – but she believed him and Jack didn't. And Jack would follow her anywhere. She was the bait: she must be saved too.

That sounds callous and calculating. Actually, Aseem's first impulse was to jump in and save them; but he had been educated as a prince so, among other things, he had learnt to put impulses aside when making big decisions – like this one.

He could see only one answer. It had worked before, with Tom the bandit; this was far riskier, but there was no time for anything else. Aseem calmly focused his mind on the hole in the lab roof. Within seconds, the soil, grit, twigs and leaves that had collected there began to stir. Fitfully at first, then faster and faster the debris swirled and circled. Now the updraught was sucking dust and smoke out through the hole. The gust caught the shadowbats' wings, tossing them this way and that, out of control.

Meena and Jack were caught off balance. He held onto the metal bar of the emergency exit; she, still on the floor, grabbed his legs. He managed to hold on, until the wind lifted Meena off her feet. Her weight had been holding Jack down; now it was an extra strain on his grip.

The remains of lab equipment flew past, shattering against the walls, the ceiling or even them. The force sucked up all the smoke and lethal fumes, but it also took much of the air. They found it difficult to breathe. Jack was dangling in mid-air, his arms weakening; Meena, losing consciousness, was barely holding on. Their attackers were trying desperately to grab anything their claws could grip, but the gusts were too powerful for them. Dashed against the walls or ceiling, they fell concussed, apart from one bat, which shot up through the aperture and high into the air. Aseem saw it was time to stop.

72

But Jack had already succumbed. He lost his grip, and the whirlwind lifted them both towards the centre of the room, throwing them about like two feathers. Now suffocating, Meena relaxed her grip on Jack just as the updraught slackened. She fell heavily onto the wooden crate, which slowly toppled over, dropping her to the ground, where she hit her head. A moment later, Jack landed on top of her.

Still breathless, Jack realised what he was lying on and got up carefully. The bang on her head had brought Meena back to consciousness, but not to her senses. A little trickle of blood ran down one side of her face, which was unusually pale, but she didn't seem concerned or in pain. She just lay there, sprawled awkwardly, staring dazedly into the middle distance. Jack looked at her helplessly, unsure what to do.

"You all right?"

Oblivious to the bleeding, Meena confusedly shook her head. "Think so … bit of a headache, though."

As the wind dropped away, there was a thud as a box fell back to the floor. Then it erupted in a series of bangs and brilliant flashes. The carton contained hundreds of old-fashioned camera flashbulbs, some of which went off, creating spectacular blue flares. Jack was dazzled by these spontaneous fireworks.

They heard a screech and saw a shadowbat motionless on the floor. Acrid, strange-coloured smoke rose from it. The others were flying around, screaming as they swooped and swerved this way and that. Meena wondered vaguely what the foul stench was.

Jack had no problem working it out. It was the smell of a shadowbat being burnt to a crisp after being hit by a camera flash. Intact flashbulbs lay on the floor. How did they work? On a shelf, Jack saw the professor's collection of old cameras, most of them fitted with flashbulbs. He grabbed two and nudged Meena gently with his elbow.

"Owwww!!! Careful!"

"Sorry. Here, take a picture."

"What? Of you?"

"No, a bat! Quick!"

Seeing the flashes, Aseem peered down into the lab and was puzzled by what Jack and Meena were up to. A shadowbat dived and Meena shook herself into action. Its wing brushed her arm as she pressed the shutter, too late.

"Get another camera! The light hurts them."

Still dazed, she picked up another camera and targeted one of the remaining shadowbats. As she snapped the shutter, it dodged behind the fume cupboard and she missed. Jack tried. He waited until a bat was flying straight at him before pressing the shutter. It had no chance to react. There was a dazzling flash, a squawk and a thud as it fell to the ground writhing.

73

The boy with the violet eyes

The shadowbat that had been sucked out now returned. The other two, having seen their comrades fall, were vengeful and reckless. There was pandemonium. As Jack grabbed another camera, all three flew straight at him, as if the flashes couldn't hurt them or they just didn't care. Jack, unnerved, pressed the shutter without aiming. Meena watched in horrified fascination.

Aseem lowered himself over the edge, first onto his elbows, then further until he hung by his fingers. He prayed and let go. Picking himself up, he glanced around. Having no idea what you did with a camera, he went for the nearest creature with his bare hands. One second the aliens were converging on Jack; a second later they split up, each taking one of the trio. Their long claws were sharp as razor blades, and their beaks could easily cut a finger in two.

Meena was the only one who had flash cameras to hand, and she used one after another to keep her opponent at bay. Aseem had forced the newcomer to the ground, using his feet to pin down its claws but unable to subdue it. Neither of them showed any sign of giving in. Jack lashed out with his foot and kicked his attacker halfway across the room. He spotted the portable ultra-violet lamp and picked it up. The enraged shadowbat hurtled back towards him, talons outstretched. Jack mastered his nerves and took aim.

The beam of ultra-violet light hit the bat. It was so close it crashed into him, knocking him over. He jumped up. It writhed on the floor, so hot that its skin began to bubble; the ultra-violet radiation had made the body cells overheat. Then it burst into flames, rapidly burning away to nothing.

Unable to reach another flash camera, Meena tried to copy Jack and kick her assailant. It was dodging, getting more confident and aggressive; Jack was terrified that, any moment, its claws might tear her face. He took a deep breath and aimed with the UV lamp. He missed; the bat turned angrily and flew at him. He aimed again, and this time it fell, caught fire and burnt.

Aseem's antagonist had broken free, and Aseem was bleeding from a scalp wound. This was the only shadowbat left, but it seemed as determined as ever. Jack was about to use the UV lamp again when an awkward thought made him pause. Meena was horrified.

"What're you waiting for? Shoot!"

He couldn't. Aseem too was an alien: if he was as vulnerable to ultra-violet radiation as the bats, it would kill him! Meena frantically grabbed the lamp and started firing. Jack was shocked.

"It might kill Aseem!"

"No! It won't – he's been flashed already," she replied confidently.

She tried again, but the creature's agility, twisting and turning, prevented her hitting the target. The shadowbat, seeing the odds against it, abruptly abandoned the fight with Aseem and flew up to the hole in the roof. It hovered there for a moment and glared at Meena before flying away.

———— § ————

Jack checked that he still had the crystal in his pocket – he could feel it digging into his thigh. Now the dust had settled, he looked around. The lab was ruined. He had no idea how he was going to explain this catastrophe to the professor, but just now he had a more important task. He went to the kitchen, got a clean cloth, put it under the hot tap, then wrung it out so it was just damp.

He wasn't sure whether this was what you were supposed to do, but he had to do something. He went back to Meena and, without saying anything, began gently to wash the blood and dust off her face, being careful not to start the cut on her cheek bleeding again. In no time the cloth was filthy and bloodstained.

"Come on," he said simply and took her by the hand.

She was so astonished that she didn't even make one of her usual sharp comments. He took her to the kitchen, which was untouched, and sat her down. He rinsed the cloth, wrung it out and went back to cleaning her face and neck. The skin was still tender, so he tried to stroke rather than rub, though she winced when he touched a nasty bruise on her forehead. Even so, she smiled.

"Thank you," she said, equally simply.

Jack now turned to Aseem, who had followed them. He was exhausted, and his face and hands had several long scratches; It had been a brutal fight. Jack put his hands on Aseem's shoulders and made him sit down too. While he was rinsing his cloth in warm water again, Meena spoke for both of them.

"Thanks, Aseem. You saved us, again. How do you do it?"

Aseem was too weary to speak, but he inclined his head and gave her a smile. He looked up to see Jack approaching, brandishing his cloth; more remarkable, for the first time he could remember, Jack had a pleasant smile. In Aseem's opinion, it improved his face considerably. This was a quite different Jack: something – or someone – had changed him.

Jack had unanswered questions, but this wasn't the time. Instead, he said: "You didn't tell me you could wrestle with bats."

"You did not enquire."

They both smiled gravely, while Jack cleaned up Aseem's face.

"What were those horrible creatures?"

"Shadowbats ... Sharfeet's minions. They came to eliminate you."

Into Meena's mind rushed a horrifying image: Jack's pale, inert corpse, sprawled like a torn rag doll, his face torn to pieces by sharp claws. She covered up her emotion by saying "They'll know not to mess with Jack again".

Jack said "I'd be mincemeat if it wasn't for you guys".

"I am hoping that bulge in your pocket—" began Aseem. Seeing Jack start to extract it, he added "Please, later. Now is not safe."

When *is* safe? Jack recalled the shadowbat's parting glare at Meena – as nasty as Sharfeat's menacing stare. Aseem had told Jack he was being hunted. If he didn't want to die, he had to know more. Aseem knew things he didn't – some of them unscientific, maybe – but he decided to trust Meena's judgement and accept what Aseem told him, not waste time questioning it.

He took a deep breath. "Okay, Aseem. You'd better tell me everything."

"Miraculous! I am gleeful to hear that – but not here. They may return."

Outside, under the trees, Aseem began to talk. "Those shadowbats are among the vilest and deadliest beasts on Ardunya – we call them omens of death. I thought they were indestructible. Now I know otherwise. They are willing slaves of the enemies of my realm – and that is where we can defeat them, with your help. Will you come?"

"Do I have a choice? No, it's time to face my nightmares." Jack looked determined.

Meena could hardly believe what she was seeing: Jack ready to face his fears and accept realities not found in science textbooks. She truly believed that the prophecy on the scroll meant Jack. That tiny portrait that looked like him, yet displayed the wear and tear of a thousand years, had caught her imagination and convinced her.

In any case, they had seen Ardunya for themselves – travelling through a wormhole, it seemed – what an adventure! What did Peter Pan say? "To die would be a very big adventure." They'd escaped that, for now. Perhaps it wasn't wise to go back – but you can't always do only what is wise.

12 Just Jack

"May we peregrinate at once?" Aseem asked.

Another word to look up, thought Jack. Guessing, he said diplomatically: "I'll be quick as I can, but I have to see the professor and check on my mum."

"That is most filial," nodded Aseem, "But mayhap we should not remain."

"Come with me," Meena, "You'll be safe at the shop."

"Good idea, Meena," put in Jack, "Except I was hoping—"

"I'd look in on your mum? Course! You go and find the professor."

"Thanks – here's the key. There's not a lot in the fridge, but be my guest."

"You are a most munificent host."

"I don't know about that. You haven't seen my house yet."

"Will your mum need something to eat?"

"She might. I think she'll just be happy to see you. Tell her I'm with the professor. That way, she won't worry."

Wow! she thought. *A new, decisive Jack – and considerate with it.*

"Let's meet at mine in, say, three quarters of an hour. You'll have to concoct some excuse for your dad."

"I can do that." She gave him a wicked smile. "No problemo!"

"You're bad! See you in a bit." Aseem and Meena watched him stride off towards the high street.

———— § ————

As he walked, the scenes of fighting and havoc in the lab kept re-running in Jack's mind. They reminded him of the dreadful end to Aseem's party – and parents. Poor Aseem! His world had been destroyed in minutes. Jack was lucky by comparison – except now he was being hunted. That problem wouldn't go away. What was it Hakeema said? "Problems, you can solve." *That's what I'm good at. But I can only solve this problem on Ardunya.*

Aseem needed him; Jack owed him. Thanks to Aseem, he'd got rid of Tom, got back from Ardunya, escaped the shadowbats, discovered his origins and seen a picture of his father. This time, when he returned – *if* he returned – he wanted to know more about his family. Before that he had to pay his debts to the prince.

Who would look after his mum? Jack saw at once there was only one adult he could be sure of: the professor. He was a man who would always cross the road to help someone in need, and he had a soft spot for Jack. But Jack first had to find some way to tell him his laboratory had been destroyed.

It was Saturday morning and the high street was busy. At the electrical store, the professor was at the counter, helping out another customer, reassembling some device as he talked to the shopkeeper. Jack loitered, inspecting LCD units; his acting would not have fooled a 5-year-old. Paul Shreddon hastened to finish what he was doing.

"Jack … what brings you here? Experiment successful, was it?"

"Y-y-yes, Professor, m-m-more or less."

"What is it? Hit a snag?"

"N-not exactly. I-I need to ask you something."

"Of course! Always glad to help. There you are, Charlie, all fixed. Now, Jack, let's pop round to Gianni's: you can ask all the questions you want while we have a little something."

At the little Italian restaurant, Jack sat, miserable and silent, while Paul Shreddon ordered a pizza, a coke and a cup of tea. He noticed scratches on the boy's face and a rip in his tee-shirt.

"Have a drink. You look as though you could do with one."

The boy did as he was told, desperately trying to think of a way to start. He felt terrible. The fight in the lab, with its soundtrack of noise, replayed across his mind. Ripples of fear and distress flickered across his face. Paul Shreddon wondered whether bullies were involved. After a pause, he said gently "I'm all ears".

"Well, it's this friend … he's just lost his parents, and he needs help. He says I'm the only one who *can* help, though I'm not sure how, but there doesn't seem to be anybody else … only he lives far away – really far away – so I'm going to be away for a bit … and I wondered what to do about Mum."

Paul Shreddon was baffled: what had this got to do with the fight Jack had been in? At that point the pizza arrived. "*Grazie*, Antonio. No, nothing else, thank you … Now Jack, get that down you, while I ask a few things so I'm a bit clearer in my mind. Just nod for yes and shake your head for no. You don't have to tell me anything you don't want to."

I don't want to tell you about the lab, but I'll have to in the end.

"Nurse Dixon comes in every weekday, doesn't she? Mornings, I think?"

Nod.

"And Mrs Whale does three mornings a week?"

Nod.

"But there's just you on Saturdays and Sundays?"

Nod.

"And this friend needs help today, is that it?"

Nod.

"If I pop in two or three times a day until you get back, would that solve your problem?"

Nod, nod, nod. Two violet eyes glistened. A smile lit up Jack's pale face.

"I'll get some groceries and call on my way home. Can your mother answer the door?"

"There's a spare key under a stone by the back door. Mum put it there in case I lost mine."

"Wonderful! It's a good reason for me to cook a proper meal. If you're going far, you'd better take this." The professor fished out some banknotes and some change.

"Are you sure? Oh thank you, Professor."

"Is that all? Some problem with your rocket?" He was not so easily deceived.

"No." There was a pause. Jack's mind was in a whirl. He had forgotten the pizza.

"Have you done something wrong, Jack?"

"No!" He almost shouted, and people turned to look. He lowered his voice. "No. It's just that … you might think I have. It's hard to explain."

"Yes, I see that. Keep trying."

Jack shifted in his seat; a large lump in his pocket jabbed at him. He took a deep breath, chose the right words and organised them into short sentences. "My crystal came out fine. But this gang saw it through the skylight and broke in. They didn't find it, but they smashed up the lab looking." He stared at his plate, unable to face Paul.

"Well, thank goodness you're all right. What about Meena?"

"She got a bit of a bump. She's gone home to get it seen to."

"Phew! That's good."

"But your lab! And your experiments. Aren't you angry?"

"Not a bit, Jack. You fought back, by the look of you. What could you do against a whole gang? Tell me, would you recognise them again?"

"No. Meena and I hid in a store cupboard." *That's an honest answer – and it wouldn't help if I told him what they looked like.*

"Very wise. Well, I'll report it to the police, though they won't do anything. The great thing is that you and Meena are all right. My insurance can repair the lab, and I can repeat my experiments. They wouldn't be good science if they couldn't be repeated."

"I thought you'd be so upset, I didn't know how to tell you."

"But luckily I know how to listen. I'll sort out the lab. You'd better see if Meena's all right, then find your friend and get off. Tell your mother I'll burn a dinner for her later on."

Jack stood up, filled with relief, bursting with things he wanted to say and didn't have words for. "Thanks for the pizza and the drink. And for being so cool." He gave the professor a big smile, turned and rushed out of the door.

The professor sat, stunned. Gianni came up with the bill and a puzzled smile.

———— § ————

The boy with the violet eyes

It was a normal, pleasant autumn day: no thunder or lightning, no torrential rain or high winds, no floods. The raksas had stopped persecuting Wellington Spa. *Because the shadowbats found me. Oh, no! In that case, maybe they've found Mum. What if—?*

He began to run, and his mind shifted up a gear. He'd always taken his mother for granted. Everyone had a mum, just as everyone had a nose. Having no mum was unthinkable. He felt guilty and despairing as he charged up the path to the back door. Breathlessly, he searched his pocket for the key, panicked when he couldn't find it, then remembered Meena had it. He got the spare key from under the stone and rushed back to open the door.

The kitchen didn't look any different, but the house was silent. Where were Meena and Aseem? Jack rushed up the stairs, two at a time, and along the landing. He flung the door open and stopped. His mother was sitting on the bed, staring. He had never seen anyone's eyes open so wide. She gazed at him in silent horror, her mouth twisted in fear, one arm outstretched with the hand up, as if to fend him off. Had she seen the shadowbats? Was she having a nightmare?

"Mum! It's me!"

She didn't move. Jack ran to the bed and grabbed her arm. It was rigid, hard as iron, unlike any human limb. It was stone. He clung to her, sobbing and cursing. Why would anyone do this to a helpless victim? *To show he's ruthless. It's a warning.* Sharfeat knew about the crystal now. The shadowbats would be back to get it and deal with Jack – and Meena, and Aseem.

He got a grip of himself. *I must find the others. I'd better leave a note for the professor.* He found pen and paper, but he wan't good with words. It took a minute more to find a way to tell the professor he wasn't needed, without making him suspicious. He pinned it to the back door.

Jack dived back inside and rummaged in the rucksack he'd taken camping. He grabbed a torch, whistle, compass, gloves, tin mug, pocket-knife, two balls of twine and a bar of Kendal mint cake. He shoved them in his pockets, closed the door, put the key back under the stone and ran down the path.

He was bitter and grim. *I nearly gave up earlier – never again. Sharfeat is going to pay for this. If the worst happens, I'll take him with me. I want justice. Why didn't Aseem do anything? I hope the bats didn't get him. Maybe he's at Meena's place. She won't give up – she'd stand up to anyone – and I've got nothing to lose.* Actually, he had a great deal to lose. We all have.

———— § ————

He didn't get far. Running along Hornbeam Avenue, past the high hedges, he swerved onto the grass to avoid someone who ran out from a driveway and rugby-tackled him. As they fell over, she cupped her hand over his mouth. It was Meena!

"Over here!" came a loud whisper.

Aseem's face poked out from behind a large evergreen bush beside the drive; he had a finger to his mouth. Meena quickly pulled Jack behind the bush, where they were sheltered on all sides. Only then did she speak, in a whisper.

"Those bats are all round our shop. They flew inside, but they came straight out again. We saw them attacking Tom and Alec. It looked nasty."

Aseem was a confused picture of guilt and sympathy. "They flitted from your residence as we arrived. I deeply grieve … we were too late." Only two days ago it had happened to him.

Meena's eyes showed her sadness. There had been just the two of them, Jack and Anita; now there was just Jack. *Well, not just Jack – he's got me.* "I'm so sorry, Jack."

He saw that she could have said much more. She was a true friend: sticking by him, staying calm, saying and doing the right thing. She gave Jack the boost he needed. Right away he looked more alert and determined. "What now, Aseem?" he asked.

"We can do naught here. If we are to avenge our parents, we must take the crystal to Macron forthwith. Hakeema will advise you how to use the crystal and end the black-flower plague. Then, with your help, we will vanquish Sharfeat."

Jack looked unusually calm. "That's not enough. I want justice. I want to see him beg for his life and then get wiped out." Meena was shocked at the violence in his words.

Aseem was diplomatic. "I too long for justice."

In a gap between the bushes, Meena noticed a lace curtain twitch at the house.

Jack said, "Right, Aseem, can we go now? I won't survive those creeps a second time."

Aseem reached inside his bundi and brought out a white tablet. Using finger and thumb, he began crushing it into powder. Over his shoulder, Meena saw the house door open; a tall, stern-looking woman emerged. Jack looked up and saw two shapes swoop and soar, high overhead, flying towards his house. He moved closer to Meena till their shoulders touched, then cupped his hands ready. She did the same, watching the woman striding down the drive. Jack noticed one shadowbat turn and head back towards them.

Aseem, reciting a verse rapidly under his breath, spread what looked like chalk dust across his palm and gave them some. He circled them anti-clockwise, muttering a spell as he made a ring with the dust. The woman was almost close enough to speak; she looked as though she might have something to say to Aseem about his white dust.

The boy with the violet eyes

He joined them in the circle. Meena and Jack felt a cold shock shoot up their spines, then a gust of freezing wind blew around them, whirling up leaves and soil until they could see nothing for the cloud of debris. The shadowbat dived. The woman opened her mouth to speak.

———— § ————

Paul Shreddon had been to his laboratory and found that Jack had not exaggerated; it might take months to put this right. He had been to the police station, where they spent half an hour filling in forms and then told him there was nothing they could do, since he had no description of the burglars, "But you'll need this case number, sir, for your insurance claim". He didn't bother telling them about his rather odd find, since he couldn't make sense of it.

He had been to the shops to get extra food and some little treats that might give Anita Cooper new strength. He carried the bags up to the house, ready to cook a meal for the two of them. When he got there, he found this note pinned to the back door:

Dear Proffesor, Mum has desided to go and stay with her sister so she ~~dusnt~~ does not need help at present. I am sory if you had to by extra food. I hope to see you soon. Your good freind Jack.

He sighed, put it in his pocket, picked up his bags and set off home. He wasn't angry, but the sight of his lab had been a shock; he'd been looking forward to having something to do and someone to talk to. He wished his wife was still alive.

Children don't realise when they make life difficult. No, that's unfair. Jack's a good boy. He's taken a few knocks today, yet he left me a note and he remembered about the shopping. I'm lucky to have him as a friend. The professor was a remarkable man.

When he had gone, Galileo tried mewing at the back door again. After five minutes, she made up her mind and headed off to 14 Hornbeam Avenue, where Mr Evans was expecting Dinah, who looked exactly like Galileo and seemed to spend a lot of time away hunting.

Mrs Evans stood open-mouthed, staring at the spot where three children had been playing in her shrubbery. In a puff of smoke, they had turned into a giant bat, which was now struggling to free itself from the cypress bush into which it had crashed. She felt vaguely that in some way this punishment, if a little bizarre, fitted the crime. *That'll teach them.*

13 Unlucky for some

Fortunately, the river turned out to be pleasantly warm and shallow, the current so sluggish you hardly noticed it. Meena loved the water. Her gilet left her arms free so, despite her jeans and shoes, she swam easily up to the surface.

Jack was still trying to work out where he was when he realised he couldn't breathe: he was under water. Though he could swim, Jack did not like water. Hampered by his coat and a bit panicky, he thrashed about until he remembered to kick upwards. Breaking the surface, he spotted Meena and swam steadily towards her.

Where was Aseem? They trod water, looking around, expecting him to surface at any second. Then Meena noticed a few bubbles nearby. As she swam to the spot, up shot Aseem like a balloon, gasping for air.

Aseem struggled frantically to stay afloat, splashing and thrashing about. His head disappeared as he turned turtle; for a few moments they saw only two waving legs, until these submerged and his face popped up again, breathless and bewildered.

Meena reached him first and held him up until Jack got there. They each took an arm, swimming on either side, and slowly got him to the shore. He couldn't get out of the water fast enough. As they staggered to their feet on the sandy beach, Aseem scurried up the bank. The other two were standing there, panting and soaking wet, when Meena shrieked.

She was staring wide-eyed at two black leeches on Jack's neck. Aseem came back. "Remain still," he told Jack and tried to peel them off, but their minute teeth were well dug in. He found a dry leaf and tried again, and this trick unhooked both leeches.

"Ouch … that hurts!" Jack rubbed his neck. What sort of place was this?

The riverbank was sandy scrubland – grass, bushes and spindly trees – but within 200 yards this turned into forest, which covered even the distant hills. Apart from scattered bird calls and the sound of them dripping, it was quiet. It was also hot. They looked in vain for the walled city of Macropuris, for *any* sign of settlement – a chimney, a cart-track. They saw nothing but virgin wilderness. Jack started to panic. *This isn't where I landed last time, so where the splat are we?*

Meena was wondering the same. "Where are we, Aseem?"

Aseem's cheeks coloured. "I regret I know not."

"What d'you mean?" Jack snapped, "You must have some idea."

"In truth, no. I think this is Ardunya, but I am not certain."

Aseem was only being honest, but it didn't go down well. Jack turned to Meena: "He doesn't know where we are! I bet this isn't even the right galaxy."

"I don't think Hakeema would make that sort of mistake," Meena responded calmly, "We're off course, but it won't be far off. She'll tell us when she gets here."

Jack was lost for words.

At that moment, Aseem yelled "Beware! We have visitors!"

High up, something was coming their way and rapidly closing. There was no time to speculate whether it might be friendly; they scattered and hid. In seconds, Aseem and Meena were tucked out of sight under bushes.

Jack tripped over the roots of a small tree and fell headlong; he had no time left to hide. He stayed put, flat on his stomach with his hands over his head. The thing flew right overhead, almost touching him. His heart hammered at his chest. But it flew on and skimmed the surface of the river, where it picked up a fish with its talons. It looked more like a dinosaur than a bird.

Meena hurried over. "Are you hurt?"

Jack lifted his head. His nose was covered in sand. "No. I thought for a minute it was one of those shadowbats."

"Just some sort of bird – very big, though."

"Yes, I worked that out … thanks, anyway." Jack got up, brushing down his clothes. Getting worked up over landing in the wrong place, then tripping over that root, had made him feel and look pretty silly. Stupid, in fact. He forced himself to calm down and then began scanning in every direction to the horizon.

———— § ————

Aseem and Meena watched. They each had great respect for Jack, despite the irritating and idiotic things he did and said. Aseem had grown up with the legend of the black-flower plague, the Barelas family, their special powers and the crystal that put everything right. He had almost lost faith in Jack, but now he was feeling more confident again; after all, Jack was a born wizard.

Meena had grown up beside Jack. They'd had lots of fun together and she knew what an extraordinary brain he had; to her, Jack was a born scientist. To anyone else, he was nobody special, but decent, just a bit weird. Aren't we all?

By the time he had turned through 180°, Jack's heart had slowed to normal. This had to be the right galaxy. He extracted his compass and took a bearing on each sun. Neither was high in the sky, though it was still hot. One sun looked to be an hour or so off setting.

"I'm sure this is Ardunya: it's got two suns, one bigger than the other, about the right size, height and position. I guess nobody lives here – this land looks too poor to farm – though we might meet hunters. This river is bigger than the one by Macropuris. If it's the same river, the city must be upstream – probably well upstream, because it's hotter here – so we won't reach it before the suns set. We'll have to bivouac."

"What is 'bivouac'?" asked Aseem.

"It's when you make an overnight camp out of whatever you find – branches, leaves, twigs, moss, that sort of thing. It's a shelter from weather and wild animals."

"Is it possible to sleep outside?" asked Aseem in a worried voice.

"Yes, of course," said Meena confidently, "I did it in Brownies."

"I know naught of Brownies," said Aseem.

"You wouldn't, you're a prince," smiled Meena.

Jack, not wanting her to tease Aseem, broke in: "And I've camped with Cubs. But *we* haven't any tents. It's hot now, but it could be cold at night. We need a fire. If we sleep in wet clothes, we'll catch a cold."

"You sound like my mum," said Meena mischievously.

"How shall we manage without clean clothes?" asked Aseem, looking alarmed.

"The same way Jack does," said Meena sweetly. It struck her that Aseem had been out of his depth ever since he arrived, whereas Jack was now shaping up well. It was the second time in two days he had got wet through, and he wasn't fussing.

"They'll dry," said Jack, taking off his top, "It's time for a Little Something." He reached in his pocket.

"What thing?" asked Aseem, reluctantly unbuttoning his bundi.

"Something to eat," explained Meena, "It's what Winnie-the-Pooh says."

Aseem's next, inevitable question was cut off by Jack handing him a piece of mint cake. He tentatively nibbled it. Meena bit straight into hers and sat down to take off her shoes.

"That's a good idea, Meena. We can leave our things here to dry while we're foraging."

"'Tis indeed a strange sweetmeat!" said the prince delightedly.

"It'll keep us going," said Jack. "Aseem, do you know what is good to eat here? Berries, nuts, that kind of thing?"

"Indeed. Hakeema has shown me the fruits of the forest."

"Great! While you're finding food, Meena and I will find a bivouac site and collect stuff for a shelter. We'll meet back here in thirty minutes."

"How?" asked Meena.

"I've got a watch. If we aren't all here in half an hour, I'll blow my whistle." He got out his knife and twine. "Tie some string to this bush and carry it with you." Catching Meena's eye, he added "The string, not the bush."

"Like Theseus in the labyrinth!" exclaimed Meena.

"Exactly. Our last job will be to collect dry firewood."

"But we have no flints," said Aseem.

"If we find really dry wood, I can light a fire without flints."

Aseem looked at Jack in amazement. This was indeed a wizard.

———— § ————

The afternoon suns were very hot, so it was a relief to discard their outer layers. The warm sand between their toes felt good too. Jack and Aseem seemed to be all thumbs in tying knots, so Meena took over and tied one end of each ball of twine to the bush. Jack made a pile of his equipment; he took the whistle and pocket-knife with him, and gave the tin mug to Aseem.

"Use this for the berries, so they don't get squashed. Good luck!"

Aseem spotted some fruit bushes and went off. Jack and Meena had to stay together, having one ball of twine between them. It was 100 yards long so that was the radius of their search, but it kept snagging on bushes. It was soon obvious that, apart from the bushes and a few hollows like bunkers on a golf course, the scrubland was flat and featureless. At least the ground was sandy, clean and dry. Jack looked at his watch.

"Twenty minutes gone, Meena. What d'you think?"

"Let's go back to that hollow. We can put some leaves down so we don't get sand all over us, and then use some foliage to make a roof in case it rains."

"Good idea. Let's tie the twine around that tree at the hollow, so we can find it easily."

"It's a good job you brought that string, Jack. What made you think of it?"

"It's the bit of scouting I'm best at, being prepared. I never could do knots and things."

"Oh, I see. So 'let's tie it to that tree' really meant 'Meena, could you tie this knot for me?'"

Jack blushed. "Yeah, sorry." He needed her; he should at least be open about it.

Meena let it go; this was no time to go off the deep end. "It's all right. It's the bit of guiding I'm best at, tying knots. I've never been very good at navigation and stuff like that."

The knot tied, they gathered armfuls of greenery and laid it on the sand; next they tore off thin branches that had plenty of twigs and leaves, and dug them into the hollow; then Jack held them up two at a time while Meena plaited them into an arch to form a little bower.

When they got back to their meeting place, Aseem wasn't there. Jack blew his whistle. The prince returned with a handful of nuts, a mugful of berries and other fruit, looking pleased with himself. "There is a goodly crop of fruit yonder. May I perchance go and pick some more?"

"Course, but let's finish what you've got first." Sharing out the nuts and berries, they ate greedily.

"We've made a shelter," said Meena proudly, "And I've tied our string to a tree beside it. Just follow that and you can go straight to it."

"It is lucky you brought that string, Jack," said Aseem.

"Luck had nothing to do with it," replied Jack sharply.

"What's that?" put in Meena quickly. Aseem was holding what looked like a blue apple.

"We call it *manjweh* – it is soft and sweet. Please share it between you. I shall find more."

"Oh, that'd be great. We'll get the firewood and kindling."

Aseem went off to forage again. Jack and Meena found plenty of really dry wood. Within twenty minutes they had a good stock and a heap laid, ready to light, about 20 ft from their little shelter. They decided to have a competition. They each picked two pieces of kindling and began rubbing them together.

"It always works in stories," said Jack after a minute's hard effort.

"I've seen it work on telly," said Meena, "But it takes time."

After several minutes' hard work, they got smoke rising, and then Meena's stick burst briefly into flame. Within five minutes they were feeding twigs and branches to a crackling fire. While they were doing this, one sun set and dusk fell. They took it in turns to look after the fire while the other put on shoes and socks again.

Aseem returned with pocketfuls of nuts, a mugful of berries and an armful of *manjwei*. The nuts formed the savoury course and the fruit made a mouth-watering sweet. Jack wondered why apples are red, green or yellow, but never blue. There had to be a reason.

As they shared out the fruit, Aseem gasped. "Alack! What misfortune!"

"Because there are 13?" asked Meena, who had been counting too.

"It is evil luck to speak that number," said Aseem in shocked tones.

"I know a cure for bad luck," said Meena casually. She took the smallest fruit and ate it. "There you go. Twelve means we can share them equally."

"You are brave," said Aseem, looking at her admiringly.

"*You* are superstitious," said Jack unnecessarily.

"I know not this word 'superstitious'."

"It's when you think little things matter, that don't really," explained Jack.

"Like covering your mouth when you yawn?" asked Aseem.

"No," said Jack, who did this only when reminded, "Like thinking something bad will happen if you don't cover your mouth."

"That is preposterous!" Aseem exclaimed.

"You could say that," said Jack.

While they were eating, the second sun set. Myriads of stars twinkled and a full moon had risen, opposite the crescent moon already high in the sky. The night looked as beautiful as it had from the ramparts of the royal palace.

When they reached the sweet course, Jack had never tasted anything so luscious. He bit off such large chunks of fruit that he had to chew with his mouth open; he gulped them down, the juice dripping from his chin. Meena wiped her mouth. She was enjoying the *manjwei* too, until she noticed Aseem. He was looking aghast at Jack.

Meena was pretty much used to Jack's table manners, which she secretly hoped to improve, but to Aseem they came as a shock. His family were particular about etiquette. Without a word, he rose, took a large fruit resembling a peach and walked off to the riverbank some 50 ft away.

"What's got into him?" asked Jack through a mouthful of fruit.

"Your table manners," said Meena briefly.

"No table, no manners," said Jack with a grin.

"Your manners are just as bad at home. You should see yourself."

"Too bad I didn't bring a mirror."

"You're a mess."

Jack saw she was unimpressed by his wit – or his manners. But weren't manners just one of those unnecessary, unreasonable things that grown-ups insisted on, like saying 'please' and washing your hands? Even when Meena told him off, he assumed it must be one of those things that girls turn up their noses at and boys revel in, like play-fights, shouting and mud.

He'd gone wrong somewhere though, because manners clearly mattered to Aseem, who was neither a girl nor grown up.

———— § ————

As they toasted themselves by the fire, Meena broke the silence.

"Aseem was really impressed by the camping stuff you brought. So was I. I never knew you could be that practical."

"I'm not, really. I'm just good at thinking."

"I know: it was great the way you worked out where we were and what to do."

"Are you winding me up?"

"I can do that anytime. But no, I'm impressed."

"Go easy! You'll make me big-headed."

"You already are. Also selfish, bad-mannered, tactless …"

"But—"

"Stubborn and argumentative."

Jack was silenced.

"Now, have you a plan for tomorrow?"

"Sort of …"

"Well, why don't you talk it over with Aseem? See what he thinks. I'm off to sleep." *So satisfying! I've been wanting to say all that for ages.*

Meena wanted to give the boys a chance to talk and get more comfortable with each other. In any case, she was overcome with weariness: the bump on her head still hurt, her bruises ached and fresh air made her sleepy. She followed the string back to their meeting place, collected their things, untied the string and reeled it in on her way back. She said goodnight to the boys and went to lie down. Their shelter was near enough the fire to feel the warmth.

———— § ————

Jack and Aseem chatted about what they should do next morning. If they followed the river upstream, Aseem thought they might meet unfriendly strangers. He was very anxious about this, but he was also keen to reach Macropuris; as a result, the more they discussed the options, the more confused the prince became.

"We must wait for Hakeema. She will tell us what to do."

"She doesn't know where we are: we went off course, remember?" Jack replied.

"She will find us," said Aseem.

"Then she can find us wherever we are." *Only, if she can, maybe Sharfeat can.* "Time is precious, you said. If Hakeema isn't here by morning, we'll set off and trust our luck."

"Surely earthlings do not believe in luck?"

"Then we'll trust to *your* luck – and be careful."

They got some sods of earth to damp down the fire, so it would stay hot longer. They went to their shelter and, thoroughly tired, settled down to sleep.

Jack began making plans. He was wondering whether Meena would insist on them washing in the river, and whether this would be a good thing or not, when he found himself back in the water, having just arrived, still wondering which way was up. Armed with 13 apples and a piece of string, he slipped easily over the border into Dreamland.

14 In the forest

Dawn came swiftly. Sunlight dappled the faces of the three children in their shelter, but they did not stir. Only when the second sun rose did Meena rise too. The others slept on, waking to see her standing by the ashes of their fire, stretching her arms. She looked fresh and lively.

"Okay, guys – what's for breakfast? I'm starving."

Jack curled up again, warm and cosy. Thankfully, there had been no nightmares. Aseem leapt up, dusting off his clothes.

"Shrubs with tasty berries abound nearby," he answered.

"Come on, Jack," said Meena, "Rise and shine!" Her mother said this every morning.

They weren't going to leave him alone, so Jack got up; he was hungry too. Aseem led them to some fruit bushes overhanging a beach. The river was spectacularly beautiful, sunlight sparkling on its ripples as though millions of tiny stars were dancing in excitement at being allowed to stay up. The air was already pleasantly warm, and only the plashing of the river broke the silence. In a near-cloudless lilac sky, two suns shone, one on each side of the wooded valley. It was like having an idyllic country park all to themselves.

"This is where I got washed," announced Meena, "You two wash, then we can eat."

Just as I feared, thought Jack. *Oh well.*

It is unseemly to perform one's ablutions openly, thought Aseem, *But it would be even less seemly not to wash at all. Oh well.*

Oh good, thought Meena, *They're not making any fuss about washing.*

Having washed, they ate. All around were fruit trees and thorny bushes covered in berries, ripe and easy to pluck. As he ate, Jack pondered how to deal with the shadow soldiers if they came face to face. He knew now that shadowbats weren't indestructible – and so did Sharfeat. They fled from flashes, ultra-violet light killed them and the noxious gas from their nostrils would burn. He needed some sort of instant fire. Would it work on shadowhawks too, like the ones that ended Aseem's twelving party?

Looking up, he saw dozens of shadowhawks patrolling, in the distance beyond the river.

"Jack, what should we do?" Aseem whispered as they crouched under a bush.

"We've got to shake them off."

"But how?"

"There's only one way. That way!" Jack pointed to the trees.

The others didn't fancy getting lost in the forest, but it seemed their only hope.

"Come on, let's get our stuff," Jack said.

They crept back to their camp and grabbed their few belongings. Jack quickly took a compass bearing on the larger sun, then on a heading parallel to the river. He would adjust their course later on. They stealthily headed for the trees.

Within a short distance, most of the sky was blotted out by the forest canopy, which let in only trickles of sunlight. In places the forest floor was clear, but much of it was covered in dark-leaved bushes and weeds. It was a jungle, silent apart from the occasional bird call high above. It reminded Meena of tales her father had told her about getting lost in the Indian jungle. It reminded Jack that they were lost on another planet, with only magic to get them home.

There were no paths, no animal tracks even; they might be the first creatures ever to have penetrated this undergrowth. It was steadily uphill, since they were following the river upstream. It was hard work, pushing through creepers, bushes and weeds. Their hands were soon covered in scratches.

After an hour, they came across some fruit bushes. While the others filled the mug with berries, Jack tried to get his bearings, but he couldn't really tell where the suns were. The best they could do was aim to hit the river; then they'd know where they were. He set the compass for their new heading, hoping his arithmetic was right. They hadn't seen any shadow soldiers, so he felt confident that Sharfeat's minions wouldn't spot them through the forest canopy.

It was dark, silent, airless and humid. Not only were they hot and tired from walking, but they perspired so much their skin itched, making them irritable. After they had plodded on for another half-hour, Meena noticed the boys were starting to trip over tree roots. It was time they stopped, before they hurt themselves. "Jack! Could we rest for a bit? My feet are killing me."

"Course. It's time for a bite anyway."

"That is most welcome and timely."

Meena and Aseem mopped their faces; Jack wiped his with his sleeve. They shared out Aseem's berries, three fruits that Meena had collected earlier – their only supply of liquid – and some of Jack's mint cake.

In the next hour, the uphill trend became more noticeable. Jack changed course again, but he often had to stop to check his bearing as the uneven ground slowed them down, forcing them to make detours around rocks and crags. They heard an occasional roar of a wild animal echoing across valleys far away. Reptiles and insects scurried under their feet. It was still very close, but not as hot as before.

Soon the sunlight seemed brighter. The forest was thinning. Each clearing was bigger than the last, and the hillside was levelling out. They were just telling each other the worst was over, when the ground under their feet became soft and waterlogged.

Within yards they were in a bog, with water nearly up to their knees. Scared to stop, unable to turn back, they staggered onwards, struggling to lift their feet, almost falling when they did. The glade that had seemed so welcome was a death-trap. They all sighed with relief as they reached firm ground on the other side.

——— § ———

There was a shriek. Meena had been only a couple of steps behind Aseem. Jack turned and saw her in mid-air, dangling upside-down from a tree. Her foot was caught in a rope trap.

Jack screamed in horror and at that moment a trumpet blast rang out. Aseem stood frozen. Before Jack could get by him to free Meena, they were surrounded by guerrillas, closing in and shouting war cries. It was an ambush.

The next thing they knew, Aseem and Jack were pinned back to back by rough-looking men wearing leather aprons and jerkins, pointing spears and daggers in their faces. Two of the band let Meena down. They lifted her off her feet and dragged her to join the others. The captives' hands were tied behind their backs and another rope linked their necks.

"Do you know who I am?—" Aseem began, outraged.

"Silence!" The voice was deep and commanding. Warriors moved aside for the speaker. The chief had a serious, stubborn face, with narrow, ominous blue eyes. It looked as though he had not shaved for a few days. There were grey highlights in his curly black hair and rugged beard. A long, deep scar ran down from his left eye to his chin, from a knife or sword fight in the past. He wore thick chain-mail as body armour. Meena and Jack were impressed.

Aseem was not. "You are committing a grave error."

The chief didn't seem interested in his error or his well-dressed captive. With little more than a glance at them, he gave a few rapid orders to the men at the rear, then strode back to the head of the hunting party, whose determined faces told a tale of their own. They were ready for some unseen enemy, facing outwards, weapons in hand, eyes scanning the forest.

One guard took hold of the rope around Aseem's neck and yanked him forward. Jack and Meena, tied to the same rope, had no choice but to follow. They set off again, on roughly the same bearing that Jack had taken. The pace was much faster, too fast. Tied together, in single file, they could see only a yard or so in front of them, with little chance to choose their footing. If they slowed or stumbled, the guards gave them a sharp prod with a spear.

There was nothing they could do. They were lost in the forest, unarmed and tied together, outnumbered by guards who were heavier and stronger. Just showing hostility or disgust might provoke them. Aseem was still angry at being ignored. How sorry their captors would be when Hakeema caught them! Meena told herself that everyone had a weakness and she had a weapon. Unfortunately, the guards didn't look vulnerable to charm. Jack was considering the evidence. Meena had been caught in a snare like a rabbit; did that mean they were destined for rabbit pie? How were they to escape and reach Macropuris?

The hunting party hurried through the woods as if there were a bounty on their heads. They seemed on edge, even afraid. They kept looking up through the treetops, as if danger lurked above. It seemed to Jack that captors and captives feared a common enemy.

Eventually, they emerged from the forest onto a track through unfenced farmland. There were still trees, but now they could see the sky. There was not a single shadow soldier in sight.

———— § ————

Their destination was marked by a high grassy bank, topped by a wooden wall of big baulks of timber, above which the heads of sentries could be seen. A deep trench around the perimeter was bridged in front of a gateway two storeys high, made of big logs like a frontier fort. Until they were underneath it, they didn't spot the watchtower high in a tree, made to blend in with the foliage.

It wasn't a fort, but a fortified village, like something out of Africa or the middle ages. The muddy track led past a tavern, smithy, workshops, meeting hall and dozens of simple dwellings, mostly of mud, all roofed with straw. They hardly seemed worth defending, yet the earthworks, palisade and sentries showed these people feared attack. The villagers, from wrinkled crones to small children, stood in doorways and watched them warily.

The raiding party stopped outside a windowless mud cabin. The chief ordered a man to untie the rope joining their necks, and they were pushed inside, Meena first. In the hovel, their hands were untied. Then the guards left. They heard the door barred. The only light was from a small opening over the door, too high for them to see anything but sky. After a minute or two their eyes adjusted to the dim light. The hut was just one room with an earth floor, a rough table, one bench and some bales of straw.

They sat down wearily, but stood up again when they heard the door unbarred. The men stood guard as two women came bringing plates of food and mugs of water. Behind stood the chief. The three sat down again with hungry anticipation. Jack decided to open communication with the chief: he gave him an exaggerated, simpering smile. The man ignored it.

"Excuse me, sir!" Meena said loudly. The chieftain turned to listen. "We are not enemies – in fact, we need your help. This really is Prince Aseem."

"I know who he is," the chief replied angrily, "And I intend to trade him for land. His father has made Serpis a place of ruin and despair. The black-flower plague was bad enough – many of us have lost family or friends – but thanks to his father's greed we are refugees in our own country."

Aseem shook his head. "This is not so. Marshal Sharfeat is the culprit. He wants to make slaves of us—"

He was cut short. "Well, let's hope he wants a slave to do his talking, or you'll have to learn a new skill. Eat up! You'll be on your way soon."

The chief stalked out and they heard the door barred again. They ate in silence. The aroma from the lamb stew did little to arouse Meena's taste buds, now *they* were the lambs going to slaughter. At least they knew their fate. Jack was seething with frustration. Thanks to Meena, he had kept his word and returned with the crystal, but his chances of using it now appeared to be zilch. Aseem ate dispiritedly, his hunger blunted by dread. Their captor was selling them to Sharfeat, who would surely kill him. Hakeema was their only hope. Where was she?

The women came back to remove the dishes. Jack began to think ahead. What would Sharfeat do with them? Meena might be a slave if she was lucky; Aseem, a rival while he lived, would have to die; Jack would be tortured for the secret of the crystal, then probably left to rot in gaol in case his powers were ever useful. The Serpian chieftain was naïve, trying to do business with Sharfeat, who would simply kill him and take over Serpis.

He just had to get the chief to see this. Well, if they went on foot or by dog-cart, there would be ample time to persuade the chief that he was walking into peril. Jack was cockily confident again. He lay back on a bale of straw, hands behind his head, one leg bent. Meena was puzzled.

"How can you relax? Sharfeat will soon be leaving us for the vultures."

"Cool it, will you? This might turn out better than you think."

This was the old arrogant, patronising Jack that she knew, the one she disliked yet admired. She hid her irritation and tried to figure out where his confidence had come from.

Aseem wasn't paying any attention to anybody. He had mentally cocooned himself as soon as they had finished eating, and now sat cross-legged on a bale of straw, glassy-eyed, presumably praying for a miracle.

———— § ————

They heard the bar being lifted. The chief pushed open the door and stepped inside. Over his shoulder they glimpsed the long-awaited visitor. A warm, breathtaking smile wreathed her soft features, and she seemed to glow with pleasure as she took in each of them. To Jack, she looked just as radiant and beautiful as the first time he had seen her. Meena, seeing his mouth open and his eyes glaze over, pursed her lips.

Aseem jumped up and rushed to Hakeema, clinging to her like a little boy lost who had found his mother. "Wherefore are you tardy? Methought you would never arrive!"

"I regret the wait, Aseem, but now I am here," said Hakeema. "I asked you to bring one earthling; it seems you got carried away – but she is beautiful, is she not?"

Meena smiled, lapping up the compliment. The timing was brilliant. Jack was taking her for granted, and she didn't approve of the way he gazed at Hakeema. It gave her a little surge of satisfaction to see him get a taste of his own medicine.

Jack was jealous: Meena was *his* friend and he didn't want her linked with Aseem. "She's with me. Her name's Meena."

"Ah, Jack! Welcome." Turning back, Hakeema added "And Meena … such a beautiful name!" She put their minds at rest. "This is Agadasu, Duke of Serpis. There has been some difficulty between Macron and Serpis, but we have now resolved it."

Jack was deflated. The negotiations he had been so cleverly planning were already over. Hakeema leaned over and whispered in his ear.

"You have the crystal, Jack?"

"I-I th-think so." He reached into his jeans pocket. Panic swept over him as he realised the familiar shape digging into the flesh of his thigh was missing. "I've lost it!"

"Say not so!" Hakeema cried.

Aseem stood open-mouthed. Meena began searching the straw where Jack had been lying.

"Here it is," she said, and handed it to Hakeema.

Duke Agadasu addressed Aseem. "Please accept my sincere apology, your majesty."

"I do accept and thank you, sir. But I do not wish to be addressed as king until I have returned to Macropuris and buried my father. Until then, I remain crown prince."

"Very well, your highness. I regret that I misjudged both your father and the king's marshal. When our delegation to your birthday feast did not return, it looked like trickery or treachery. Sharfeat told us that the king was behind it, and I believed him. Hakeema has now apprised me of what happened, with the evidence of her own eyes. Like you, I too have been forced from my home. I wish to offer you and your attendants all the hospitality I can."

Jack decided he didn't mind being taken for Aseem's attendant as long as he wasn't going to die. Meena felt this would be good training for Jack in case she ever decided to take him on as *her* attendant.

15 The pilgrimage

No longer prisoners, the three went outside for some fresh air, though the air was hot rather than fresh. A gaggle of giggling children followed them round, staring and pointing. Jack and Meena were the first creatures from outer space they had seen. Serpis didn't get many visitors.

Duke Agadasu abandoned the idea of setting out for Macropuris, aware now that he would never return if he did. Instead, he put all sentries, lookouts and scouts on the highest alert, in case of a raid or even invasion. Then, knowing he had a lot of indignities to make up for, he escorted his guests to a timber-framed house at the end of the village. It had a central hall, with rooms on two storeys at each side. A young woman opened the door; the duke introduced her.

"These are my temporary quarters, since Macr— ... ahem ... Sharfeat took my palace and my best land. This is my daughter, Radel, who will serve you. Now I must go to organise this evening's banquet for my honoured guests."

Radel showed them the house and then took them around the village, which was coming to life. People were going to and fro with tools, benches, food, clothes and decorations; there was chatter, laughter and singing coming from the houses; and the people who stared at them now smiled. Aseem was happy to be stared at; he was used to it. Jack enjoyed the novelty of it. Meena really didn't like being stared at by people she didn't know.

When they got back to the hall, they were invited upstairs. There were low tables with glasses of cold water and savoury titbits. They sat on big cushions covered in soft fur, and the room was pleasantly warm and comfortable after the heat outdoors.

"This is the sular," Radel explained, "Because it catches the small sunlight. The solar, at the other end of the house, catches the light of the great sun."

Below they heard people giving instructions, moving furniture and setting tables, preparing the hall for the evening. Meena asked Aseem why he looked worried.

"If the duke gives an oration, I shall have to reply – and I am unskilled in rhetoric."

"That's no problem. Just be yourself – you're always charming. Tell them how pleased you are to be here, how kindly they welcomed you, how good it is that Macron and Serpis are friends again. You can end by saying this splendid feast will get cold, so we should sit and eat."

"How do you conceive such wise words? You must be an orator!"

I'd be tongue-tied if I had to stand up and speak. But it might be fun to try. Meena smiled.

15 The pilgrimage

Very soon they were invited down to the hall, where everyone else was already seated. Long tables down the sides and the high table across the end were piled high with food. The musicians at the far end of the hall played quietly. Aseem was led to a seat between the duke and duchess. Hakeema sat on the duke's other side.

Meena was shown to a seat between Radel and her young cousin Ramu, opposite Aseem – who naturally was treated like royalty. Looking every inch a prince, he was enjoying his leading role. Meena could almost see him fluffing up his plumage, his peacock's tail on display.

Jack was to sit beside the duchess, but even before he sat down he was picking at delicacies that he fancied. Little Ramu began copying Jack's table manners but got told off by the duchess, who gave Jack a meaning look. The meaning was lost on Jack.

There were no speeches, to Aseem's relief. Instead, the music changed and the older girls entered, wearing colourful costumes. They formed sets in the middle of the hall for some very energetic country dancing, with some slower solo dances halfway through. Everyone watched, entranced; even Jack stopped eating for a minute.

When the dancing was over, the duchess tried to make conversation with Jack, but got nowhere. Young Ramu listened to Meena and Radel, who were getting to know each other and exchanging experiences. Hakeema joined in, and soon she and Radel were gossiping away. Meena said something to Aseem, and they began chatting too. Jack, having ignored everyone while he gorged himself, found he had nobody to talk to. He wondered why.

Candles were lit, small children were taken off to bed and the musicians played classical pieces. First one moon rose, then the other, shining in the windows. As the evening drew to a close, Aseem declared himself tired and Duke Agadasu willingly escorted them, not to a mud hut this time, but to a small, comfortable house.

As she dropped off to sleep, Meena was wondering which unlucky family had been ejected for their benefit. Aseem was so happy and exhausted that he hardly had time to think anything before he fell into a deep and dreamless sleep. Jack was lovingly constructing his own personal fantasy when he drifted off, dreaming he had found Hakeema wounded and unconscious in the forest and was carrying her to safety, but she woke and smiled at him, and the next thing he was plunging into a bog, sinking deeper and deeper.

Hakeema was lying awake, running through her plan for the next day. She was relieved that the earthlings had not mentioned her accidentally sending them slightly off course; the witch Jemima's instructions were not always clear. Aseem had done remarkably well to lead them out of that wilderness. Until today, she would not have thought he had the survival skills to lead them out of a sandpit. He must have been truly inspired yesterday, perhaps by that earth girl, who clearly adored him. She also wondered why Jack hadn't asked the obvious question, which must surely have been on his mind all evening. Well, he would know more tomorrow.

——————— § ———————

It seemed they had been asleep only five minutes when they woke to birds chirping and the smell of cooking. A quick breakfast of scrambled eggs, bread and honey gave Jack very little time to gaze at his idol, but it gave Meena a chance to ask a question that bothered her even more than him.

"Hakeema, how does Jack fit into the prophecy that Aseem showed us?"

"Yes, what's special about me? Is it that I'm good at science? And what's the crystal for?"

"There is one who knows more than I: a priest, my old teacher of divine wisdom and magic, who is fighting the raksas. He will answer your questions – and mine."

"But I thought you knew where to find all knowledge?" said Aseem.

"I see part of the picture; soon I shall see more. We must depart. We have some hours' journey ahead, and Sharfeat will be searching for us."

They were confused. If this priest taught Hakeema, he must be very knowledgeable. But some hours' travel each way? It might be too late for Jack to stop the raksas, while the journey exposed them to the risk of capture. *And dust*, thought Aseem, gloomily accepting that Hakeema knew best.

Jack wanted to know the secret about himself, but he was afraid to probe. Finding out might be like opening Pandora's box. As Meena said, not all knowledge is good. *If you let bad things into your mind, you can't get them out again.*

Duke Agadasu had taken care of everything, picking out animals and packing provisions; young warriors were already mounted, waiting to escort them. They might meet wild animals or Sharfeat's men. Unlike yesterday's forced march, today's mode of travel was grander, quicker and safer. They rode high up on soft, silky seats in howdahs mounted between the humps of a *huppos*, one of the dark blue, elephantine creatures. An experienced mahout drove their animal, under orders from Hakeema.

Soon they left the farmland behind. The forest here was more like parkland, one glade after another with no sign of people. Meena and Jack were awed by the beauty of this strange land and by the sense of so much space.

There was no track, but Hakeema seemed to know her way, every so often directing the mahout. They learnt that the black flowers had not bloomed yet in this out-of-the-way place, but were reported not far off. They came across wild animals, including some wolf-like creatures squabbling over their kill, but these kept well away from the *huppos*. Nonetheless, their escort remained vigilant.

The ride was surprisingly smooth and they covered mile after mile with nothing to distract them but beautiful, unspoilt forest. They fell to talking about Sharfeat and why he had chosen to destroy what that was good, torturing and killing people, enslaving others.

"What did he have to gain?" asked Aseem, "He had power, privilege and riches. His position was second only to my father."

"Exactly," rejoined Hakeema, "He could not bear to be second. He wanted all power for himself."

"Not all power," said Meena, to everyone's surprise. She had not spoken for some time. "I don't think he wants the power to do good – only bad."

"That's true," said Jack thoughtfully, "All he's done is destroy, take people's homes—"

"And their freedom," added Meena.

"Is that what I have to sort out, Hakeema?" asked Jack.

"I trust you will," was the answer.

Talk moved to the task of defeating Sharfeat. None of them had any idea how – Hakeema refused to be drawn – or any confidence. It all seemed to depend on her old teacher.

———— § ————

After two hours, some flat-topped hills came into view. As they got nearer, they saw that the plateau was fronted by cliffs. There were a few ledges big enough for a thorn bush, but they could see no way up. They stopped at the base of the cliff, in a place where the rock formed a steep natural staircase. Hakeema left the young men with the animals, explaining that she did not fear an attack here.

They had something to eat and drink, and then Hakeema took Aseem, Jack and Meena up the steep rock stair. There were a few tall yellow flowers and patches of grass. In places, it was so steep they had to help each other up; elsewhere, crags or boulders blocked their way, but ancient steps led around each obstacle.

After half an hour they reached the top, hot and out of breath. There was nothing there. The plateau was bare desert, a sea of dusty stone broken by little gullies and cracks in whose deep shadow a few tiny weeds grew. *This can't be the right place*, Jack thought. *Has the sun gone to her head?* Tired, they sat down on the rocks, despite the scorching heat, waiting for Hakeema to explain.

"Aseem, you must be on your best behaviour. I require the highest respect for my teacher," she warned, with no indication where this teacher was to spring from.

"I won't let you down, Hakeema, I promise."

She spoke as if he was a mischievous little boy. Jack couldn't believe it. Aseem had kept going when he was afraid and still been patient, tactful and kind. That was grown-up. He'd shown amazing self-control when he had just been abruptly robbed of the building blocks of a happy childhood – loving parents who could do anything, a wise tutor who knew everything, a serene and orderly world. That was really grown-up. He'd gone alone to another planet, found an alien and got him to co-operate. That would be beyond most grown-ups.

Even when we landed in the wrong place, it wasn't Aseem who threw a tantrum, was it? If anybody was childish, it was me. Even if you're a child, you don't have to be childish.

Meena felt the same: *Hakeema misjudges Aseem. I know he's a boy, but he's so sensible. He's as grown up as anyone I know. Not like Jack. Or me? I wonder what he thinks of me?*

What Aseem was thinking of her just then would have made her very embarrassed.

———— § ————

Hakeema settled her mind and began to concentrate completely; she knew that this difficult feat really needed much longer preparation. At first the children were too hot and tired, and too busy thinking, to notice that she was staring at something that wasn't there. Then they heard her chanting in a low voice, in a language even Aseem did not recognise. She was using her hands to squeeze and shape something in the air in front of her. They gazed, rapt. She began to run her fingers up and down an invisible railing.

A few yards away a pillar appeared, as though being sketched lightly by a pencil, wavering a little until the shadows were pencilled in. As it became solid, a second pillar materialised. The roof joining them threw a shadow over the doorway, a vague shimmering alongside became a wall, a low roof emerged and gradually the whole edifice – some sort of shrine or temple, perhaps an ashram – took shape and became real.

It was a rambling group of low buildings, the size of two or three bungalows, topped off by a small stone dome. The shrine looked as ancient and as solid as the rocks it stood on. The paint was peeling off in places, wind had eroded the stonework at the base of the columns and the heavy wooden door was dry and deeply seamed with cracks.

Jack tried to explain what his eyes were telling him, and failed. He found himself bewildered. Logically he could not have seen what he had just seen. Since he could not come up with a rational explanation, Jack decided to accept it for now as bizarre and unexplained.

Meena was just as astonished. Only Aseem was unamazed. This was magic: that was all the explanation he needed. Magic, to him, was like electricity to us: mysterious, but quite normal. He stood up and followed Hakeema; the others, a little uncertainly, tagged along behind.

Without speaking, she climbed three dusty steps to the portico and went up to the time-worn door, which creaked slightly as she pushed it open. It was as solid and heavy as it looked. Inside, their footsteps echoed in the broad, stone-flagged passage. The walls of green marble were so polished that they shone, every doorway carved with geometrical shapes or stylised vines and creepers.

A bar of light across the passage marked an archway to the centre of the temple. In the bare, circular space under the dome there was nothing but a low column, topped by a rounded stone with a central hole and handle. A man in a white robe stood, praying. Hakeema edged a few feet to one side, her back to the wall, gesturing to the children to do the same. They waited.

It was hard to say how old the priest might be, since time here didn't seem to be quite the same as on Earth. Indeed, everything on this planet seemed mysterious or unpredictable. The priest was slim and fit, his face was tanned and alert, but the wrinkles around his mouth and the crows' feet beside his eyes suggested great age. So did his long, white hair and his equally wild beard, reaching almost to his navel. The white cloth he wore had no shape or stitching; it was more like a bedsheet than a garment.

The priest opened his eyes and turned to Hakeema with a welcoming smile. She bowed and opened her arms wide in a gesture of peace. Then she stood straight and spoke.

"Master *ji* … forgive this intrusion. The black flowers are in bloom and a devil-worshipper has usurped the throne of Macron." She gestured at the children. "*Guru ji*, you have heard me speak of Prince Aseem. This is Jack, last of the Barelas family, and his friend. Jack has the crystal. We will do our utmost, but we need your wisdom to outwit the demon and his puppet." She remained in a respectful posture, while her old teacher considered.

"You bring your own answer. You have wit and the will to undo this evil. But keep your wits and weapons to yourselves until you are ready to strike the decisive blow. Take heart! Now I have words for the Barelas boy alone."

The sage sat cross-legged on the mosaic floor and courteously invited Jack to do the same. Hakeema and Aseem went out, and Meena reluctantly followed them. They moved down the passage, out of earshot. The master began to tell Jack about father's family.

"Four millennia ago, your ancestors were nawabs of a little principality famous for alchemy. Their badge was a dodecahedron, the shape of a rare crystal of many colours, which a priest gave to the first nawab. The nawab's son found he could do strange magic with this crystal, and his daughter made a second crystal by transmuting a blue stone found in a remote cavern.

"After centuries of peace and prosperity, it is said, the demon of the black mist came from another planet. It haunted the nawab's dreams, made his beloved wife die in childbirth, caused storms and floods, infested people's minds with malice and spread disorder. The black flowers bloomed. The nawab busied himself building a ziggurat in memory of his wife.

"The plague spread and many died; people blamed the demon, but they also blamed the nawab for doing nothing. Gangsters became warlords, who made their own laws and ignored his ministers, so he sacked them and tried to do everything himself. Instead of storms, now there was a drought. Frantic days and sleepless nights made the nawab weary and ill.

"He consulted a priest, who urged him to pray daily but be practical too. The nawab recalled his ministers, took their advice and sent envoys abroad. His calm faith inspired people, but they needed help; the rivers were drying up. The Lord of Macron offered food and soldiers if the nawab accepted him as his overlord. The nawab had to agree. What else could he do?

"Seeing his little son making a ziggurat with his toy bricks gave the nawab an idea. He climbed to the summit of the new pyramid, which was topped by a good-luck symbol made of crystals. He added the crystal of many colours to the pangram and used the ethereal charge in his body to give it life and redirect it. Within hours Black Mist had fled to another planet.

"Within weeks the plague was over, but the nawab had died. His young son should have succeeded him, but the Lord of Macron wed the nawab's daughter and united the two states as one kingdom. The rains never returned, the land became a desert and the survivors moved to Macron. The nawab's son became a cooper and so took the name Barelas, though everyone knew he was the rightful nawab and had power to end the plague, among other things. The royal apothecary recorded all births and deaths in the Barelas family. They lived modestly yet were highly respected; they even married into royalty, making you and Aseem distant cousins.

"No one knows how the nawab's daughter made the crystal. In the fairy tales that preserve the story, the secret came to her in a dream."

Jack gasped. "My father told me about the crystal in a dream!"

"So it is true. I heard another version of the tale from a very learned witch in Serpis. She said the last nawab had one title that died with him: 'Lodestone of the Land'. I think it referred to the Barelas family's special powers, which the king did not inherit."

"What is a lodestone?"

"Do you not have these on your planet?"

"I don't know. What does it do?"

"It is a stone that knows which way it faces."

"Like a compass?"

"I know not this word 'compass', but perchance it is the same."

"Did my father know all this?"

"Your father knew that he had special powers, but not what they were."

Jack fell silent, fixing in his mind all he had heard: dreamed instructions, dodecahedron, crystal-topped pyramid, ethereal charge, pangram given life, lodestone giving direction. He hadn't much to go on, so he treasured every word.

"Did you know my father?"

"I ... met him once."

"What was he like?"

"In some ways he was very ordinary—"

Jack sighed.

"Handsome, decent, a little careless, not particularly brave or confident—"

Wry smile.

"Not much good with women – or men either. He could be very obstinate. He practised alchemy in a small way. He thought for himself, though he thought more of others."

Interesting.

"But he was sad. He became a fugitive, hunted by the raksas. I believe it caused his death."

"I think it's hunting me."

"Most like. That is why we priests are in hiding, scattered. We tried to warn the king that Sharfeat would sell his soul to the devil for more power, but Jonda and his advisers were too trusting. In every soul, in every kingdom, on every planet, in every age there is a wrestling match between good and bad. Today that struggle has become a war – but with prayer, fasting, soma and your crystal, the devil will again be defeated."

"What do I do with the crystal?"

"Only your father can tell you. Yet use your wisdom. Believe in yourself. That is all."

The priest smiled gravely, bowed and resumed his meditation. Jack believed in science; he didn't have much faith in himself. And he still didn't know what he was meant to do.

He got up and made his way outside, where the others were waiting. Meena and Aseem began firing questions, but Hakeema stopped them.

"We must go," she said. They walked down the steps, then instinctively turned for one last look at the shrine: it had gone. The plateau was as rocky and deserted as when they first saw it.

———— § ————

In thoughtful silence, they trudged in single file back down the steep path in the burning heat. When it was wide enough for two abreast, the questions began again. Aseem got in first.

"What is the secret of the crystal, Jack?"

"Just that: a secret." Jack didn't want questions – he was thinking over all he'd been told.

Hakeema thought he now knew all he needed. "So what are you going to do?"

"I've no idea!"

Meena asked, "Did you find out what's special about you?"

"I don't know what my special powers are. I learnt one weird thing, though: my ancestors were nawabs, rulers of a little kingdom."

"Wow!" said Meena.

"That is well known," said Hakeema.

"Well, nobody told *me*." Jack was a little angry. Why would nobody tell him anything?

"I assumed you knew," responded Aseem.

Jack was exasperated. "Well, I don't! I'm new round here and I'm not grown-up. If no one tells me, how am I supposed to know?"

"I see," said Hakeema, though she didn't.

"What else did the priest say?" Meena asked.

Jack turned to her. "What's a dodecahedron?"

"It's a regular, twelve-sided solid. Why?"

"It's the badge of my family. It was taken over by the King of Macron."

"Of course," said Aseem, "That is—"

"Well known," finished Jack bitterly.

"Did you find out anything else?" put in Meena.

"The priest told me about a pyramid."

"There is a pyramid in the old palace; no one knows its purpose," said Hakeema.

"Where is this old palace?"

"In the old capital. It was abandoned in the Dark Aeons when the river dried up."

——— § ———

Duke Agadasu's men were waiting for them at the bottom of the hill. Under Hakeema's orders, they all set off swiftly back to the village. The clear blue sky had turned a dark grey. A breeze sprang up and before long it became a fierce wind. Horizontal lightning flashed across the width of the sky, making the *huppos* fearful and uneasy. A few seconds later, a series of loud thunderclaps unleashed a heavy downpour of rain. The mahout struggled to control the animal, which was frantic with fear. Jack wondered what – or who – had caused this extraordinary change in the weather.

Within minutes, the downpour stopped and the wind dropped, the clouds thinned and dispersed across the wide sky, letting sunshine through again. Even though the heavy rain had left them soaked to the skin, Jack nodded off.

Meena laid a silk scarf over his head to protect it from the strong sunshine. Sprawled on the satin cushions of the howdah, he slept.

In his dream, he was delivering Mr Patel's papers when Galileo pointed out that he was being chased by Tom Atkinson. As he got close, Tom turned into a shadowbat. Jack pointed a finger at him, and he instantly shrivelled up and fell to the pavement. Jack's father picked out a paper for him to drop in the next letterbox, but Jack began reading it instead. It had drawings and instructions for making some weird device. He weighed the ingredients on the kitchen scales.

He thought he knew what he was making, but he wasn't sure, so he just did what it said, following the diagrams. It was good that he had a photographic memory, because his father had rolled the paper into a tube and put it to his ear. Mr Ji was telling them something very important, which Jack couldn't quite hear because he was a ghost. That was strange, since ghosts are supposed to be cold and he felt very hot. And why was his mum waking him when he was comfortably asleep?

"Wake up, Jack, we're getting near the village."

"I want to look at the paper again," mumbled Jack.

"What paper?"

"The one .... Where—?" His father, Mr Ji and the paper had vanished. Jack remembered what the old priest had said about a dream or a vision. The mahout, Hakeema and Aseem, to judge by their bland, unmoved faces, had noticed nothing; Meena was retrieving her scarf.

"You've been asleep, Jack," she said.

16 The bottom of page 9

"Only just happened ... puff of smoke ... horrible ..."

Mrs Evans was all confused, and Mr Evans didn't like this at all. He put on his boots and stomped down the drive, looking for youngsters playing with fireworks and Halloween bats. Instead he found his part-time pet, Dinah, staring uneasily at a nasty gash in the cypress bush. She looked accusingly at Mr Evans. Seeing three children on the common, he shouted at them, but they were too far away to hear.

"I'm worried about Meena and Jack," said David.

"What was that puff of smoke?" said Andromeda.

"Some idiots throwin' fireworks, I guess, frightenin' that cat," said Lloyd.

"They can throw some at that man then," put in David.

Andromeda said "Let's leave him to his fate. I bet his star sign is Cancer, he's so crabby."

"That's unfair," David said. "Come on, let's see if Meena's down at the shop."

"Yeah, let's," said a nasty voice. It was Tom Atkinson, still scratched and bruised.

"We got some questions," added Alec, behind him.

"What do you want to know?" said David nervously.

"Where her boyfriend is – him and his science tricks," said Tom, "He's set bats on us."

"'Snot right," said Alec sulkily.

"It isn't," said Andromeda, "It's not fair, ganging up on someone like that."

"Jack wouldn't do that," said David, "If you want him, he's over there, talking to that lady."

"Any time you need our help, just ask," added Lloyd cheerily, "Bye."

Tom and Alec were still standing there open-mouthed when Mr Evans finished telling them off. If he had looked up, he would have seen hundreds of giant bats circling overhead. Earth had similar creatures, so Sharfeat was sure the natives would suspect nothing.

———— § ————

The professor saw the bats as he left the Coopers' house, after reading Jack's note. He found them disturbing. Not that they were impossible exactly – at least one bat, *Pteropus vampyrus*, had a wingspan of 1.5 m or more, but that lived in the East Indies. The largest European bat, the rare *Nyctalus lasiopterus*, which catches birds on the wing and eats them, only reaches 45 cm and had never been seen in Wellington Spa. He could see hundreds of *these* bats – and it was still daylight.

Paul Shreddon believed in keeping an open mind, and he suspected these odd events must be related; yet what theory could account for freak weather, an earthquake, epidemics, poisoned water, giant bats and the strange, burnt organic matter in his laboratory? He decided to go back there and see if he could find anything to connect these phenomena.

As he neared the lab, he saw even more bats. One flew close, and he saw with a shock that its dog-like face seemed to be inspecting him; there was something odd about its feet too. As he unlocked the door, more bats joined it. This was unpleasant, but not alarming; few bats are carnivorous, and none is big enough to cause real harm to humans. Just then, one of them appeared to dive-bomb him. The professor nipped smartly inside, put down his shopping and made a mental note to check the habits of bats.

He emptied one bag and piled all the shopping into the other. He went down the steps, stood in the doorway of the lab and looked at everything systematically. Eventually satisfied, he clambered over the rubble and used the plastic bag to scoop up the burnt object. Next he went over to the emergency exit, where he had noticed one of his old cameras lying, the flash bulb used; checking, he saw that half his old cameras were missing from their shelf. They were lying on the table, the floor, all over the place, and all the flash bulbs had been fired. On the floor were several more blackened scraps and his ultra-violet lamp.

He went round picking up every camera he could find and then took them through, two at a time, to the dark room. This, thank goodness, was undamaged. He spent an hour processing the negatives and developing the prints. As the first print appeared, he was shocked at what it showed. By the time the last one had dried, he was in desperate haste to get home. He needed to think this through. He picked up his UV lamp and shopping bags, and set off.

Bats loomed out of the darkness and vanished again. Under the street lights, he could see better; there were several bats overhead. He put down his shopping and rested his arms for a moment. He took out his UV lamp, switched it on and pointed it upwards. There was a flurry of wings, and one bat was bathed in a violet spotlight; for a moment it hung there, glowing brightly and breathing out vapour, until there was a pop and it seemed to explode. What was left of it fluttered to the pavement. After waiting a minute or so for it to cool, the professor scooped it into the bag containing the bat remains from the lab.

On the way home, he bought an evening paper. As he came out of the shop, he saw several bats circling above the door. He walked rapidly away, but their circles remained directly over his head, but lower. Was he becoming paranoid? When he got home, he found with relief that he was not suffering from an unreasonable fear of persecution; the bats really were nasty, according to the local paper.

SCARY!

GIANT BATS TERRIFY TOWN

Halloween has come early to the small town of Wellington Spa, still reeling from yesterday's unexplained natural disasters. Flocks of aggressive giant bats are reported to be flying around the common.

A dog has been savaged by one of them, several people have been attacked in broad daylight and the streets are now deserted.

Horrible

Mrs Anharad Evans, 42, of Hornbeam Avenue, found a bat stuck in her cypress bush. "It was horrible," she told our reporter. Mrs Evans was not able to describe it, but eyewitnesses say the bats have foxy faces and are not afraid of humans.

Several people have tried to shoot the marauding bats, but without success. They are reported to have a wingspan of 5 ft (1.5 m) or more, though this seems likely to be an exaggeration.

Batty

The largest British species are the greater horseshoe bat (*Rhinolphus ferrumequinum*), the noctule bat (*Nyctalus noctula*), which is known to fly in daylight, and the long-eared bat (*Plecotus auritus*), but none of these has a wingspan of more than 15 inches (38 cm).

Mr Eric Spode of the wildlife trust said, "I don't know what they are, but they're not local. We don't have bats like that in Wellington Spa."

Advice

The police advise people not to venture outside, to keep all doors and windows closed and keep pets indoors. They are seeking expert advice on how to deal with these dangerous pests.

The advice to boil drinking water remains in place, because of the mysterious poisoning of the river, from which Wellington Spa takes its water. The dead fish have been carried away by the floods, which are now rapidly subsiding. The clear-up continues, and most homes now have electricity again. Householders should ensure sockets are dry before they are used.

There was more, but the professor had read enough. Every photograph he had developed showed a bat flying straight at the camera – in other words, attacking – and one showed Jack ducking, so Meena had taken that photo. It proved that the reports had not exaggerated, because the bat's wingspan was about the same as Jack's height. Most of the pictures were out of focus, but in several the bats' nostrils were flared, as if they were snorting. It looked nasty.

No wonder Jack hadn't explained himself very well over lunch.

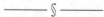

Over the next half-hour, the professor made telephone calls to a couple of former colleagues, wrote some notes, made a 'to do' list and then sat for a moment, wondering how to handle the next call. He could convince people if he could get them to look at the photographs. That was the tricky bit. They would be under pressure, and they might by now have had enough people telling them the bats were monsters from outer space, or zombies, or a figment of their imagination – the usual, unhelpful things that some people always say.

An ally would help. Since it was Saturday, he rang the council's emergency number and asked for the pest-control officer. When he explained what it was about, he was told the man was already down at the police station. Poor man.

The professor put on his coat, picked up his notes, the photographs and the plastic bag of evidence, and set off. The streets should have been full of people going out for the evening; instead, they were full of giant bats going out for the evening. One swooped so low its feet brushed his hair. *Which I didn't.*

At the police station, everyone looked harassed and hurried, though they didn't seem to have anyone in custody. A door opened and a soldier emerged with a gun; he stared at the professor without speaking and went out. Paul Shreddon went up to the counter and rang the bell. A weary-looking constable appeared.

"I am Professor Paul Shreddon. I can help with this bat problem. I've brought some evidence your superiors ought to see." He waved his bag and the photographs.

"I'll see if anyone's available, sir," said the constable, in a voice suggesting this was unlikely.

However, the professor's name evidently carried some weight, because the young man returned and invited him through to an interview room. Within seconds the inspector strode in, abruptly announcing that he could give the professor three minutes and it had better be worth his while – if the bats were from another planet, he didn't want to know.

After five minutes, he called the constable and gave him a message for the desk sergeant; after ten minutes, the desk sergeant and an army officer entered.

"Everything under control, Sergeant?"

"Yes, sir, Constable Perkins is on the phone now, working down the professor's list."

"Good. Ah, Captain Wilkes! How did you get on?"

"Not too well, Inspector. It's chaos out there. My men are trained snipers – never miss more than one shot in five – but they haven't managed a single kill yet."

"Driving you bats, eh?" remarked the inspector.

"They may have astonishingly quick reactions," said the professor, "But they can't beat the speed of light, and that's how we'll get them."

"I know bats like the dark," said the captain, "I didn't know light could kill them."

"It doesn't, of course, normally. But these bats are different. When they attacked my laboratory, my assistants used camera flashes, and they didn't take to that. While the electronic flash was recharging, my people used the old-fashioned flash bulbs on some cameras from my collection. That drove the bats away and gave us these photographs. When the bats did return, my assistants tried an ultra-violet lamp on them. It burnt them to a crisp."

"I'd like to see that, sir, to be convinced."

"Here you are." Professor Shreddon extracted the remains of shadowbat no. 2 from his shopping bag. "This is one I bagged earlier, on my way home."

"Unbelievable!" said the captain, shaking his head, "Well, that definitely gives us something to work on."

"It'll do me," said the inspector briefly. He stood up. "We still don't know what they are or where they came from, but I just want to get rid of them. Thank you, Professor. Well, Captain, this should do the trick."

———— § ————

There were no drunks or rowdy gangs on the streets of Wellington Spa that night. Instead, the police, the army and pest-control officers were picking off shadowbats with their new weapons. They had commandeered every short-wave, battery-operated ultra-violet lamp in the town – from vets, tanning salons, factories, the hospital, individuals – and they soon had an effect.

Although the creatures were burnt, there was little, if any, fire. The rapidly increasing red glow after a bat was hit indicated to the professor that a chemical reaction was spreading rapidly and producing heat. He guessed that their blood cells would burst, then their internal organs, until their bodies largely vaporised in the intense heat. What mattered was, it worked.

Within a short time, the charred remnants of Sharfeat's army had crumbled into powder – and even that gradually oxidised. The specimen from the lab was already disintegrating before Professor Shreddon reached the police station, so it was just as well he had by then 'shot' a replacement.

By the time the zoologists and people from MI6 arrived, early on Sunday morning, there was nothing left. By Monday morning, Sharfeat's extraordinary invasion of Wellington Spa had left only a memory, some intriguing photographs and a short paragraph in *The Times* at the bottom of page 9.

17 The nadir

Even before the village came into sight, they sensed something was not right. It was too quiet. Hakeema signalled to the mahout to stop and to the escort to keep strict silence.

They paused just inside the forest. The tilled furrows looked neat and carefully weeded; the pasture was green and healthy. There was no one in sight, but perhaps they were at a meeting. There were no animals grazing, but they might be elsewhere. There were no birds to be seen or heard, but then in the distance a hawk appeared, circling lazily.

In alarm, Aseem pointed at the gadget on his belt. Hakeema ordered them to take cover and dismount. The forest was thick enough to conceal them from prying eyes overhead, but at ground level the flattened undergrowth showed all too clearly the way they had come.

"That's got to be a shadowhawk up there," whispered Meena.

"And I bet there'll be more of them. Sharfeat is closing in."

"Why haven't we seen any soldiers?"

"I don't know, but we can't stay here and be sitting ducks."

"So what's the plan?"

Just then, Hakeema asked a young warrior to go to the village and do some reconnaissance. Jack stepped forward. "I'll go too. I want to study these hawks at close quarters."

"No, Jack, it's too dangerous. I'd never forgive myself if anything happened to you."

"We're already taking risks. What's the alternative?"

Meena spoke up. "You're both forgetting: Jack is the only person who can make the crystal work. So it's very brave of you, Jack, but you can't take afford to take risks."

"Why is everybody treating me like a little kid? I can look after myself."

"So could the captain of the night watch, and the shadowhawks killed him. Remember?"

That grim scene flashed across their minds. Jack took a deep breath. Meena's face was firm, but pink. No one spoke. Aseem knew Hakeema would never let *him* go – he too was needed. Now his parents were gone, Macron would rally round him. In any case, he had no appetite for another fight. Hakeema saw that Meena was right, but she was at a loss.

"Then I cannot send this young man to his death either. We must find Duke Agadasu. There is naught we can do here."

"There is one thing," said Meena decisively. "We can do what Jack suggested."

Jack looked at her, half-annoyed, half-bewildered.

Hakeema looked entirely bewildered. "You said it was too risky."

"It *is*, for Jack. We can't replace him, or Aseem – or your knowledge. We need the mahout to control the *huppos* and we need every soldier we have. That leaves me." Meena was really surprised they hadn't worked this out.

"You?" said Hakeema doubtfully.

"You want to go on your own?" asked Jack, concerned.

"We're all taking risks now. You said."

"But what can you do?" exclaimed Hakeema, "You're a girl!"

"So?" said Meena indignantly, "I've practised hiding and tracking, and moving silently, in Brownies. I'm small, so they may not notice me. And, if they do, fine: I'm just a girl."

Aseem prayed that Hakeema would forbid Meena to go. Hakeema just stared at her. Jack's feverish imagination had already substituted Meena as victim in place of the captain of the night watch. He forced the scene from his mind by answering her question.

"Actually, Meena, you'll be just as good as me." *I don't want you to go, but I can't say that. It's true you're expendable and I'm not. I can't say that either. Stop talking to yourself, Jack.* "Hakeema, she's clearly the best man for the job."

Jack felt about in his pockets, brought out the Kendal mint cake, selected the piece with the least fluff on it and gave it to Meena, along with the compass and his precious pocket-knife.

Hakeema was still gaping. Meena spoke.

"You need the compass, Jack; I don't, really. But I might need the knife. Thanks."

Two troubled violet eyes met two determined hazel ones.

———— § ————

As Meena worked her way along the forest edge, she glimpsed shadowhawks patrolling. She decided to move deeper into the trees, which meant pushing through tall plants, clambering over fallen trees, ducking under branches and disentangling herself from brambles and burrs.

She noticed a clump of tall spikes, topped by black flowers, and then another. There were whole banks of black flowers on woody stalks. Large mice ran up and down them. After 20 minutes, she smelt smoke and headed for the edge of the wood. She took out Jack's sweet, removed the fluffs and popped it in her mouth. Something ran over her foot, and she jumped. It disappeared. She took a deep breath, leant on a tree trunk and cautiously looked out.

Smoke and flames were rising from the far end of the village. Because of its defensive earthworks, she could only see the roofs. What had happened to its people? She couldn't see any soldiers: where were they? She had to get a closer look. There was no fire around the nearer gateway. Could she reach it without being seen by the hawk eyes above?

She watched them for a full minute and saw they were spreading out and moving away; was the village empty? They were not searching any more. Had everyone been captured? She was taking a chance, but she had to know. Luckily the field in between had a tall crop.

Meena got down and began to creep across it on all fours, peering ahead. Something ran up her leg, and she stifled a scream. It jumped off. A rat scuttled past, and another. There were dozens of rats, but they weren't interested in her: they were eating the crop, stalks and all. Meena began crawling again. It was very hot. As she got nearer the gateway she could hear flames crackling and sheep bleating.

Near the gateway, a large tree offered shade. Someone in a hurry had left their fleece – a sheepskin made into a long jerkin – with their packed lunch underneath. Meena wolfed down the pie, saved the nuts for later and put on the fleece. It was much too big, which made it easier to pass herself off as a sheep. She looked around carefully. The shadowhawks were further away than ever and there were no sentries in sight; she set off, down into the dry ditch, under the log bridge and up the bank to the gateway.

She took three deep breaths, then trotted slowly through the open gates. Many houses in the village were on fire. Nearby were some sheep in a pen, bleating in terror. Still on all fours, Meena went to the pen and undid the rope holding it shut. Several sheep knocked her flat in their panic to get away.

Meena scurried down a back lane where fire had not yet caught hold. The doors were wide open; every home had been ransacked. Their one ally had fallen to Sharfeat's soldiers; their only refuge was being burnt to the ground; all their hopes of helping Aseem had come to this. Even Meena began to lose heart.

Now very hot under the fleece, she looked up: at least the sky was clear. Reaching the back of the duke's hall, she heard voices. Putting her head down like a grazing lamb, she edged around the hall until she could see. In the main street was Sharfeat himself! Mounted on his horse, he was facing rank after rank of shadowhawks and, behind them, ordinary soldiers. In front was the monster Khabish.

Sharfeat sounded nasty. "There's nobody here, Khabish. Your invincible army outnumbers the Serpian rebels, yet they've outsmarted you and slipped away. If you can't bring me that traitor Agadasu, dead or alive, I shall have to replace you. Black Mist does not tolerate failure."

He was threatening Khabish, insulting him in front of his soldiers. The beast was 80 times his size and quite unafraid of the marshal, but he *was* afraid of Black Mist. The shadow soldiers fidgeted, glancing around. Sharfeat and his bodyguards rode off grimly without another word.

Khabish's body glowed red with fury. The moment Sharfeat had gone, his anger erupted. With a frightening roar, a small fiery tornado came spinning out of his mouth, and another and another. The great beast grabbed the fireballs one at a time and flung them at his soldiers. Meena shut her eyes; she couldn't bear to watch anyone, however wicked, getting burnt. But an explosion made her open her eyes again. When a fireball struck the shadowhawks, they reeled back – before exploding with a bang. Khabish was making an example of some of his troops, to show the others what further failure would mean.

Meena did not wait to see or hear any more. She retreated discreetly back down the lane, keeping her head down. The fire had spread to part of the palisade now, and smoke billowed above it. She followed some madly bleating sheep though the gateway and across the bridge.

Reaching the tree again, she allowed herself one minute without the fleece to get her breath back and wipe off the perspiration. She took a final look around. The sky was empty. So were the fields: the rats had gone and the crops with them. She took a deep breath, put the fleece back on and set off again on all fours. The field seemed endless, her legs were tired, her knees were sore and she was still hot, but at last the little lamb reached the shelter of the forest.

Discarding the fleece, she pushed on to rejoin the others. She had good news. First, Agadasu had evacuated the village, and Sharfeat had no idea where he had gone. The duke had proved much shrewder than Meena had given him credit for.

Second, there was real tension between Sharfeat and Khabish. Each was under pressure to achieve victory, each was using threats and both feared Black Mist. If their partnership were to succumb to the pressure, it might well end dramatically.

Meena's third and best piece of intelligence was that the shadowhawks too were vulnerable to fire. They had kept away from the burning houses, not just on the ground but in the air too, and Khabish could destroy them in an instant with his fireballs.

The bad news was that their little band now had nowhere to go for friends, supplies or shelter – and the black flowers were in bloom even here.

———— § ————

There was tremendous relief on everyone's face when she returned. They crowded round.

"I have good news and bad. I didn't see the duke or his people; they abandoned the village before it was attacked. Sharfeat is there, and his men are burning it to the ground. But he has no idea where the duke has gone."

"The duke is cleverer than Sharfeat!" said Hakeema, "But how did they not detect you?"

Meena told them about the sheepskin. They all stared at her, impressed, especially Jack.

"We too have good news," said Hakeema, "Agadasu has sent word. We are to join him."

Meena had been looking forward to travelling in a howdah – so had Aseem – but they were to go on foot. Soon the shadowhawks would be scouring every inch of the jungle, and the tracks of a *huppos* and a company of cavalry would be obvious, so the mahout had been sent another way as a decoy, and the horses had been turned loose.

Their guide did not navigate by compass bearings. Instead, along the way he looked for certain shrubs, trees, rocks or soil. He kept his eye on the two suns, and followed scents and markings and the lie of the land. At one point they went astray, until the guide realised his error and they retraced their steps. The duke's men seemed to have no sense of urgency. They walked steadily and unhurriedly, their only concern not to give away their position, since their small company could hardly fight a horde of shadow soldiers.

As they walked, Jack asked Aseem about the little column in the temple.

"It is a quern, a little mill, to grind wildflower seeds for soma – those tall yellow flowers we saw on the way. Soma is a sacred drink that makes the priests more godlike, so the raksas cannot harm them."

"Can we have some?"

"No, Jack. It is too strong for ordinary mortals."

Aseem turned to talk to the guide, so Meena told Jack about Khabish.

Jack said, "Sharfeat is stupid to threaten Khabish: that monster could bury him."

"I wouldn't say 'stupid'," Meena said pointedly, "Sharfeat's clever enough to see that Khabish is scared of Black Mist and will keep doing what he's told."

"What about his soldiers?" Jack asked.

"The shadowhawks were fidgeting and nervous the whole time. They were scared of the flames because, when Khabish threw fireballs at them, the ones who got hit just exploded and burnt to nothing."

Jack smiled. "Now we know how to get them, thanks to you. You're a hero!"

"The word is 'heroine', but thanks."

"I have a feeling that, if we wait, Khabish will self-destruct. But I need to work out how to deal with the shadow soldiers. Just don't mind if I don't talk for a bit."

"I won't say a word," said Meena.

The boy with the violet eyes

After ten minutes, Jack looked across at his friend. "Meena? I'm struggling a bit with the science on this planet, but this is where I've got to. Listen, and tell me what you think."

Telling her to listen was typical Jack; asking her opinion was excitingly new.

"You remember the watchmen? Their swords went right though the shadowhawks as if they weren't there; and one hawk turned into a shadow to kill the captain, then it turned back and flew off. And in the palace they were grabbing people and ripping them with their claws."

"You can skip the details." Meena was squeamish.

"Well, they must be solid to do all that, like the shadowbats. But if they want to get out of the way, it's like us moving a computer file out of the way. They minimise their bodies to look like shadows or holograms, and they're safe unless the attacker finds the tiny spot where their minimised body is. But they have to be normal size if they want to attack. What d'you think?"

"It makes sense," said Meena, "But it means we can't hurt them until they attack us."

"Right. That's what happened in the lab. The stuff they squirted didn't hurt us, but it did catch fire. I guess it came from the gut – maybe methane gas or methanol – and it was meant to suffocate us."

"So we need some portable fire," said Meena thoughtfully.

"Brilliant! I just need to think how to make it in the wilderness at short notice."

"No problem for a wizard with your talent."

"I wish."

──────── § ────────

They had been walking through scrub up a valley perhaps half a mile wide, whose sides steepened into white crags that formed the skyline on each side. Where the valley bent to to the left, a dense wood forced the stream and their path under the cliffs on the right. When they emerged, they saw about a mile away the head of the valley. It ended in another cliff: there was no way out.

They stopped and looked at their guide. Was this a trap? He pointed to a vertical slit at the base of the crags: Agadasu had taken sanctuary there in a cave. When they asked the name of this place, he told them it was called Dead End. They blanched. It didn't sound a lucky choice.

This retreat needed no watch tower. It gave a perfect view of any attackers: there was only one approach with no ground cover, only greensward. The duke had gone on the run as soon as his neighbour had unexpectedly invaded Serpis. Now, with only a small force and no base, he was reduced to evading the shadow soldiers. He keenly awaited Hakeema's arrival. He hoped she would bring reinforcements and a plan of campaign.

As they approached, he came out to welcome them, quickly ushering them inside in single file. The winding entrance was the height of a house, but very narrow. The cave was packed with the duke's people; there really wasn't room for the newcomers. No sunlight penetrated the cavern; the only light came from oil lamps. They emitted a foul smell and smoke, which made Meena cough and Jack's eyes water. The cave was crowded, claustrophobic and airless.

"Hakeema, we cannot go on any longer. I hoped you would bring men, weapons and supplies. The people of Serpis want what any nation wants: peace, order and independence. Now I am ready to yield for the sake of my people, but I will give you time to get away before I surrender to Sharfeat."

Before Hakeema could reply, Jack jumped in. "Thanks to Meena here, I think we can beat the shadow soldiers."

The duke looked irritated. What was the boy blabbering about? Defeating the shadow soldiers? This was just fantasy.

This is the usual reaction to an original idea. If it doesn't fit with what people expect, they dismiss it. And the easiest way to dismiss it, is to say it's impossible. Children are full of ideas, because they do a lot of thinking. Most grown-ups can't cope with a lot of thinking.

So Jack wasn't surprised. Besides, in this land the sword was still the mightiest weapon. But Hakeema was an apothecary, so he hoped she would listen; Meena had learnt chemistry with him and she would take him seriously. He thought it wise not to mention his dream.

"Yesterday we fought off some shadowbats on our own."

"And today I saw shadowhawks killed," added Meena.

"I know what to do," said Jack, "But I need raw materials. If we go outside, I can explain."

On a ledge in front of the cave, Jack used a white pebble like a chalk to draw on a flat rock. He drew an upright box for the shell, with a few small circles inside it whizzing round like stars, surrounded by small dots for the black powder. Attached below the box, he drew a small square containing the lifting charge, with a long tail beneath, representing the fuse.

Fireworks: Jack's favourite thing! If he could get the materials in time, Jack planned more sophisticated aerial fireworks with extravagant effects. How? He had seen fireworks, of course, and been fascinated. The professor had a book on how to make them, he had told Jack about his father's fireworks, and Jack had made a rocket of his own. Judging by the baffled faces of Hakeema and Agadasu, they had never seen a firework. He tried to explain.

"It will shoot up into the sky and make a very bright light – and, if we wish, a bang. Do you have such things?"

"I have never seen such a contraption," said Hakeema.

"What is it?" asked the duke.

"It is called a firework," said Jack, with no sign of impatience. He needed the duke on his side, and he realised all this was hard for an Ardunyan to take in. "I need special salts and ores. I am hoping you know where to find them."

"What do you require?" asked Agadasu.

"Potassium nitrate, carbon, sulphur, sodium chloride—"

"I know not these substances," said Hakeema, "Mayhap we know them by other names?"

"Potassium nitrate is saltpetre, carbon is coal, sulphur is brimstone, sodium chloride is salt."

"The salt we use at table?" asked the duke.

"Yes, chief."

"That is easy. For the rest, I know not."

"I can describe them," said Jack. "Sulphur is a yellow powder – I think it's found as yellow crystals."

"I have some in my workshop," exclaimed Hakeema. "What else?"

"Carbon. That's coal, or charcoal."

"Charcoal we have," said Duke Agadasu, "And can get more."

"We need lots of saltpetre," said Jack, "If you hit it, it makes a bang."

"There is noisy rock in a cave near here. I can get someone to show you," said Hakeema.

"Great! Do you have calcium chloride? It soaks up water."

"Yes, yes," said Hakeema enthusiastically, "I have some."

"And do you know of a strange oil that wells up from the ground? It has a strange, sharp smell and catches fire."

"I shall fetch it. I have many such curios. Also, I know places where curious matter is found or the ground bubbles open. The duke's men can show you, if I tell them where."

"Could you tell them now? We need to move fast."

"Of course!"

He turned to the duke: "Sir, may I have some soldiers with sacks to collect the noisy rock? They must handle the sacks gently, and put them in a separate cave. It mustn't blow up yet."

"Very well, youngling. If Hakeema sees merit in your strange ideas, I shall give what help lies in my power."

"Thank you, sir. With these weapons, we cannot lose!"

"God grant it, boy. I go to instruct my people."

The children were left alone, with the two lookouts nearby. Jack turned to Aseem. "We may have to fight before nightfall. Has the duke any more soldiers?"

"The rest of his men are scattered across Serpis, acting as simple peasants."

"How quickly could they get here?"

"Mayhap within a short time. I shall ask." He turned to go.

"Thanks. … Meena, I can do the chemistry; you'll have to do the physics."

"You mean height, weight, range and so on? I'll do my best. But you seem to know a lot."

"We did that project on Guy Fawkes. Remember?"

"I've forgotten most of that!"

"So have I, to be honest. But the professor made fireworks with my dad. I nagged him for ages and he's been showing me how to make them. The rest came to me in a dream today."

"What, when you fell asleep in the howdah?"

"Yep." Jack didn't feel the need to have secrets from Meena any more. It was such a relief to be able to tell her things. With this new idea, he was excited and suddenly confident; the world of science was his home ground. Now he was busy working out the details; he hadn't stopped to think what might happen if things didn't go to plan. Meena usually did that.

———— § ————

Aseem and Hakeema returned together. Aseem assured Jack that the rest of the Serpian army were on their way. Hakeema had given directions to the soldiers. The duke wanted Aseem by his side, so he was soon off again. Jack gave Hakeema a list of the substances he wanted, with quantities and notes on how to identify them.

"Right. These are the must-haves. These are substitutes that might work. These are useful extras – and you'll need leather gloves, because this, and this, will burn your skin."

"Very well. I shall bring all I can."

Hakeema was given half a dozen soldiers as escort. Jack and Meena saw them set off and followed their progress. A little way down the valley, Hakeema's small company turned to climb a gully. Only when they were out of sight did Jack realise that Hakeema might not come back – and she had the crystal.

There was no time to think about that now. Meena had lots of questions for him. Had he test-fired his rocket? What angle did he intend to launch it at? How far did he want it to go before the flash was set off? What speed should it reach? What materials would he suggest for casings and fuses? What weight of flash powder did they need? In ballistics she was the expert; he was reduced to estimates, don't-knows and guesses. She suddenly felt very responsible: it would be horrible if the rockets didn't work; it would be worse if Jack started worrying about it. She had to keep him positive and focused on the task.

"We'll be firing the rockets from the base of these cliffs," explained Jack, "So they'll fly more like arrows, up a bit first and then straight."

The boy with the violet eyes

"I know the path of a projectile is a parabola," said Meena, "But I don't know what formula we need. An arrow takes the same time to reach the ground whether you fire it or just drop it, so the range depends on the speed – and I'll have to guess that for now."

"Just do your best, Meena. When I get back, we'll make one and try it out."

"Okay. You see what materials you can find. I'll start doing the sums."

A junior officer led Jack and their company, armed with sacks, up a side valley. Where the crags were lower, they turned to climb a steep cleft. The plateau was dry and stony; they headed for some low, steep-sided hills.

As they came nearer, there were patches of mist and a faint but pungent odour. Jack took a deep breath; the soldiers covered their noses and looked at him in disgust. It was the distinctive stench of rotten eggs – hydrogen sulphide. *Surely it can't be that easy?* The smell suggested they might find sulphur, which he needed; and one place you find sulphur is in areas of volcanic activity. That would explain the 'mist', probably from a hot spring or a fumarole.

The duke's men began cursing when they saw where this alien was leading them. Even their officer looked unhappy. Jack explained that the planet was bleeding from a slight wound and it would help the planet if they removed some pus from the wound. Even so, only one soldier volunteered to come to the edge of the fumarole. The hole was filled with steam and gases, the edges were bright yellow and the smell of rotten eggs was everywhere. The soldier was promptly sick. Jack was too busy to be sick. He gathered as much sulphur as he could and the soldier, recovering, was shamed into helping fill the sacks.

Leaving these under guard, the officer led them to a fissure in the hillside. Jack told them not to strike a flint: sparks might kill them. Sunlight reached only a short way into the cave, just far enough to show that the crumbling walls were green. Jack scraped off a minute amount with his knife and took it outside to ignite it.

His instinct was right. This wasn't white or ochre-coloured like saltpetre, but it was just as volatile, exploding with a small puff. This was the main ingredient, like flour in a cake, and there was plenty of it. They mined as much as they could, filling the sacks. Meanwhile, Jack scouted around and found a dry lake bed with various interesting deposits, which his assistant scooped up or scraped off into separate bags. If these were not suitable, he would use whatever Hakeema brought. Jack wanted the fireworks to be really flamboyant, with more colours and special effects that would get the enemy rattled.

These substances were evidently rare on Ardunya, yet they were all coming to hand. Andromeda would have said it was all fated. Lloyd would have said Jack's guardian angel was looking after him. Aseem would have said he was lucky. *What would Meena say?*

When the sacks were full, they set off back to their hideout. They had so much 'noisy rock' that Jack had another idea. On the way back they went to the woods further down the valley. Yes, the trees had slim, straight trunks with no branches near the ground. He asked what the trunk was like inside. The answer was better than he hoped.

The soldiers went to dump the sacks in a cave and returned with axes. They chopped down a small tree. It took a great deal of effort, confirming that the timber was tough, yet the heartwood oddly was soft and not difficult to scoop out. The older trees were hollow right through, but there was a bit of work to do before they could be used as cannons. Following Jack's instructions, the officer ordered his men to chop down a number of trees, cut them into two lengths, clean out the insides and make tapered plugs, with a handle, to fit one end. They set up a work camp where the weaponry would be assembled, under a dense canopy of trees.

Meena had worked out times for three trajectories, steeply up, flat and down into the valley. They decided on a range of 50 yards and between them they worked out the weight of the charge and the length of the fuses. With two young helpers, they quickly built a few simple rockets and then set off down the valley, up the gully and across the plateau to the low hills near the salt lake. Here, out of sight, they tested the rockets. There was no pyrotechnic display – they didn't want anyone to know about that yet.

They worked! On the steep trajectory, though, the rocket was too slow and fell back. It would need a bigger charge. On their way back, Jack told Meena about the cannons, and asked her to calculate how much powder to use in the charge. She reminded him she would also have to work out the length of fuse for them and for the flame-tipped arrows. After that, she would try a bigger charge for the steep-trajectory rockets and test one up at the salt lake.

While Meena got started on that, Jack showed some women how to make black powder – the gunpowder. He got them to work in twos and threes, well separated to avoid accidents. The children made paper packets of salt, rolled up tight, for the 'stars' – the coloured display – in the fireworks. A few older girls did the same with the green powder; Jack wasn't sure what it was, but presumably it contained copper and would burn with a green or bluish flame.

The children also prepared rocket bodies and casings, carried messages or ran round with food and drink, which the oldest people prepared. The younger children cut up candlewicks and tissue paper for fuses. The older people made arrows or hollowed out saplings for launch tubes. Everyone helped in one way or another.

While all this was going on, Jack explained his plans to Duke Agadasu. Dead End valley was ideal in having only one approach, but it also had only one way out. They could be trapped – or so Sharfeat would think. But the narrow valley gave the shadow soldiers little room to manoeuvre, and the crags had many clefts and caves from which unseen Serpians could fire.

As the rest of the army began to arrive, they were set to dig three trenches across the valley, with only a narrow track to cross by. Other men dragged the first cannons up to the base of the crags, overlooking the trenches, or carried sacks of saltpetre, sulphur and charcoal to the firing points. Soldiers, armed and briefed, took up battle stations below.

Meena had made one flame-tipped arrow – though it would be firework-tipped until Hakeema returned with the oil – and set the boys to make more. Then she set off to test the new rocket fuse. The duke had some fine archers, and Jack explained what they were to do. He even got them to modify their bows so they could fire two arrows at a time.

Jack had done all he could. He sent scouts to look out for Hakeema, but there was no sign of her. She should have been here by now. He looked up and saw the first of Sharfeat's shadow troops in the distance.

18 Fireworks

Aseem, thanks to the device on his belt, had warned the duke, but everyone looked stunned; they were only half ready for battle. The hundreds of soldiers, armed with halberds, swords, spears and bows, knew from experience that such weapons were useless against these creatures. Three shadowhawks hovered high up, inspecting the forces they faced.

Jack was standing outside a cave, showing some women how to assemble the fireworks, when he heard a warning cry. He turned to see the three hawks flying straight at him. His blood turned cold and he froze. They swooped down, on course to snatch him up.

Instead, they stopped abruptly in mid-air, their sharp talons a few feet from his face, ready to seize him. They hovered, as if to mock their prey before the kill, staring expressionlessly into his violet eyes, wide with fear. But then, inexplicably, they flew up and away.

Why had they not attacked him? Sharfeat must know that Black Mist had tracked down the Coopers and killed them all, save Jack. The prophecy depended entirely on him. Without him, the Serpians would give up, and the last threat to Sharfeat would be gone. He tried to reason it out. The shadowhawks had singled him out, so they knew who he was. Were they under strict orders only to reconnoitre? Well, they would be back.

The Serpians had set up dozens of cannons, prepared hundreds of rockets and arrows, and wearied themselves digging trenches, ready to stand their ground. With these new weapons, they might win; if they lost, well, every Serpian child believed it was better to die free than be a well-fed, living slave, or worse: for a raksas needed meat, and childmeat was particularly tender.

———— § ————

Jack finished explaining how to build up each firework and asked some women to instruct the other groups. He ran panting back to the main cave, where the duke and his officers were finalising strategy and tactics. Now feeling bolder, the earthling told them about the shadowhawks.

"How did you repel them?" one officer asked.

"Obviously I'm not as good-looking as I thought," said Jack.

The Serpians looked baffled, and glared in disapproval at a messenger boy of about 14, nearly choking as he tried not to laugh.

Aseem was there, but his mind was elsewhere. "Why is Hakeema so long? I fear for her."

"She'll be fine. It's the shadow soldiers that give me the chills."

"How will you repel them?" asked an officer.

Jack's face was now serious. "They're scared of fire, so they fly away from it. They won't get the chance. When they attack, they'll fly straight into our aerial fireworks – except I'm waiting for Meena to tell me the fuse length and Hakeema to bring the rest of the stuff."

"We have the cannons," someone pointed out.

"Yes," said Jack, keen to explain, "But they can't shoot upwards; we use them against the ground troops. I was hoping to have flaming oil for the arrows, but for now they're tipped with small fireworks. It's the best we can do."

"These weapons are new to me, I admit, but I know something of war," said Duke Agadasu with a polite smile, "Mayhap you will allow me to plan the battle."

Jack blushed. He was being told off, in the kindest way, and he was glad; he couldn't plan a battle. The duke spelt out his orders.

"We are no match for Sharfeat's army. Attack is too risky. Instead we force them to attack. We eliminate as many as we can and hold out as long as possible. They are far from base, so eventually they must retreat or wait for supplies."

The duke's finest warriors, armed with swords and spears, were the first line of defence against Sharfeat's ground troops; behind them were the halberdiers, ready to join hand-to-hand combat. As soon as the enemy tried to cross the three ditches, they would come under fire from the cannons and archers.

The cannons were hidden under the crags – some loaded with sacks of black powder and salts, with a delayed fuse, others with sacks of pebbles and packets of gunpowder. The former faced slightly upwards, the latter were trained on the trenches below. Most archers were stationed in caves below the crags, with small numbers in the valley. Each had one grown-up or two younger assistants.

Other pairs of youngsters were stationed in clefts and crevices, ready to launch rockets at incoming shadow soldiers. Jack had tested some tissue paper, and it made a good fuse; Meena had roughly calculated the length of fuse – the lift charge to get the rocket into the air – and the break charge to actually set off the firework. She was away testing the prototypes.

Jack's rockets were ready for final assembly. Most fireworks contained just sodium chloride, but some had green, blue or orange powder too. Women were hard at work completing this task while men were filling sacks of grapeshot and adding the packets of black powder.

When the time came to retreat, Duke Agadasu said, they would withdraw to the higher ground at the sides. The old and very young would hide in caves. Clearly the duke assumed they would not win the battle. He was blunt: anyone not fighting should surrender unconditionally when defeat came. The duke looked sombre, but he finished by thanking Jack.

"Without you, Sharfeat would play hide-and-seek with us and then kill us anyhow. This way we die fighting. For a youngling, you have a great mind and a great heart."

Jack coloured up, very proud of such praise from a grown-up he had come to admire. He wished Meena was there. "With Hakeema's materials, chief, and a bit more time, we could give Sharfeat a fight to remember."

———— § ————

Before they could say anything else, they heard an urgent cry: "The enemy is in sight!"

"To your stations, men! You know your duty," called the duke confidently. Everyone ran to their position, leaving Agadasu and Aseem at the cave, with a few staff officers and messengers.

Jack ran to join his designated helpers in a crack halfway along the cliffs. His job was to ignite the rocket fuse at the right moment as a signal to the others. He was too busy to think of being afraid; he just wished he felt sure his weapons would work. They could see the shadow soldiers in the distance, rank after rank of them, advancing.

The lookout's voice was heard again. "The wise woman is in sight!" Jack scanned the valley and there they were, Hakeema and her soldiers, clambering down the gully that broke the line of crags on the left. Jack was thrilled: soon he would see her beautiful face again, and her men had heavy sacks on their shoulders. *My shopping list. At last!* There was a stranger with them too, though he seemed familiar.

Then Jack noticed ahead of them a small figure carrying rockets. Was 'the wise woman' Meena? The duke sent men to escort them inside their lines. Jack was excited to see Meena again and desperate to get the fuse specifications and the extra raw materials. He ran down to the spot where the men were hurriedly dumping their sacks. Officers, men and messengers were gathering, awaiting orders. Jack was panicky and anxious, hardly knowing where to start with Meena's fuses and Hakeema's sacks.

"What took you so long? Sharfeat's breathing down our necks."

Meena was weary. "I couldn't get here any faster, Jack." She looked reproachfully at him.

Suddenly Jack felt sick: Meena thought he meant her. He meant Hakeema, forgetting she had trekked miles across wilderness and hurried back without a rest to bring what he asked.

Hakeema broke in. "I see you did, Meena. Are we too late, Jack?"

Jack tried to cover his blunder with an awkward smile. "You guys did well. Let's see what you've brought, then?"

"I brought what seemed best," said Hakeema, "But I have only modest amounts of each."

"There's plenty! Now we should be able to stockpile enough rockets, if there's time."

"I've checked all the fuses, Jack, and the lift charge is enough for the steep trajectory."

Hakeema looked at Meena, astonished.

Jack tried again. "Thanks. You must be tired. Why don't you both have a bite to eat and a rest?"

They set off up the hill. Jack told the officers where the men should take the sacks, pressing them to be very careful handling the explosives. He asked a messenger boy to bring him a supply of flints. Meanwhile he went round the firework makers, taking one volunteer from each group. He showed them how to make flame-tipped arrows and spears. They were to stand behind the archers and soldiers on the battlefield, and only pour and ignite the oil when it was needed.

Then he set off to run from one firework site to the next, reminding them to pack the 'stars' tightly, close up, add the time-delay fuse and a packet of black powder, and seal the rocket before moving to the next one. The women were quick, soon stockpiling hundreds of rockets. Every minute enlarged their arsenal, but the attack might come at any moment.

———— § ————

Instead, Sharfeat and Khabish approached with their personal bodyguards. A messenger girl came up to tell Jack that the duke wanted him for the parley. His young assistants took charge, and he and the messenger set off.

As they ran, she explained that no battle ever began on Ardunya until the two sides' heralds had met to see if they could negotiate terms. But Sharfeat had come in person. Jack was to accompany Duke Agadasu and his officers on horseback to hear Sharfeat's conditions.

The girl assumed he could ride, but Jack had never been on a horse in his life – and Ardunyan horses looked rather bad-tempered. The girl helped him mount, but she could see he was clueless, so she smiled at Jack, put the reins in his hands and told him to sit upright and grip the horse gently with his knees. Jack just wanted to make sure he didn't fall off.

He tried to look calm and confident as they rode out through the ranks of Serpian soldiers and into the open. The two sides faced each other, yards apart. This was the first time Jack had come close to his arch-enemy since their encounter on the palace stair. He hoped it would be the last.

Sharfeat gave them a wicked smile. His face showed a man who cared for nothing and nobody but himself, a man who would smile as he sliced open your face. Jack was trembling, unsure what Sharfeat might do, but he tried to put on a brave face. The duke seemed extraordinarily calm.

Sharfeat spoke directly to Jack. "You are to surrender at once, without any conditions. If you bring all your people into this open space, with their hands in the air, I will overlook the mischief you have caused. I may even be lenient in punishing you."

This was not negotiation. *If we bring people out in the open, they will be sitting ducks. This is just a ploy to set up a massacre.* Jack was tense, and his voice came out as a high-pitched treble – but to his surprise he found the right words.

"They are Duke Agadasu's people, not mine. You'd better talk to him."

The duke spoke. "We have seen your 'leniency', Sharfeat. In any case, you are a fake: you have no right to power and you will not have it much longer. You will lose this battle and Black Mist will not accept excuses. I imagine Khabish already has his orders what to do with you."

"Do I look worried?" asked Sharfeat. He looked utterly confident. "*You* should. You will be enjoying my hospitality when this is all over."

Agadasu turned pale. Khabish showed no more emotion of any kind. Jack and the duke turned their horses and headed back to their own lines, followed by their officers.

—————— § ——————

The duke expected a traditional battle first, and his men were in position. When the shadow soldiers joined in, he would need the new weapons, but there were not yet enough of these. Could they delay the start of fighting?

Just then there was an explosion. At one of the projectile work-sites, someone had mishandled a sack of grapeshot, the black powder had exploded and the battle had claimed its first casualty. Outraged that the Serpians had dared to attack when the parley was barely over, Sharfeat and Khabish hurried to rejoin their army. Sharfeat signalled to the shadow soldiers, and the fighting began.

The shadow soldiers went through the first line of the Serpian ranks like a hot knife through butter. The warriors put up a brave fight with their lit arrows and spears, but their enemies were too agile for them. The duke, alarmed, gave the order to fire the cannons.

"No!" yelled Jack, but his voice was lost in the roar of a dozen cannons. They launched heavy sacks, which were blown apart by the first charge of powder as they fell, dropping hundreds of pebbles in mid-air. Jack saw them fall on the duke's soldiers below. Men shouted, the injured screamed, others lay silently where they fell. Smoke from the cannons mixed with clouds of dust from the ground to create a fog over the battlefield.

At first, the shadow soldiers flying overhead were taken aback by the explosions, but they soon saw that the weapon had turned on its creators. They waited for the smoke to clear and attacked again with renewed ferocity.

The boy with the violet eyes

Jack ran down the slope as fast as he could. The soldiers were disciplined, but they were confused and angry at being hit by their own side. Many lay concussed or bleeding. Through a clear patch in the smoke, Jack saw Agadasu.

"Chief, don't use the cannons yet! They're only hurting our men."

"When do I use them?"

"Not while our people in the way. Those men need to be under the crags, and the horses behind the trees. Only then can you fire the cannons. First we must use the arrows."

"Very well." The duke gave orders, and the pull-back began. It was rather disorderly, since no one had prepared for this, and the sides of the valley were soon overcrowded. The shadow soldiers saw the retreat as an act of panic: they had the Serpians on the run. They chased them up the slopes.

Once their own stragglers had reached safety, Jack signalled to the archers, who let fly their flame-tipped arrows. The first shadowhawk that was hit exploded in a ball of flame and fell to the ground, burning fiercely to nothing. Others flew into crags or cannons and were injured or killed. As the archers picked off more, the enemy became wary. Within a minute, the shadow soldiers had withdrawn.

A cheer went up. This time the duke's men could see some benefit in the new armoury. As the smoke and dust began to settle, they saw Sharfeat's ground forces marching forward. This was the opening manoeuvre the duke had expected, and now he knew just what to do. He sent a messenger to the cannoniers.

There was room for only a few men on the track. The rest had to scale the ditches. These were dry, but Sharfeat's men still had to climb down into them and back up the other side; men had to wait while those in front scrambled down, or up, the slope. When the front line reached the third trench, the cannons opened fire with grapeshot.

This time they did their job. The rain of stones knocked out or injured the enemy soldiers, while the flashes, bangs and smoke frightened and confused them. Those clambering up fell back on the squirming pile of troops behind them. Within a minute, they stopped advancing. As their casualties mounted, Sharfeat's men – what was left of them – saw they would have to retreat.

——— § ———

Having rested and eaten, Hakeema joined Duke Agadasu, and Meena sat with Aseem at the mouth of the cave.

"I can't see what's going on. Can you?" said Meena.

"I am supposing our enemies are regrouping," replied Aseem, "But they are hidden by the trees and that bend in the valley."

"Let's find Jack," Meena suggested.

128

Jack was waiting with two assistants to launch his rockets, but there was no enemy in sight. He was pleased to see Aseem and Meena. He told them about the shadowhawks who could have killed him, but didn't, and suggested they climb to the top of the crags to get a better view of the battle. The other two were keen, and began scrambling up a cleft in the rocks.

This crevice had footholds and the odd stunted tree they could grab, until they reached a short pitch of smooth rock. They did not fancy going back down, so they had to find a way up it. Meena the gymnast quickly found the right solution.

She leaned back against one side of the crevice and began to walk her feet up the other side until they were opposite her shoulders. The boys watched in alarm, but Meena was quite comfortable. Using her elbows and hands to support herself, she moved her shoulders a little way up, wedged herself and then walked her feet up a bit further.

After a minute or two, she reached the top of the cleft. She found a foothold, carefully transferred one foot to it, then hauled her shoulders up again. Now she could put more weight on the foothold and push herself upright. She scrambled up on top of the crags.

Aseem and Jack could feel the challenge hanging in the air. The prince set off, copying Meena exactly; Jack supported him until he could no longer reach, but by then Aseem had got the hang of it. At the top, Meena helped him find the foothold, and he climbed the last few feet on his own.

Jack tensed himself, concentrated hard and moved very, very cautiously. The other two kept quiet, sensing that he was only just keeping panic at bay. At the speed of an agile snail, he inched his way up. Finally, Meena guided his foot into place at the top, and encouraged him gently until he was able to stand and clamber out.

On top of the crags was grass, with a dry, stony plateau beyond. Grass under his feet had never felt so wonderful. They had a superb panorama here, but the bend in the valley still obstructed their view. The answer was to walk along the clifftop, keeping back from the edge so they were not spotted, until they reached the place where the valley changed direction.

Below they glimpsed Sharfeat's injured foot-soldiers straggling back along the narrow path on the other side of the valley past the dense woodland. In the great wood straight below them, previously unsuspected, was a lake in the middle of a broad marsh. To their right, beyond the trees, the rest of Sharfeat's ground troops were milling about in the open; only the shadowbats were still in good order, hovering low. In a space among the confused mass of soldiers they saw the great beast Khabish, glowing deep red with anger. Jack, standing between Meena and Aseem, pointed out Sharfeat nearby, in the midst of a knot of officers on horseback, deep in discussion.

The boy with the violet eyes

Something made Meena look round. A shadowhawk was swooping down on them.

"Jack!" she yelled.

Jack froze, but Aseem pushed him sideways. Jack fell against Meena. The shadowhawk grabbed Aseem in its talons and flew straight on, over the edge of the crags and above the valley. It circled and landed beside Sharfeat and his officers, still grasping Aseem, pinning his arms to his sides.

Jack helped Meena to her feet. They gripped each other tightly and stared down at poor Aseem far below, now Sharfeat's prisoner. Jack and Meena looked at each other, still in shock. Life can be like that: we don't know what's around the corner. And this corner was dangerous – what had happened to Aseem could happen to them. They looked around wildly for somewhere to hide: the plateau was bare, apart from the short turf.

Meena spoke first. "Let's get back, before they come for *us*."

––––––– § –––––––

They could not identify the place they had climbed up, and Jack was not sure he wanted to. It took them some time, hunting back and forth along the cliff top, before they found another way down with more footholds.

When they reached the cave and told their news, Hakeema was devastated, tears running down her cheek. Jack silently cursed himself for not foreseeing what would happen. He felt even worse because Aseem had sacrificed himself. *For me or for Meena? Well, if he saved me just because of Meena, I'm still grateful. And, if she admires him more than me, she's right. How odd: I don't mind.*

The prince was proud, yet he never made you feel bad. Jack was proud, but he often upset people. It was a different kind of pride. Aseem was always courteous, considerate, kind and … modest. That was it! It was modesty that made Aseem – and Meena – so attractive. *I'm not Aseem and I never will be*, he thought. *But I can learn from him. Unless it's too late.*

Meena couldn't share her thoughts with Jack, not yet anyway. She was still sorting them out. *If I hadn't shouted, Aseem would have been safe. He did it for me. Well, perhaps for Jack too, but mostly me. He was wonderful, and I feel awful.*

Word of the capture of the Crown Prince of Macron spread through the Serpian army. But this was no time to be sad, as the duke well knew. He had lost hundreds of his people, and they still had to face the shadow soldiers. Now that he held the crown prince, Sharfeat was in a strong position. Macron was less likely to fight back. The duke was a practical man, and his task now was to rouse everyone to resume the struggle.

"The enemy hopes we will surrender. Why? To become slaves? No, let us copy the prince's example. He risked all to save the earthling, who alone can end the black-flower plague. We must be ready to risk all to save Serpis!"

––––––– § –––––––

The duke was concerned about his troops confined in the hot, airless caves, wondering how much longer they could stand it. A fitful breeze sprang up, causing eddies of dust. It gave Jack an idea, and he quickly explained it to the duke, who sent messengers to the two cannon crews furthest away. With great effort, they turned their weapons to face down the valley and loaded them with smaller sacks of grapeshot and a bigger charge of powder.

When they fired, one hit part of the enemy camp; the other landed just short. Dust and smoke enveloped the troops, who began to choke and rush around in panic. Seeing these soldiers were now useless, Sharfeat sent in his shadow soldiers, bats and hawks.

The shadowbats stayed low, where they were not spotted until they were very close. The other cannons fired, creating clouds of dust and smoke, forcing the shadow soldiers higher, where they were more easily seen. Some were ignited by gunpowder flashes and rapidly burnt to nothing.

The shadowhawks dived from up high, and the duke's archers fired flame-tipped arrows from caves and crevices in the crags, picking off their targets. There were terrible shrieks as the shadowy shapes caught alight, burnt and fell like black rain. One archer in particular never seemed to miss: this was Indar, Aseem's weapons tutor, the familiar stranger who had returned with Hakeema.

For close-range defence, Jack had shortened the rocket fuses to finger length. This was dangerous for the crews, who had to dive behind the rock the moment they launched them, but the rockets had to meet the attackers in mid-air to cause maximum impact. The archers were running out of his flame-tipped arrows, and the whole of Dead End valley was now filled with attacking shadow soldiers.

Jack gave the signal, and every member of the rocket crew ignited their fuse. In a series of detonations, dozens of rockets shot into the sky. The result was spectacular. Ardunyans, who had never before seen any fireworks, were given a display that earthlings could hardly imagine. They were astonished. Yellow fireworks burst and showered patterns of palm leaves, roundels, zigzags, polygons, serpentines and spirals, followed by afterbursts in magnificent shades of yellow, green, blue, orange, turquoise, purple and colours that had never yet been named.

Jack watched with his mouth wide open at this, the ultimate firework display. He had long dreamt of making a rocket of his own that might throw a single shaft of colour into a dark sky. He had never imagined he might produce a spectacle like this, in the midst of a battle, using materials gathered on a faraway planet.

Dad would be proud! He recalled his father's face from the scroll, as he watched the evening sky turn bright and dazzling. Thousands of shadow soldiers popped like balloons as they collided with fragments of the falling stars, unable to get out of the way. Within minutes, most of Sharfeat's dark army had burnt to a crisp. Fires broke out in the woodland, illuminating the dazed remnants of the enemy force.

Sharfeat watched in disbelief. No one on Ardunya had ever imagined such weapons or such devastation. His army had been almost annihilated. The last few shadow soldiers flew off. They were all gone by the time the smoke from the cannons and fireworks cleared.

19 The monster in the swamp

Meena ran to congratulate Jack. She found him thanking Indar and the other archers and the rocket crews, saying how well they had done. *Wow!* thought Meena. A knot of soldiers and youngsters gathered admiringly around their new hero.

Khabish bellowed at his soldiers, but they were no longer listening. As they fled down the valley, a great cheer went up among the Serpians. Their joy was short-lived. Khabish was loping towards them on his hind legs, in a towering fury. His glowing, red-hot body showed his mood.

Those on the battlefield, carrying away the dead and injured, scattered in all directions. Their spears bounced off the beast like matchsticks; flaming arrows and fireworks were equally useless against a beast that breathed fire; his fireballs had already killed two of the duke's men. Khabish lumbered straight past them.

Seeing Jack, he roared triumphantly and charged. Jack was terrified. How to elude this formidable beast? Indar pointed, Jack grabbed Meena's hand and the three ran towards the trees, where the undergrowth would slow their pursuer and hide them.

Khabish gave chase, coughing out whirling fireballs and lobbing them into the trees. Soon the woods were engulfed in flames. Burning branches fell in their way, slowing them. Fire did not bother Khabish. He ran in huge strides, leaping over fallen boughs, closing the gap on Indar, Jack and Meena. The crashing and splintering noises were getting nearer.

They emerged from the inferno onto soft ground. To the right was a lake. In front and to the left was a marsh hundreds of yards wide, but they dared not stop. A furious roar told them that Khabish was close behind. They set off across the bog, leaping from tuft to tussock. The water welled up around their feet.

They could hear splashing and slurping noises behind them as the beast began to wade through the marsh. Water rushed over the top of Jack's shoe. Instead of being burnt, they were going to drown, if Khabish did not tear them limb from limb first.

Indar was ahead, but he was struggling. "Do not follow. I am sinking past my ankles!"

But Jack shouted "Keep going! This is our only chance!"

Far ahead, there were some drier patches that looked firm enough to stand on – if they made it. Meena, picking her way carefully, had fallen behind. Khabish was lumbering through the bog twenty yards behind her, but his burning eyes were fixed on only one person.

"Jack!" she yelled.

The boy with the violet eyes

A fireball shaved Jack's head, frizzling the top of his hair. His foot slipped off the flattened rushes, plunging his leg into the marsh above the knee. It didn't matter. With each step, Khabish was sinking deeper.

There was a prolonged sucking noise as the beast heaved a huge foot out of the tangled growths in the bog, and a great splash spattered them with mud as the foot went in again. The beast was hardly moving at all and the bulk of his gigantic body sank further, until after a few laboured steps he could no longer lift his hind legs. Thrashing about, Black Mist's enforcer had no thought for his enemies any more. He was no longer the hunter.

For there was life below the surface. The silent swamp awoke, and ripples appeared here and there. The snouts and eyes of reptilian creatures broke the surface, and made towards the splashing, plunging beast. They ignored Meena, Jack and Indar, who made smaller and fewer splashes as they reached firmer ground.

Khabish's luck had run out. The swamp had him in its grip. The water snakes circled, and one darted in, ripping a piece of juicy flesh from his tough hide as the beast stumbled. Khabish grabbed the snake with his front paws, tore it in two and flung it away. It gave one terrible shriek before falling under the water, lifeless.

Jack, Meena and Indar had reached firmer ground. They turned and watched as Khabish pounded away any fresh ripples that appeared before him. A water snake would screech and disappear into the depths of the swamp, only to be replaced by two more.

"What are we waiting for?" asked Meena. She tugged at Jack's sleeve.

"Wait, Meena … look!" Jack pointed to the lake behind Khabish, where bigger ripples were forming a circle, like a whirlpool. The water snakes fled as a rumbling noise beneath the water grew louder. Something was pushing its way to the surface. The ripples were now waves. Khabish stopped struggling, waiting to see what was causing this turmoil.

The whirlpool boiled over and a creature erupted from the water. It was as big as Khabish or bigger. At first, seeing its scales, they thought it was a giant fish, or a crocodile, but it had several heads with one eye each, and they were snake heads. Meena had seen such a beast, in a book about the Hindu gods: could this be Shesha, the seven-headed serpent king? It moved swiftly towards Khabish, its seven necks erect, its seven heads showing seven intimidating eyes and many fierce teeth.

Khabish stared in disbelief. There was no fire in his belly any more. Even if he had been free to escape, he could not have moved a muscle. He cringed, expecting the marsh monster to strike.

But the serpent was staring too: it had seen Khabish before. Black Mist had sent him here to take one of the serpent's babies, to kill it and extract the vile black liquid that had poisoned and petrified King Jonda. The serpent remembered. Its seven eyes glared and its mouth opened, showing long, deadly fangs. They struck Khabish with the speed of lightning.

The trapped beast roared in pain and pounded the serpent with his fists; but the venom was already working its way through his body. He gasped. His heartbeat weakened, from the thumping of an engine to the ticking of a clock. Khabish stopped in his tracks, the colour draining from his body.

The water serpent reared up and struck again, this time meeting no resistance. All seven fangs penetrated the hide, and the effect was like an electric shock. Paralysed, Sharfeat's beast swayed once or twice, and then began to topple. The great grey carcass hit the water sideways with a crash, coming to rest with just one great flank still visible. Jack, Meena and Indar watched, horrified, as the last bit of the corpse sank slowly from sight.

The great serpent turned and swam away, submerging as it went. Its last three heads sank below the surface with a few small ripples. When those had gone, the swamp was as still and silent as before. They could hardly believe what they had seen.

———— § ————

"I rejoice to have witnessed the end of that evil beast Khabish," said Indar as they walked back.

"Me too," said Meena, "But that Shesha-thing nearly scared the life out of me. What if it attacked one of us?"

"Jack would make some white magic to drive it off," said Indar seriously.

"The way he drove off Khabish, you mean?" Meena couldn't help being mischievous.

Indar was puzzled. "Did you drive the beast into the swamp, Jack?"

"Yes, by running away like a chicken. But Aseem didn't bring me here to do impressions."

Meena looked at Jack. "How are we going to rescue him?"

"Search me," he replied. "It's one thing after another: we land in the wrong place, get dragged off to prison, fight a war and that beast nearly had us for breakfast. I just want to know what this crystal does – and then get out of here."

"It will come to you," said Indar.

"It'd better come quick," said Jack grimly.

When they returned to the battlefield, the duke was up at the cave dealing with the aftermath and sending people to forage for supplies; Hakeema was in the valley attending to the injured. They went over to tell her the news, but she already knew.

"Yes, we heard his death cry."

"He fell to the seven-headed King Shesha," Indar added.

"So this creature exists," said Hakeema wonderingly, "I never believed the tales before."

Duke Agadasu joined them, and they recounted Khabish's end. After the duke had marvelled at their escape, he broached his own concern.

"With your help we have accomplished a miracle, but Serpis is not yet free."

"Nor is Macron," said Indar.

"Neither is Aseem," added Meena.

"I am," said Jack, "What do I do now?"

"I thought you would know, being a Barelas," said the duke.

"My father might've known," said Jack quietly.

"Mayhap the prophecy will tell you?" offered Hakeema. She recited it slowly.

> *When black flowers the land shall overwhelm*
> *And rats eat up the blossoms, crops and seeds,*
> *When black shadows cross the royal realm,*
> *Double darkness shrouding darker deeds,*
> *Then will come the famine, plague and treason,*
> *Evil magic, slavery and war,*
> *The end of peace, but only for a season:*
> *A barrel-maker shall the land restore.*
>> *A cooper, one named in this family history,*
>> *Born to yield power to the jewel of mystery,*
>> *A youngster, but wise – no hero, but brave –*
>> *The pyramid will light and the whole kingdom save.*

"Serpis knows full well of the flowers and rats," said the duke, "Famine, plague and war."

"Macron has seen dark deeds, treason, black magic and slavery," said Hakeema.

"I'm the young Cooper with the jewel," said Jack.

"And you're wise and brave," said Meena, "But no hero."

"It is passing strange that you say so," said Indar, "After all Jack has done."

Meena looked down, realising she had made one sharp remark too many.

"There was nothing about a pyramid when Aseem read the prophecy," said Jack.

"Did my old teacher not mention it?" asked Hakeema.

Jack shook his head. "I don't think so … Wait! The master *ji* mentioned a ziggurat, but he did once call it a pyramid. He said nothing about double darkness, but the prophecy does link it with the black flowers – and I'm some kind of lodestone …"

"That's all clear, then," Meena said acidly.

"Not all." Hakeema missed the sarcasm. "But the pyramid is in the old city, Macropolis."

"It is near a day's march," said the duke, "There is no water or pasture: you cannot ride."

"What if Sharfeat spots us?" put in Jack.

"We don't have a choice," Meena insisted, "This is what we came for."

"A small group on foot might not attract remark," said the duke.

"Could we travel at night?" asked Jack.

"In the dark we would not be seen at all," mused Indar.

"'Tis your only chance," said the duke. "Go at second sunset. I shall march on Macropuris, before Sharfeat can regroup his forces. I am sending messengers to every part of Serpis, telling of our victory and your mission to end the black-flower plague. If we act now, we can triumph."

"I go with Hakeema," said Indar, "I ask only two men to protect the earthlings."

"Granted," said the duke, "And now I leave you. Farewell! Let us meet in Macropuris!" He picked two men as escorts, ordering them to make up packs of food and fill waterskins. The six retired to a quiet cave for a couple of hours' rest.

None of them got much sleep. The soldiers refought the battle in their minds. Hakeema tried to recall what she had read or heard about the black-flower pestilence, its accompanying disasters and how exactly the cooper ended it. Meena wondered what was happening to Aseem. Would Sharfeat torture him? Or kill him? How were they to find him?

Jack slipped into sleep. He was back in the professor's lab with the crystal in his hands. Form 9G were there, sitting at their desks. They were talking and laughing, and he wanted to make them stop, but he didn't know how. His father leaned over, murmuring "Use your personal magnetism, Jack!" and gave him an encouraging smile before vanishing. Jack stared at the class, then down at the crystal: it felt very heavy, and the class had gone quiet – or very far away.

While they slept, the Serpian army packed up and the country folk started back to their village, taking the injured with them. Hakeema woke to hear the army setting off.

———— § ————

King Sharfeat and his demoralised army were making their way back to the capital. Yesterday he had rounded up sons, daughters, dogs and goats as live bait for the raksas, and burnt down homes as a warning to the Serpians. Now he was leaving Serpis in his enemy's hands.

Sharfeat feared that Macron might rebel when people heard of the Serpian victory, but he feared Black Mist even more, for he had promised the demon victory. What was left of his army now knew he was not invincible. The fire weapons had destroyed his shadow soldiers. Khabish had gone. Rats had eaten the crops, and people were starving or dying of plague. He could no longer feed the livestock meant for the raksas. Black Mist was hungry. But why bother with the demon? He was king; he held the crown prince and the capital. His enemies were disorganised. People were afraid of him.

How to keep power? He remembered what Hakeema had said – how easy it is to acquire power, how difficult to maintain it. He had to prove her wrong. If he captured Jack, he could learn the secrets of the crystal and the fire rockets. And where Jack was, Hakeema would be. He wanted her for himself. What woman would not want a man as rich and powerful as Sharfeat? She wouldn't resist, especially if something unpleasant might happen to her precious Aseem. The crown prince's capture was a masterstroke. For now, heavily guarded, he was leading Macron's army home.

———— § ————

Hakeema woke the others. After some bread and cheese, and a drink of water, the six set off down the now deserted Dead End valley and turned left to scale the ravine. When they came out on the plateau, they paused for one last look. Jack spoke.

"Hakeema, can I have my crystal back?"

"Indeed, it is properly yours."

They stopped while she got it out of her pack.

"Thanks." Jack eased it into his deep pocket. "Do you know anything about the pyramid?"

"There was no 'pyramidal light' in the version Aseem read," put in Meena.

"Mayhap not," said Hakeema airily, "There are several versions."

There was a startled pause. Meena said, "But Jack needs to make sense of it."

"How can he until he knows what it means?" Hakeema replied.

Jack and Meena exchanged a glance and tried not to look as exasperated as they felt.

"Do you know what the pyramid looks like?"

"I once read a description, but it was very muddled. One passage said the pyramid was in darkness, another said the sun bathed it – and it lay inside a maze. I planned to reveal all on our arrival."

Why wait? Jack said, "I don't see what the pyramid has to do with the black flowers."

"Oh, that reminds me," interrupted Meena, "My dad told me about the *mautam*. It's like the black flowers. In the forests of India, the bamboo flowers every 48 years, then there is famine for a year. He said the *mautam* was a mystery, but I looked it up on the internet, and scientists think they know why it happens."

"Scientists?" said Hakeema, "Wizards, you mean? Isn't 'science' your word for magic?"

"That's right," said Meena, with a sly look at Jack, "Well, the wizards think the rats like the bamboo seeds and they have lots of babies – no, not the wizards, Jack – and the baby rats eat all the crops and spread fleas, which bite people and give them plague so they die of that or starvation. I think that's what happens with the black flowers."

"So how's my crystal going to help?"

"I don't know," said Meena, "But it seems very like what happens here."

"In any case," said Hakeema, "With the crystal, you can drive any raksas from the planet."

Why didn't she tell me that before?

———— § ————

Sharfeat's army were beginning to look mutinous. General Galman, the second-in-command, ordered a halt and distribution of rations. Sharfeat rode up to ask him what was happening.

"Why have you stopped?"

"Sire, the men have marched all day and fought a battle. They are exhausted."

"Did I order a rest? I want them moving in five minutes." Sharfeat signalled to a senior officer. "It's no wonder you didn't win the battle, Galman. Tie him up!"

The marshal was frustrated and fuming, still unable to believe he had been defeated by a box of tricks dreamt up by two 13-year-olds. But he had to blame somebody, and who better than his second-in-command? Poor Galman would pay dearly for taking on Jack.

Sharfeat turned to a young captain. "Take a dozen men: find Hakeema and the earthlings. Search the old city," he growled, "I intend to deal with them myself, so track them and keep me informed … or else."

———— § ————

The moons rose and night creatures awoke. With only double moonlight to guide them, the six had to tread carefully to avoid stumbling. There was no talk as they crossed the stony desert in the dead of night.

By first light, they reached a line of gentle hills, seamed by ravines whose streams petered out in the dust of the desert. They followed one of these; it gave good cover and fresh drinking water. At one point they heard a movement and froze, but then a night bird flew off.

"So far, so good, Hakeema," Jack whispered.

"Yes, we have been fortunate," she whispered back.

Indar seemed on edge. He was constantly scanning the horizon in every direction, though there was nothing to see.

—————— § ——————

Behind the palace in Macron's capital city, the royal dove keeper was woken by one of his birds returning. He got out of bed to collect Colum's message. He was not supposed to read it, but he always did.

In shock, he read it twice. 'The king' and his shadow soldiers had suffered a setback, they were returning to regroup and would require breakfast when they reached Macropuris. The dove keeper rushed to wake the chamberlain, who would take the necessary action, but on his way back he had a word with the housekeeper, the duty chambermaid, the night watch and the boots boy, who gladly left his post for an hour to visit his sick mother in the city.

Luckily, she was well enough to get the news to every street within the hour. Beadles on night duty sent word to their colleagues; the city gatekeepers did the same and changed the password. The night watch went round the palace speaking to every officer, soldier, clerk and servant. After half a dozen words, few made any fuss about being woken; those who did fuss were politely encouraged to stay in their rooms by several lengths of rope.

At the royal dovecot, the keeper did not go back to bed, but gave Colum extra corn. Thanks to one pigeon, a whole city had come alive again.

—————— § ——————

Three hours behind Sharfeat's army, Duke Agadasu was pressing on towards Macropuris. His outriders were able to track Sharfeat's men without being observed. The duke had also sent a group of cavalry ahead by a moorland route, shorter but more difficult, which would bring them out on the track again close to Macropuris – ready to ambush Sharfeat's army.

The Serpians were still outnumbered, but they had just won a battle – and, if they didn't fight on, Sharfeat would come back to kill or enslave them. They had nothing to lose but their lives and everything to gain.

20 Crystallised

In the pale dawn light they reached the top and saw that the hills dropped away much more steeply on this side. Far below, the old city of Macropolis stood on an island of rock reached by a bridge over a deep gorge. The broad valley around it was patterned with fields, paths and cottages, on both sides of the meandering river bed; but everything was dry as dust. There had been no water here for hundreds of years.

As they hurried down to the deserted city, the second sun rose and it grew warmer. Even near the foot of the slope, they were still well above roof level, but now in the bright sunshine they saw that most of the buildings were ruins, and some even had stunted trees growing where roofs had once been.

Hakeema pointed. "You see the market place? On this side was the palace, around that courtyard."

Jack peered down. "Is that the pyramid, by the tall tree?"

Hakeema shrugged. "I know not."

Meena studied the scene. "It's like a ziggurat, only polygonal. I thought pyramids always had a square base. And look – there is a bridge from the top to that tower. I wonder why."

"What's that, Indar?" Jack asked. He pointed at a small cloud of dust in the distance.

"Such fortune was too good to be true," said Indar grimly, "We must reach the pyramid before them. Run!"

As they stumbled down to the city gates, they heard the faint drumming of horses' hooves. It echoed the frantic beat of Jack's heart. Meena was not going to panic, but even she felt a bit sick. She had talked him into coming all this way with the crystal and now he and it were going to be captured, just when they were so near their goal. And, if they were captured by their arch-enemy, what would he do with them?

Sharfeat's men were less than half a mile away as the six raced across the bridge. The tall city gates, though shut, had begun to rot in places. They clambered over fallen planks and heavy beams, stooping to squeeze through where the bottom of a plank was missing. No horse would pass this barrier.

The sky seemed overcast as they ran down the main street. Turning left into the deserted market place, they saw the open palace gates. They rushed through and stumbled to a stop in a polygonal courtyard about fifty yards across. Each side had a shadowy archway at the centre of walls four storeys high. They could not see the pyramid any more.

"That's the tall tree!" shouted Meena.

"Let's check those two archways," said Jack.

The boy with the violet eyes

"We three will guard the gate," said Indar.

Meena chose one arch, Hakeema and Jack another, and began searching. The sky was growing darker. Indar hid a soldier on either side and took up his stance in the courtyard. His loaded bow faced the gate. He heard footsteps.

Behind Sharfeat, a dozen armed men guarded Aseem. Relief swept over Indar as he understood that the marshal expected a parley. Hakeema and Jack emerged from one of the archways, hastily finishing their discussion.

"It's the boy I want, Hakeema," Sharfeat shouted. "Macron will show you its gratitude for finding him, but I take over now. And look who I've brought: your Prince Charming. He is your responsibility. Give me the earthling in exchange."

"You betrayed his father; you will betray Aseem too," replied Hakeema.

"Kings cannot be traitors," said Sharfeat smoothly.

"And traitors cannot be kings." Jack's violet eyes blazed. "I accept the swap – if you accept my conditions. You must let me use my crystal. And then let the rest go, including Aseem."

"You impudent rascal! You dare make conditions?"

"It's your call."

"Do you take me for a fool?"

"I wouldn't take you for a million pounds. Now make your mind up."

Sharfeat's eyes bulged; he spat in Jack's direction before responding. "I accept the terms, with one proviso. When your task is done, you and the rest go free, but" – Sharfeat turned to Hakeema – "*you* come with me."

She turned pale. There was a pause before she answered. "Very well, Sharfeat."

The men released Aseem, and he ran to the arms of his tutor and his newest friend.

——— § ———

Meena found herself in a dark, stone-flagged lobby with several ancient doors. The first opened with a groan, and she stepped into what looked like a small, smelly farmyard with a manure pit.

She retreated and tried another door. This one revealed a twelve-sided room with no windows, lit by a dome high above. She screamed as a large cobweb fell across her face. The spider scuttled away, but Meena had gone.

The third door was ajar, but jammed; she edged through the narrow gap. Just twenty yards in front of her was the pyramid. It rose steeply, in terraces – like an Aztec temple. Everything was in twelves. Meena ran round and counted twelve sides, twelve storeys high. Each terrace had twelve stone steps running sideways up to the next level. She climbed up to the first terrace, from which stairs led up to the left and the right. But one flight of steps ended halfway; the other way ended in a wall. This was a giant puzzle.

Meena decided to run back to tell the others. On hearing the raised voices in the courtyard, she hid and listened. *Why is Jack putting himself in Sharfeat's hands? Hakeema too! They can't trust him.* There had to be a reason.

"Very well, boy," said Sharfeat. "Do your magic with the crystal, but I am right behind you."

"Show me the way to the pyramid, then," said Jack.

Sharfeat's eyes narrowed. "This is some trick. You know where it is!"

"No, he doesn't," said Meena, stepping out. "But I do. Follow me."

Sharfeat pushed Jack forward.

"It's this door here," Meena told them. "Jack, give me a hand: it's a bit stiff."

She slipped through the gap and pulled Jack after her. Sharfeat pushed, but the heavy door wouldn't budge. It hadn't moved in centuries. He swore and took a run at it with his shoulder; the door stayed stuck. He called his men.

"Don't worry, Mr Sharfeat," Meena said sweetly, "We can manage."

"We'll be fine," said Jack. He stared at the pyramid, awed by its steepness and size – the height of a cathedral.

"It's like a maze in 3-D," said Meena, "We just have to work out the pattern."

Sharfeat was raging, trying to force open the door. Jack bit his lip. Meena, fascinated by this vertical labyrinth, seemed unconcerned; she chose a place and they began to climb. It was very steep, and Jack tripped. Why was it so dark, even outside? He looked up. One sun was nearly eclipsed, the other now showed just a ring of fire behind its moon. This was the double darkness! They started up the next flight of steps.

Sharfeat's men were taking turns to batter at the door. Jack tried to keep up with Meena, but the steps were a foot high and with each step he felt weaker; he struggled up to the next terrace, but each way it ended in a blank wall. They were trapped: there was no way up! Meena went to the lower of the two walls, jumped up, grabbed the top of the wall and scrabbled up onto it. Jack jumped up, but fell back. He tried again, and scrambled over.

It was the top of another stair that stopped halfway. Jack used his hands to make a step for Meena until she got her elbows onto the next ledge. She pushed up, straightened her arms, brought up one knee and scrambled onto the shelf. She gave Jack a hand up. They heard the door below beginning to give. Jack looked down and nearly toppled off. Meena grabbed him.

"I can't stand heights," he said breathlessly.

"Just concentrate on climbing," she said, "Don't look down."

He struggled up the steps to the next terrace, feeling slightly dizzy. They heard a loud bang as the door gave way, and a clatter as Sharfeat started in pursuit. It was dark as night now, so they could not see him – nor the black mist forming.

———— § ————

The top was a paved dodecagon, 12 ft across. *The shape of my family's badge.* In the middle was a small stone table of the same shape with a raised rim. It was filled with metallic crystals, exactly the same shape and size as Jack's, sitting in liquid. They tessellated, so it looked like a child's toy truck neatly packed with blocks. *This must be the pangram the priest mentioned.*

There didn't seem to be any pattern to it. Where did his crystal fit in? As soon as Jack asked himself this, he saw a gap. He dropped it in the slot: it fitted perfectly. Nothing happened. They could hear the scrape of boots somewhere below them. Jack began to panic.

"What now?!"

"I think you need to make the right pattern." Meena was scared too, but she had to keep it together for his sake.

Jack thought hard. It was like those pocket puzzles where, to move a tile, you first slide another tile out of the way. What should he move? He tried sliding a brick, but nothing happened. He slid it back and tried another. Still nothing. What was *meant* to happen? "Use your personal magnetism," his father had said. *I am a lodestone, a compass. Magnetism aligns a compass. I have my own magnetic field: the electric current in my nerves. If I solve this puzzle, my electricity might make the circuit work!*

An idea came to him. Taking a deep breath, he tried again. As fast as he could, he started sliding his own crystal nearer the centre. Having got it there, he moved round to the other side, filling in the gaps behind, moving the crystals to make a chain, a sort of dodecagonal spiral. As he slid the last crystal into place, a sharp electric tingling began to surge down each arm and through his fingertips. When he tried to pull his fingers away, his whole body came alive and in the gloom there was a flash. An arc of intense white light joined his fingers and the crystal.

His fingers would not move. His whole body was tense and excited. His crystal was getting hot and the other crystals glowed too, forming a circuit diagram. Jack could feel his body forming part of the circuit. The water began to bubble.

Meena gripped Jack's arm. He looked up to see Sharfeat. "You little rat … I will end your life with my bare hands," he roared. This man was dangerous. His red eyes were on Jack, his face twisted with rage, his hands ready to grab. But now he was staring at Jack's fingers.

The crystal throbbed with the charge flowing through Jack. It shone in the darkness. The forces stabilised and Jack felt his crystal weld itself to the dodecahedra around it. Everything stopped moving, glowing with heat. He pulled his hands away, knowing instinctively that his part in the process was over. It was time to move.

The crystals glittered and gleamed with unearthly colours. Wisps of vapour in three colours – lilac, rose and graflim – rose from the bubbling water. Only later did they learn why there were three vapours: lilac to kill the black flowers, rose to bring back the king and graflim to drive off the demon.

Jack and Meena did not stay to watch. As Sharfeat edged round the pangram, they turned and ran across the bridge. They sprinted to the tower door – but it was locked! They banged, pulled and pushed, but it stayed fast. There was no escape.

——— § ———

The double eclipse made it too dark for those down below to see what was happening on the pyramid. When the guards saw a spark, they expected fireworks again and either hid or fled. Then the ethereal glow emanating from of the crystals outlined Meena and Jack as they crossed the bridge.

Hakeema could just see Sharfeat's head, until the clouds of coloured vapour obscured him. Her eye was caught by the children coming back along the bridge. *The tower door must be locked!*

"Indar, I am going up the tower. Defend my back!"

Indar notched an arrow as Hakeema blundered from door to door in the dark, until she tripped over a step and stumbled up the stairs.

"The enemy is escaping! After her!"

Indar fired his arrow and the guard fell. As his companions tackled the other guards, the archer looked for another clear shot. He never saw the spear coming. It pierced his side and he crumpled silently.

Sharfeat turned back; he would deal with the brats later. He must have that crystal. He tried to prise it free, but it was like trying to pull a brick out of a wall. Intense rays of violet light played on his face and he was breathing in the vapours, but still he struggled on. Jack and Meena saw that he was on his knees, gasping. Meena saw their chance.

"Let's climb down the tree," she whispered, "There's a bough right below."

Jack looked aghast. "You're joking!"

She climbed over the parapet, letting herself down onto the bough. She grasped it with both hands and carefully lowered herself until she was sitting astride it.

"Now you, Jack!"

Jack looked over the edge and felt immediately very sick. He sank to the ground again, unable to contemplate the long drop. Moments from suffocation, Sharfeat hauled himself up and staggered onto the bridge. Behind him, Black Mist was gathering. It was time for revenge.

The boy with the violet eyes

"I'm not finished, boy! I'm taking you with me," Sharfeat screamed. Jack stood unsteadily, feeling sick and scared. This was like waking from one of his nightmares, only this was real. Black Mist was here too. He felt his eyes began to sting.

He backed away until he felt the wall of the tower behind him. He could do no more. He slowly slid to his knees. It was not a heroic way to die, but then he'd always said he wasn't a hero. Was this his destiny, to do one good deed and die? *I never said goodbye to Mum. I didn't say sorry to Paul. I left Meena on her own. Oh well. I did my best.*

Meena dared to peep back over the parapet and saw Sharfeat standing over Jack. His hand went inside his waistcoat and brought out a dagger. Hearing a scraping noise behind Jack, he hesitated. The door opened to reveal Hakeema. Behind Sharfeat, a black shadow took shape.

"Really, Sharfeat, your memory isn't what it was," said Hakeema carelessly, "Don't you recall? The boy goes free if I stay."

Sharfeat tried to look as though this had slipped his mind. "Ah yes, Hakeema. What would I do without you?"

"Run along, Jack! Behind me is the way down."

Jack was dazed. His thoughts chased each other. He got up shakily, backed around the door and started down the stair.

"I never thought you were serious, Hakeema," said Sharfeat with a grisly smile.

"I was never more serious – but of course I'm not coming."

"And the boy has escaped. You are clever! Beauty with brain – a rare commodity." He grabbed her by both arms.

"Take your hands off me, marshal!" she shouted, pushing him away.

"Not 'marshal' but 'your majesty'. Still, I like spirit in a woman. We could be a great team."

"Over my dead body!" She dug her fingers into his cheek.

"If you wish," he snapped, "It will be a warning to your pupils." He thrust the dagger at her, hilt first. "You are taller, so your blade should be that much shorter. It's only fair."

Hakeema did not want to attack, but with only a dagger she could hardly defend herself. Sharfeat drew his sword and slashed. She tried to parry, pitting her desperation against his lifetime of practice. Her arm was swept aside and he got in another stroke while her guard was down – a swift jab to her leg drew blood. As she bent to fend off another blow, Sharfeat lunged, and this time his blade gashed her side. He pulled it out with grim satisfaction.

Hakeema clutched the wound, trying to stop the bleeding with her free hand. As the colour drained from her face, she dropped the knife and tottered sideways, falling heavily against the door. The tyrant watched with vengeful pleasure. She groaned; her eyes flickered and rolled up, showing the whites. Then she lay still.

"You heartless pig!" screamed Meena, looking over the parapet from the bough.

"Now you, brat," said Sharfeat. He turned, but Black Mist filled his field of vision.

"Fooooo!" rumbled a voice like thunder. Jack had heard it many times in dreams. "You failed. I must go, before I am destroyed by the spirits released by this crystal, and so must you. I have plans for you ...."

Sharfeat did not wait to hear what Black Mist had in mind. He clambered onto the parapet and jumped. There was a gloop as he hit the manure, and two nasty cracks as he broke an arm and a leg. Black Mist plunged down to the farmyard after him. Meena could hear Sharfeat yelp in pain as he tried to stand up, until the black mist blotted out all sound. It formed a twisting whirlwind that chilled her and nearly sucked her off her perch. She glimpsed Sharfeat being sucked up by the rumbling tornado shooting into the blue sky. The raksas had vanished, taking his henchman. The two suns were half uncovered.

Light was returning to Ardunya.

——— § ———

The three coloured vapours were still billowing from the top of the pyramid. Meena wanted to get away. When she moved along the bough, it dipped and she no longer had the strength to pull herself back up and onto the bridge.

Jack had been listening on the spiral stair. When all went quiet, he pushed at the door against the weight of Hakeema's body. Sharfeat was nowhere in sight. Jack didn't look down; instead, he saw the sunlight catch Meena's glossy brown hair behind the parapet. He went to give her a hand up; then they rushed to Hakeema. In the hot sunshine, she looked like a pale, bloodied doll. They heard footsteps on the stair, and Aseem burst through the door.

"Good news!" he cried, "The people have taken Macropuris in the king's name ... and Sharfeat's army has surrendered." He faltered, seeing their faces, and turned to look.

"She saved me," said Jack.

Aseem's face crumpled as he stared down at Hakeema's lifeless body. She had been almost like a mother to him; now she was gone too. "I wanted her to see me crowned," he said sadly.

"She must be buried with honour," said Jack, "Can we get her down the stairs?"

It was slow and laborious. When they eventually reached the foot of the tower they found one soldier supporting Indar and the other washing his wounds. Aseem was gently lowering Hakeema onto the step when he heard a whispered "Thank you". Her eyes were open, trying to focus on him.

147

Joy lit up his face. "Hakeema!"

Meena used most of their water to clean Hakeema's wounds, and Jack tore his tee-shirt into strips, which Meena used for bandages. Aseem encouraged her to sip the last of the water.

Sharfeat's guards had gone, all but three who waited, shamefaced, outside. Anxious to make amends, they offered their horses for the ride to the capital. Hakeema and Indar could travel only at a walk, so Aseem ordered one soldier to lead their horses.

The messenger awaited orders. Aseem gave him a note for the chamberlain, and the rider set off post-haste. Then he mounted the third horse, with Meena and Jack behind, while the others followed at a walk. They made their way slowly back to Macropuris.

21 I never did

When they reached the palace, they were dusty and saddle-sore. The guards saluted and grooms helped them dismount. The chamberlain greeted them, telling the good news as he led them through the great indoor garden.

"Strange clouds have passed over the city with miraculous effect. You will see!"

He explained how, when the lilac vapour touched the black flowers, they shrivelled and dropped their petals; when it touched the plague victims, they began to recover. When the graflim-coloured cloud arrived, people saw the last shadow soldiers suffocated; and, when the rose vapour reached the palace, it enveloped the petrified king and ate away the stone crust.

"Yet, though the king looks alive, he has not moved. Come quickly!"

The doors at the end of the garden opened as if by magic: they were expected. Aseem ran straight to the far end of the hall, where a huddle of courtiers and servants surrounded King Jonda. He was not breathing. A nurse stepped forward.

"I see the trouble," she said and clapped the king on the back. She put a wooden spatula in his mouth and scooped something out; the king coughed and gasped for breath. Those present gasped in wonder and relief. Soon, though weak, the king could focus and speak.

"Aseem? ... Where is Sharfeat?"

"He has been defeated, Father, and fled through a worldhole."

The king took a sip of water. "Methinks I slept. Son, where is your mother?"

"She is in her room," said the prince delicately, "I shall go to her, Father."

"Do so, Aseem. The chamberlain can enlighten me about all that has passed."

———— § ————

Aseem beckoned to Jack and Meena, and they followed a courtier up the great stair. The prince looked sombre as they padded along the thickly-carpeted corridor. Through the doorway of the queen's room, they could see the queen's body lying on a catafalque between four tall candles. The courtier stood aside.

"I shall wait here, sire."

"So will we," said Meena, taking Jack's arm and drawing him aside.

As Aseem went to his mother, Jack looked at Meena and realised what she meant. *If you've just lost your mother, you want to be alone. What about* my *mother, though? Maybe I can still save her.* "We have to go home, Meena."

"Yes, we need to see to your mother, and my parents will be wondering where I am. But we have to say goodbye first."

Aseem emerged, his cheeks tear-stained. As Jack opened his mouth to say goodbye, Meena spoke first: "We're so very sorry about your mother, Aseem."

"Yeah, we're really sorry," said Jack awkwardly. *I didn't think, did I? It never hurts to think.*

"I am lucky to have such friends," said the prince, sniffling and dabbing his eyes, "And my father lives. Forgive me."

"Do you think your father is well enough to say goodbye to us?" asked Meena.

Sheesh! How does she always say the right thing? She's like the best sort of grown-up.

"For certain he will wish to say farewell, though he is weak. Come."

On the corridor they met Hakeema and Indar being helped to their rooms. The ride had opened up Indar's wounds. She had bound them up again though, and he would recover. He could say only a few words, and she looked frail. Their goodbyes were affectionate but brief. They both needed treatment and rest.

The king gave Meena and Jack a warm smile. "Friends ... mere thanks cannot suffice: Macron is indebted to you, and Serpis too. I thank you from the bottom of my heart."

"That's what friends are for, your majesty. Jack did what any true friend would do."

There was a pause as everyone looked expectantly at Jack. Were they expecting a speech? That wasn't quite what they got, but for once Jack did think before he spoke.

"I'm not sure I was a true friend: you see, I wanted to know about my dad, I didn't want to look useless, I didn't want to get hurt, I was angry with Sharfeat and I knew I'd never be safe till I found how to use the crystal. I liked feeling important, of course, and I enjoyed making the fireworks. But Meena had to make me do everything. If it hadn't been for her, I wouldn't be here at all."

Everyone laughed, Meena blushed and Aseem smiled through tears. Jonda said: "Honesty is not amiss between friends, child, but you are too hard on yourself. You did well. And, if you did all this because of Meena, you did not think only of yourself, did you?"

Jack felt overwhelmed. He had survived, he hadn't messed up, he'd even done some good – but he'd never expected praise from someone he admired. Jack's violet eyes looked gratefully into the grey eyes of King Jonda. "Thank you, king. We really should go home now."

"Naturally ... but tarry a moment." Jonda beckoned the herald, who gave him a small, shiny, black stone. He placed it on Jack's palm. "This is the Nawab's Amulet, your forefather's. No raksas can harm whomsoever holds it. I give it to you because you are most precious; but also it is yours by right. Keep it ever on your person."

"Thank you," said Jack. He slipped the jewel into his pocket and bowed.

"I yield it gladly," added Aseem, smiling.

Jonda turned to Meena. "But for you seemingly, Jack would still be at home, studying alchemy and playing games. You must have some very powerful magic!" He smiled knowingly; so did she. "Alas, I have no keepsake to give you, child. So I offer you the simplest and best gift." He opened his arms wide, and Meena went to him, looking very happy. He gave her a big hug, she gave him a kiss. Everyone said their goodbyes and so they parted.

———— § ————

They walked through the palace and out into the hot sunshine. As they walked down the curving high street, people smiled; a fruit seller gave them a ripe *manjweh* each. As Jack ate his, a thought struck him.

"Before we go, Aseem, can we go back where I landed?

"Of course. Yet why?"

"I want to see if the black flowers are really dead – and pick up something."

From the spot where he had hitched a lift with the dead man, they walked up to the wood. A sickly, sweet scent hung in the air; under the trees the ground was strewn with black petals around rotting stems. No flowers, no rats, no plague: the crystal had ended it. At the edge of the wood they found the crossed twigs. Jack's blazer and tie were dry, but Meena shook the beetles off before he put his blazer on. It was time to go.

Once more, the prince took a white pellet from his bundi, powdered it, gave them some and made a circle with the rest. He chanted the spell and joined them in the ring. The sudden, bitter wind made them shiver, the whirling dust blotted out the peaceful landscape and they lost touch with the ground, moving blindly through freezing fog.

As it became warmer, they glimpsed the lights of Wellington Spa. Moments later they were standing a little shakily on the common. It was night-time. It was also time to part, and Aseem looked sad and happy together. So much had happened in such a short time. Jack and Meena were old friends; now they seemed like old friends to Aseem too.

Meena put her arms around him. Jack wasn't jealous any more.

"Will we see you again?" she asked.

"It's my birthday on November the 1st. Can you come?" jumped in Jack.

"Delighted! Hakeema will work out the earth-date."

Meena let go. Aseem turned to Jack, who put his arm out to shake hands, just as Aseem opened his arms for a big hug. *Oh well, why not?* thought Jack.

The prince began preparations. Within a minute his circle and incantation were complete, he vanished in a whirlwind as his words died away in the night sky: "Farewell, dear friends."

——— § ———

Meena broke the silence. "We're going to miss him … he became a best friend."

"Yes, he did … has, I mean. We'll see him again."

"I hope so. Now, we'd better get home."

"Will you come with me first?"

"Course, but I can't stay long." They started walking, too tired to run. Jack had no magic vapour to free his mum, even if she had survived.

"How long have we been away, do you reckon?"

"I was just working that out – and how much trouble I'll be in. We were there for two and a half of their days, but I reckon their hours are about 36 of our minutes. I think we've been away 35 or 36 hours. It must be Sunday night now."

Opposite 14 Hornbeam Avenue they met Dinah, who recognised Jack and mewed.

"Hey, Leo, did you miss me?"

Galileo didn't answer, but padded along behind them heavily. Dinah had eaten a very good dinner; they did you well at No. 14, but they didn't play with you. She toddled up the path.

"Here's your key," Meena said.

She followed Jack into the house and put on some lights. Without a word, Jack ran straight upstairs, bursting through the bedroom door, dreading the sight of his mother. She was still there in bed but, to his utter astonishment, no longer petrified. She looked feverish, her eyes were closed and she was moaning, but she was alive!

How? Surely it couldn't be the crystal? Or the vapours from Ardunya? Or the amulet in his pocket? Had the professor done something? *I can't work it out, but who cares?* Jack was just overjoyed. She moved slightly and opened her eyes.

"Is that you, Jack?" Mrs Cooper looked weak and confused.

"Yes, Mum. You're looking better." He was desperate to ask her what had happened, but now was not the time – and he needed to consult Meena first.

"I've had a terrible nightmare. I thought I was dying."

"You too? Nightmares must be catching!"

"Did I pass out?"

Jack should have planned what he was going to say. Before he could say anything, Meena spoke from the doorway.

"You had a nasty attack, Mrs Cooper, but you'll be fine."

"Meena, could you make Mum a nice cup of tea?" He had to make it all seem perfectly ordinary, or his mother would start asking questions, like: what was Meena doing in her bedroom in the middle of the night?

"I've had a few adventures, Mum. I'll tell you later."

"Where have you been?"

"Finding out about Dad."

Anita Cooper looked startled.

"But I want to hear it from you as well."

She nodded slowly, searching his violet eyes. "We'll talk tomorrow," she said.

Meena returned with tea and biscuits, plus the *manjweh* she had saved. She put the tray beside Mrs Cooper and smiled. "The fruit will give you energy."

"Thanks, Meena."

Jack kissed his mother on the forehead.

"I have to feed Galileo and walk Meena home. Won't be long."

———— § ————

The church clock struck twelve. The streets were quiet, but their minds were busy.

"What are we going to say, then? Come on, bright spark."

"We could tell the truth," said Jack.

"I don't think so. My dad would never let me out again. Anyway, who'd believe us?"

"The professor will."

"Parents are different. We've got to tell them something they *will* believe."

Jack stared up at the night sky and grinned. "Something bad, you mean? Right!"

"I know. Your mum was afraid of the bats, so we took her to stay with her cousin in Ayr."

"And on the way we stopped at Gretna Green."

"In your dreams. Let's stick with the cousin, shall we?"

Meena had no key, so they knocked and waited. Mr Patel opened the door in his pyjamas. He called to his wife, who came downstairs two at a time in her dressing gown. She folded Meena in her arms, looked questioningly at Jack and frowned at Mr Patel.

"Praveen, put on your nightgown!"

In the kitchen, the questions began.

"Where have you been all this time?"

"I was fearing the worst," said Mr Patel, putting the kettle on.

"Meena, you realise we called the police?"

"We—"

153

"Don't interrupt," said Mrs Patel, "Anyway, the police were no help. They said 'It's all a bit difficult'. I said 'My girl is missing, and all you can say is "It's a bit difficult"?' I was angry."

"You were upset," explained Mr Patel.

"This policewoman said bad things about you, Jack."

"I—"

"Yes, she said 'Boys are funny at that age'. Which I know. I myself was a boy."

"Praveen! You're as bad as that policewoman. I'm sure Meena can explain."

"We—" said Meena.

"Quiet!" said her father, "The police said: 'Perhaps they ran off together'."

"Why didn't I think of that?" jumped in Jack, coming to Meena's rescue.

The Patels were momentarily silenced.

"Jack's mum was frightened of the bats, so we took her to stay with her cousin."

"Meena was safe with me," added Jack, "Thank you for trusting me, Mrs Patel."

"Jack was great," announced Meena, getting up, "You see: he brought me home, safe and sound. But it's long past his bedtime."

"Goodnight, Mrs Patel ... Mr Patel." Jack felt more cheerful than he had for a long time.

As Jack and Meena went to the door, Mr Patel seemed to wake up. "There was a gang here today asking for you, Jack. I do not like to see you mix with no-goods."

Does he mean Tom's gang? "Was the leader curly-haired and rather large?" He didn't want to say 'fat' – even of Tom.

Mr Patel looked stern. "Yes. If you wish to go on seeing my daughter, you must promise not to associate with such low life any more." He paused. "Well?"

There could be only one answer. "I promise, Mr Patel."

Mrs Patel couldn't speak for a fit of coughing, but her eyes twinkled.

Meena took over. "That's good. I'll see you to the door, Jack."

At the door, Jack said "You realise I'm giving up Tom's gang for you?" They stifled their giggles. More soberly he said "I think that knock Aseem gave him has worn off. It's going to be tough."

"And you've proved you can be tough. You were great."

For a moment, Jack forgot everything he had learnt. "I know."

"I wonder if you should see a doctor? I think your head's beginning to swell again."

Ruefully he laughed at himself. "It's often like this. I believe the technical term is 'fathead'."

"See you in the morning then, fathead, and don't be late. Sweet dreams!"

"Thanks. I've had enough of the other sort."

Jack walked down the street. At the corner, he turned and waved to Meena before heading home to his own bed. What is it they say about dreams coming true?